A Rob Wyllie pa
First published in Great Britain in :
Derbyshire, United I

RobWyllie.com

The Maggie Bainbridge Series

The Loch Lomond Murders

Rob Wyllie

Chapter 1

It was raining of course, but then by repute it was always bloody raining up in these parts so there was no reason for him to be surprised. And it was damn cold too, although this being the 1st of October and 6.30 in the morning that too was only to be expected. But these facts of nature, or was it geography, irrefutable though they were, weren't doing anything to improve Yash Patel's darkening mood. It hadn't helped that yesterday's journey up from London had been a bit of a nightmare, the plane delayed for two hours before it had even left Heathrow due to some unspecified technical fault, and then the bloody taxi driver had wanted an extra fifty quid to deliver him to his crap hotel here on the so-called bonny bonny banks on the basis that it was twice as hard to drive in the dark. The delays meant he'd arrived too late for dinner, although to be fair John the chatty proprietor had knocked him up some borderline-acceptable cheese sandwiches, accompanied by a couple of so-so malt whiskies that Yash suspected were something other than what the respected label on the bottle claimed. But he was here for a story, a story that his gut told him was going to be bloody huge, so if there was to be some discomfort, it had to be endured. There had been just one car in the car-park, an upmarket SUV with a private plate, which struck him as vaguely odd since for some reason he pictured his boat-guy driving a battered pick-up. But the bloke was a local and probably could walk here, or maybe he even lived on his boat. Whatever the case, now Yash was making his way along the rickety jetty, half-expecting his ferry not to be waiting at the end of it as arranged, but no, there it was, or at least he assumed it was the one. Through the gloom he could just about make out the name painted neatly on its bow. *Lady Rose.* Yep, that was the one. As he got close, a bearded figure wearing a bobble hat popped his head out from the shelter of the wheel-house.

'You'll be the man from the newspaper then?' the man said, unsmiling.

He nodded. 'Sure, that's me. Yash Patel, from the Chronicle. And you must be Ally Russell.'

'Aye, I'm Russell,' the man said. 'I'm hearing you want to be going to Inchcailloch.'

'That's the general idea, yep. John at the hotel said you could take me.'

Russell shrugged. 'It's no' allowed, you do know that don't you? They've made it against the law. Out of bounds.'

So here we go, Patel thought. The ritual mating dance before the all-important question was asked and answered. *How much?*

'Sure, everybody knows that,' Patel said. 'But my paper believes it's in the public interest that the truth about the disaster is told. That's why they've sent me up here.' That made him smile to himself. *Sent? As if.* Yash Patel, crack investigative reporter, fearless seeker of the truth and multiple award-winner, didn't take orders from anyone. He didn't like to be pissed about either, but that didn't mean he didn't know the value of a bit of tactical schmoozing. 'And Ally, I've heard you know these waters better than any man on the loch. At least that's what John at the hotel told me. He said you were the *man*.'

'Aye, and he'd be right in that,' Russell said. 'So okay, I'll take you. But it'll be four hundred pounds, cash. In advance.'

Patel gave the man a look. 'Yeah *sure* mate. What is it, a mile and a half? Less? And you want four hundred notes from me?'

The boatman shrugged. 'That's my price. Take it or leave it.'

He had to hand it to the guy, straight to the point and no dancing around the subject. *Four hundred quid, take it or leave it.* He didn't like it, but right now he didn't have any other option but to take it. And besides that, he had to get out of this bloody rain before he caught a dose of something.

'Fair enough,' Patel said. 'Just as well I went to the cash-point yesterday. But I'll give you two hundred now and the other two hundred when you drop me back at this jetty. That's *my* offer. Take it or leave it.'

'What, you think I might leave you stranded on that wee island?'

The thought had occurred to Patel but he decided to keep it to himself.

'No no, I'm sure you wouldn't do that mate. It's just business, that's all. Half up front, half when the job's done. Standard stuff.'

'Aye all right then,' the boatman said, briefly breaking out a half-smile. 'Let's just get you on board and we'll get off before the loch wakes up.' He extended an arm, Patel taking it to steady himself as he stumbled over the high side of the little boat. 'Come on, you can squeeze in the wheelhouse alongside me and keep yourself dry. It's pretty rain-proof.'

'Thanks,' Patel said, giving the ramshackle structure an uncertain look. 'That would be good.' Rain-proof or not, it did a good job of keeping the biting wind off him and for that he was grateful. Having squeezed in as instructed, he watched Russell pulling back on the throttle, stirring a throaty roar from a diesel engine buried somewhere behind them. So much for keeping things nice and quiet.

'We can give it some welly whilst we're heading south along this shoreline,' Russell said in explanation, as the boat spun away from the landing stage. 'There's no restrictions along this bit. But then we'll turn it down to an idle, spin it round and let our momentum drift us up to the island. I know a wee inlet we can slip into that's well-hidden from the disaster site.' He gave Patel an amused look. 'There's no jetty mind, so you'll be getting your feet wet.' *Soft southern Sassenach*, that's what he'd be thinking no doubt. But Yash could put up with that, having heard a lot worse in his time. Sad though it was in twenty-first century Britain, it came with the skin tone.

'Sounds like you've done this before then Ally?' he said.

'Like John at the hotel said, I know this water like the back of my hand. I was taking the tourists and bird-watchers onto Inchcailloch for years before they built that bloody tower.'

That bloody tower. The bloody tower that on a stormy New Year's Eve almost two years ago had crashed down onto the craggy surface of the tiny island, killing seventy-four souls in the process.

'So what did the folks around here think of it?' Patel asked. 'Before the tragedy I mean, obviously.'

Russell spat out the words. 'A bloody carbuncle, that's what we thought. One of the most beautiful places on earth and they had to go and build a bloody *observation* tower, like it was Niagara Falls or something. And look what's happened now. It's ruined the place for ever. After thousands of years of tranquillity they've ruined it for everybody.' All of this he said without once looking at Patel, his head craning forward to see ahead through the rain-splattered windshield.

And it was perhaps true, Patel reflected. He'd felt a little the same way when he'd checked into his hotel. Before the tragedy, guests would have been looking forward to spending time in what Russell had accurately described as one of the most beautiful places on earth. Now it seemed disrespectful to even be here, almost as if you were trampling all over the graves of those who had lost their lives in the disaster.

'We'll be heading east in a minute. And then it's just half a mile to the island.'

'Don't they have patrols then?' Patel asked. 'Boats I mean.'

Russell shook his head. 'Not at this time in the morning. They're running a strictly nine-to-five operation. Fact is, they're relying on visitors treating the place with respect.'

'And are they? Are people treating it with respect?'

'In the main. And anyway, you need a boat now since they've closed the new bridge from Balmaha. So it's no' so easy to get there nowadays.'

Patel smiled to himself. It taken him less than five minutes to find someone who would take *him* there. But then again he thought with characteristic lack of modesty, not everyone was an award-winning journalist on a national newspaper, equipped with a persuasive tongue and an even more persuasive cheque book.

'I see they've taken to calling it the Lomond Tower again,' he said.

Russell gave a snort. 'Aye, that's the Scottish Government's doing. But it's still the McClelland Tower in most folks eyes and it always will be. Doesnae' matter how much our esteemed First Minister and her thought police try to persuade us otherwise.'

By his tone, Patel guessed Russell probably wasn't a fan of Sheila McClelland, and that probably meant he wasn't a supporter of Scottish independence either. But that, he knew, was an emotive subject best avoided in this neck of the woods.

'Imagined in Scotland, Designed in Scotland, Built in Scotland,' Patel said. 'I looked it up. That was the big slogan, wasn't it?'

'Aye that was it,' he agreed. 'Bollocksed-up in Scotland more like. The usual tub-thumping crap from these guys.'

Patel smiled. 'But Sheila McClelland has had her own share of tragedy too. I expect people felt sorry for her after everything her family has gone through.'

Russell gave him an apologetic look. 'Aye, I suppose you're right, it was a terrible thing for her right enough. And they've still no' found the body. Poor lassie.'

Now the engine had become almost inaudible as the boatman throttled back and began to rapidly spin the big wheel. On command, the little craft began a ninety-degree turn and soon the strong westerly wind was behind them and for the first time, the single windscreen wiper started to have some effect.

'That's Inchcailloch, straight ahead,' Russell said softly. 'You can see it now. Bloody awful sight it is too.'

And now, in the dank gloom of the autumn Loch Lomond morning, Yash Patel could indeed see it. The shattered stump of the McClelland Tower, still rising about a hundred feet above the ground, looking for all the world like a great oak shattered by a lightning strike, shards of twisted steel girders painting grotesque shapes in the sky. He shivered as he pictured the scene on that fateful night. Families enjoying a traditional Scottish Hogmanay, looking forward to the bells and to *Auld Lang Syne*, none of them aware that they wouldn't see another year. Twenty-to-twelve, that's when it had happened. Survivors described hearing a deafening crack as, four hundred feet below them, the concrete and steel superstructure gave way, in the process severing the power cables and plunging the revolving restaurant into darkness. And then as if in slow motion it began to topple, before crashing to the ground and bursting into flames. Seventy-four lives lost, including twenty-one children. Bodies so badly burned that only a small proportion of the gruesome remains were ever properly identified. His paper like all the others had run the story for weeks and he vividly remembered the front page that carried a photograph of each of the victims. No wonder the Scottish government and its First Minister were trying to swerve responsibility for the tragedy, because who would want something like that on their conscience?

'We're just coming up to the wee inlet,' Russell said, pointing to the left.

Patel peered out the side window. 'But that looks like a landing stage.'

The boatman grinned. 'Aye, I was just winding you up earlier. But it's on its last legs so you'll need to watch your step. And it'll be slippery.' As they approached, he tweaked the throttle and gave a deft nudge to the wheel, causing the boat to drift on a diagonal path towards the wooden jetty.

'I'll give you thirty minutes maximum and then I'm out of here,' Russell said as he docked. 'They do foot patrols from about eight o'clock and I don't want them finding me here. It's a five-grand fine.'

Patel shrugged. 'Sure, but I don't want you keeping the meter running, okay?'

And so at last he was here, setting foot in the place that would be at the heart of his next big story. He had no particular plan in mind for his short visit but that was the way he worked. He had to have been there, in this instance for no other reason than to be able to tell his readers what it looked and felt like. He'd take a few photographs and make a few notes but already he knew this was a place that once visited could never be forgotten. Eighteen months after the tragedy, First Minister Sheila McClelland had stood up in the

Scottish Parliament and announced that the islet of Inchcailloch was to be declared a national memorial to those who had died, and that the remains of the tower would be left to decay in whatever manner nature might dictate. Soon there would be the public enquiry, the standard establishment whitewash that would run for years and cost millions and conclude that it had been a terrible act of nature although some small mistakes had been made in the design and construction but that lessons had been learned and it couldn't happen again.

With just thirty minutes there wasn't much he could do other than take a walk around, take in the scene, try and imagine what it must have been like that terrible evening. As he got closer to the wreckage, he noticed that it was still partially surrounded by striped tape, rattling forlornly in the stiff breeze. *Crime Scene - Do Not Pass.* Yeah, it had been a crime all right, but who had been responsible? That's what he meant to find out. And then, out of the corner of his eye, he saw something that pulled him up short. It was a wooden cross, no more than eighteen inches high, crudely constructed and bearing no plaque of identification. Next to it lay a small posy of flowers, pansies he thought although he was no expert. It seemed that somehow a friend or loved one had made it onto the island and in defiance of the lockdown rules, had erected their own rather poignant tribute to a loved one. With a smile of satisfaction he took out his phone and photographed the pathetic scene. That was the front page, sorted. His work done, he made his way back to the jetty, composing the story in his head as he went.

Imagined in Scotland, Designed in Scotland, Built in Scotland. He bet they wished they hadn't said any of that, and now the whole debacle had moved into its next phase. *Covered Up in Scotland.* Yes, there was no doubt about it, the cover-up was now in full swing, starting with the decision to stop nosey-parkers like himself poking their noses around the island. But that wouldn't stop him. He meant to uncover the truth, to find out what had caused the terrible tragedy, and more importantly, who was responsible.

Because there was nothing Yash and his paper liked more than a good witch-hunt.

Chapter 2

For Maggie it had been by any measure the most unsettling of days, the sort of day that sent your head spinning and wondering how on earth to react. Two phone calls in the space of five minutes, calls of such ridiculous happenstance that she began to wonder if her mother's deeply-held belief, that everything that happened to you was not mere fate but part of a master plan handed down to you at birth by God, might actually be true after all.

It had been Frank who'd called first, ringing from his car on his way to some meeting or other with his boss DCI Jill Smart. *How do you fancy moving to Scotland? Maybe only for a wee while.* She hadn't been sure how serious he had been, because with Frank it was never easy to tell. Which in actual fact was one of the reasons she had both fallen in love with him and agreed to marry him too. She had long known that it was Frank's mission in life never to say anything to anyone that didn't make them feel better, and it worked on her as well as anyone in the world. Just *looking* at him made her feel good, his soft open expression radiating a bonhomie and charm that was both comforting and beguiling. The fact was, she would move to Timbuktu if he asked her to, not that she had a clue where that was. Definitely not in Scotland at any rate.

And then seconds after she had hung up on Frank, the second call had come in, this one from her best friend Asvina Rani, go-to family law solicitor for the rich and famous. *I've got a huge case for you and Jimmy. You'll need to drop everything because the client meeting's at 3pm today. Oh, and by the way, it might mean moving to Scotland for a bit.*

Jimmy was waiting for her inside the atrium of Addison Redburn's Canary Wharf glass palace, the swish tower-block where Asvina plied her lucrative trade. And as had been the case for the last two weeks or more, she saw that his face wore an unmistakably downbeat expression. Spotting her emerging from the revolving door, he made an obvious if not entirely successful effort to smile.

'Afternoon boss,' he said. 'This has all been a bit of a rush, hasn't it? What's it all about?'

She smiled. 'Yeah, Asvina was pretty cagey on the phone. As for what's going on, all she said was it was big and important and pretty sensitive. In fact, the only thing I know is that it's connected to your homeland in some way.'

He gave her a wry look but made no comment. As they made their way over to the elevators, she squeezed his arm and said quietly, 'And anyway how are you? I mean, with everything that's happened? If you don't mind me asking?'

He shrugged. 'Oh fine fine. All fine here. It was always going to happen and now it has. So I'm fine.'

They stepped into a waiting elevator, she sensing that perhaps it would be better to park that line of conversation for now. *Plenty of fish in the sea, especially for a great-looking guy like you*, those were the words that had come into her head but she was glad she'd managed to keep them to herself, recognising at the last minute what a crass cliché it was. And anyway, the fact that something had obviously gone badly wrong in the relationship of Jimmy and Terezka Berger was actually none of her business. As to his divorce from Flora, well he was right, it *was* always going to happen but having been through a marriage break-up herself, she knew that didn't make it any easier to deal with. Perhaps later, in a quieter moment, she would try to get him talking because in her experience that always helped.

Asvina was waiting as they stepped out into the vast open-plan office, tall, slim and beautiful as ever. Maggie often thought her friend could easily have been a supermodel, but of course she was making about five times as much in her chosen career. She smiled warmly at them and gave Maggie a hug, then more formally, extended a hand to Jimmy.

'Thank you both for coming in at such short notice,' she said, speaking quietly so as not to be overheard by the general office. 'The case been referred to us from our Edinburgh branch. You'll find out why in a moment. Suffice to say, it's a rather difficult and sensitive matter.'

'We're intrigued,' Maggie said, smiling. 'As usual, you never give us the easy ones.' Earlier she had speculated as to what the matter might be, perhaps some big Scottish film star going through a bitter divorce or maybe the boss of one of these huge Edinburgh financial services firms waging a battle over a multi-million pound inheritance. That was the kind of affair that was meat and drink to Asvina Rani and she and Jimmy had worked on plenty like that in the past. But nothing could have prepared her for the shock when she found out what *this* one was all about. As Asvina led them into a corner room, Maggie immediately recognised the attractive and perfectly-groomed figure sitting stiffly in one of the meeting room chairs, her hands on the table and clasped tightly in front of her.

'This is Mrs McClelland,' Asvina said, smiling. She gestured towards the tall balding man sitting alongside. 'And this is her husband Andrew.'

A third man, smaller and casually dressed, sat opposite the pair. Uninvited he said, 'Aye, and I'm Willie Paterson. I'm the father. The *real* father.' He made no attempt to hide his antagonism towards the other pair. This is going to get interesting, Maggie thought.

'Pleased to meet you all,' she said, unsure as to whether they were expected to shake hands or not. Opting against it, she pulled out a chair beside Paterson and somewhat uncertainly, sat down.

'Aye, good to meet you all,' Jimmy said, settling his big frame in the chair next to Maggie.

'So if we're all sitting comfortably, I think we'll get started,' Asvina said briskly. 'The First Minister has an Edinburgh flight to catch in just over an hour so time is short. So Maggie and Jimmy, I've already explained to our visitors how Bainbridge Associates helps our firm with our investigation work, but it seems your reputation precedes you.'

'We've done our research,' Andrew McClelland said. 'As you might expect. We were quite impressed by your track-record. And now I hope you can help us too.'

He spoke with that easy self-assurance that Maggie had often witnessed in people with wealth and power. But it wasn't just his position in society that gave him such presence. Six-two or six three, with broad shoulders and a muscular look, he emitted an aura of powerful physicality. Mrs McClelland too had a commanding aura, her soft attractiveness such an asset in her ascent to the top of her profession. But she was clever too. Maggie had heard Sheila McClelland speak often on television, even though she was only vaguely aware of Scottish politics, and had always thought the woman talked a lot of sense, unlike a lot of politicians she could mention. But today it seemed First Minister McClelland was to take second fiddle to her husband, which Maggie found interesting. What Paterson's role in the matter was, she assumed would emerge as the meeting progressed. As it turned out, she didn't have to wait long.

'So Maggie - you don't mind if I call you Maggie?' Paterson said.

She nodded her assent.

'Aye, great. So Maggie, you need to know that this pair are only here because I threatened to go to the papers about the whole shebang. I don't know about Andy the big lap-dog here, but our Sheila puts her bloody political reputation ahead of everything. Even her own daughter. It's bloody shameful. But the fact is, the police have been absolutely crap and now her government just want to sweep it all under the carpet as if nothing had happened.'

Sheila McClelland gave a disdainful shake of her head but said nothing.

'So maybe a wee bit of background would be helpful?' Jimmy said, smiling. 'Bring us up to speed and all that.'

'Of course,' Andrew McClelland said smoothly. 'You will have heard about our poor daughter I expect?'

'She's no' your daughter,' Paterson interjected. 'She's mine, and don't you forget it pal.'

'You walked out on her when she was a baby,' Sheila said, with undisguised bitterness. 'It's a bit late to be playing the loving father now.'

He spat out his reply. 'Juliet and I made up and you bloody know it. And my daughter had more of my time in the last few months than you ever gave her. You and your stupid *cause,* it's all you ever think about.'

'Folks, perhaps it would be helpful if I ran Maggie and Jimmy through the background,' Asvina said. 'It's obviously a very painful matter for everyone and I totally sympathise with what you all must be going through.' Maggie smiled to herself. She was brilliant, her old friend, with her inherent amiability able to bathe even the most difficult situation in a soothing calmness. Without waiting for an answer Asvina continued,

'So I expect you will both know of the heartbreak of Juliet McClelland's disappearance. It's a terrible thing and of course the family here has been suffering greatly as you can imagine.'

'I *can* imagine,' Maggie said. 'It must be awful for all of you. I do remember the story at the time. This I think was what, about two and a half, three years ago?'

Asvina nodded. 'That's right Maggie. It was April the twenty-third to be precise. But to cut a long story short, and as Mr Paterson said, the police investigation into her disappearance has been unsuccessful and the family would like us - that's you, Maggie and Jimmy - to pick up the baton and find out what happened. There is of course a very good chance that she disappeared of her own volition and she may still be alive. That would naturally be the most fantastic outcome, if you could track her down. That is the hope of the family.'

'Of course,' Maggie said, nodding, although instinct told her the chances of that happening were about a hundred to one against. She only had the vaguest recollection of the case, because at the time it was unfolding she had been immersed in her own overwhelming problems and had no room in her head to think of anything else. About three years ago that would have been, although what were the exact circumstances of Juliet McClelland's disappearance she could not recall. Presumably Asvina would imminently fill in that gap.

'So, the bare facts,' Asvina said, on cue, 'and I'm sorry if this is painful for the family to hear again. Juliet was - is - a medical student, in her third year at Glasgow University. A bright girl and very beautiful, just twenty years old at the time of her disappearance. Like many students, she supplemented her income by working as a waitress. On the evening in question, she was scheduled to work a shift at the Auchterard Hotel on the east side of Loch Lomond. She never arrived and has not been heard of since. As I said, that's the bare facts.'

'That's awful,' Jimmy said. 'I feel for you all, I really do.'

'Well the police were bloody useless as I said,' Paterson said. He stabbed a finger at his ex-wife. 'Despite all the shite *she* talks about Scotland's world-class services and how bloody marvellous we all are and how amazing everything would be if we could just get shot of all you English. No offence ladies', he added, directing an apologetic half-smile first at Maggie and then Asvina.

'It was complicated,' Sheila McClelland said, her tone serious. 'By the Denis Northcote case.'

'What's that?' Maggie asked. 'I don't think I've heard of it.'

'They were desperate to fit up Northcote for Juliet's killing,' Paterson said scathingly. 'To keep everything nice and tidy. But I told the copper in charge again and again that the MO was totally different.'

'Sorry Willie,' Jimmy said, looking puzzled. 'I'm still not following you.'

Asvina smiled. 'Maybe I can help. You see, around the time of Juliet's disappearance, there had been three other murders of young women in the city. The police eventually apprehended and charged a council refuse worker called Denis Northcote with the killings, and he was tried and sentenced to life imprisonment.'

Maggie nodded. 'Ah yes, I think I remember now. And the police suspected he'd killed Juliet too?'

'It was probably a reasonable assumption,' Asvina said. 'It's highly unusual to have two serial killers operating in the same city at the same time.'

Paterson shook his head. 'No no *no*. Northcote was a bloody narcissist, leaving his stupid little sign in blood on their foreheads. He *wanted* the bodies to be found, he *wanted* to read all about it in the papers. And when he got caught, he was boasting about what he'd done to anybody who would listen. There's no way he killed Juliet. No way.'

'Well, whatever actually happened, it'll all be a complete waste of everyone's time of course,' Andrew McClelland said. 'Despite what Willie here says, the police did a thorough and painstaking investigation at the time but sadly were unable to bring the matter to a satisfactory conclusion. My wife knows my feelings in the matter but for the sake of Juliet's father, we are reluctantly prepared to support this initiative.'

'Aye, but you two are only *supporting* it because I threatened to tell the whole world that you were actively blocking it.' Paterson gave Maggie a conspiratorial look. 'You see Maggie, that's what you're going to be up against here. It'll be like a bloody obstacle course with everybody who was involved told to keep their big mouths shut.'

'That's nonsense Willie and you know it. Miss Bainbridge and Mr Stewart are assured of our complete cooperation,' Sheila McClelland said. Maggie turned her head imperceptibly, caught Jimmy's eye and smiled. She knew what he was thinking. *Cooperation? Aye sure*.

'Well, that's good to know,' she said, smiling. 'Specifically, I assume the Scottish police will be made aware of our assignment and will help us in any way they can.' She posed it more as a statement than a question, although she guessed what Frank would be thinking if he were here, this being very much in his line of work. Their first instinct would of course be to cover up and obfuscate, and that was going to make their task ten times harder. But no matter, they'd dealt with that kind of thing plenty of times in the past.

'Naturally,' Sheila McClelland said. 'I'll speak to the Chief Constable personally.'

'Brilliant,' Jimmy said. 'And who's going to be our main liaison? You Mr McClelland or you Mr Paterson. Or all of you?'

'That'll be me,' Paterson said, jumping in before the other pair could answer. 'It's me that's driving this. So you talk to me first, okay?'

'Everybody happy with that?' Maggie asked. Andrew McClelland stole a glance at his wife, evidently looking for a sign of her consent or otherwise.

She nodded. 'Juliet's father can be your first point of contact,' the First Minister said, 'but as I said, you will have our full cooperation.' She moved as if to stand up, then said to Asvina. 'So Miss Rani, if we're all done here, I have a plane to catch.'

To Maggie, it sounded cold and uncaring, but she knew Sheila McClelland wouldn't be feeling that way inside. No mother would be, with a daughter missing and not knowing what had happened to her but fearing the worst. And even having only met Mrs McClelland for this brief period, she could tell she was a decent person. She thought of her own Ollie, to her the most precious thing in all the world, and remembered the indescribable agony when she was separated from him for nearly six months back in those dark days. No, for the First Minister, if it came down to a choice between the reputation of the Scottish police force and by extension her government, and finding out what happened to her precious daughter Juliet, then that would surely be no contest.

At least, she hoped it wouldn't.

Chapter 3

Right now everything was pretty bloody marvellous in the life of Detective Inspector Frank Stewart and he was hoping that nothing his gaffer DCI Jill Smart was going to tell him in their upcoming meeting was going to screw that up. Because he could tell from her tone when she'd called him earlier telling him to get his arse over to Kensington police station and a bit sharpish too that this wasn't to be any ordinary meeting. Like a naughty schoolboy, he'd immediately racked his brains to think of anything he might have done wrong, at the same time wondering if he'd offended any of the brass in recent weeks, but no, nothing obvious sprang to mind. He'd asked her of course what it was all about and all she had said was it was important and then added cryptically, and maybe we'll be moving you back to Scotland. *Moving you back to Scotland?* What the hell was that all about he wondered?

What *was* a bit of a pain though was both the day and the time of the meeting. *Half-past four on a Thursday afternoon*. Didn't Jill know that was the day he met up at the Old King's Head after work with his brother Jimmy and his fiancé Maggie Bainbridge? *His fiancé Maggie Bainbridge.* His heart skipped a little beat as he repeated the phrase to himself. Yep, it was true. Miss Magdalene Bainbridge was his actual fiancé, the woman he was actually going to *marry* in the very near future, although no exact time or place had yet been arranged. But him, marrying the fragrant Maggie Bainbridge? How the hell had that happened, to him of all people? Truly, the sun must have started shining on the irreligious. He'd given her a quick call from the car on the way to Kensington, casually mentioning the Scotland thing and deliberately curtailing the conversation before she had a chance to answer. The chances were it wouldn't come to anything anyway, so it was probably nothing to bother about.

On arrival, the desk sergeant informed him that Jill had booked one of the anonymous interview rooms buried in the depths of the station, a dank and featureless box deliberately designed to put suspects ill-at-ease. A curious choice he thought, given they could just as easily have met in her spacious corner office with its picturesque view of the car pound. The door was closed when he got there, but like all these wee rooms it was equipped with a one-way glass panel allowing him to take a quick dekko through to see who he would be meeting with. *Flipping heck* was his immediate reaction, a phrase he had recently and involuntarily picked up from his Yorkshire-born love. Because here standing in the corner of the room leaning against the wall was none other than Assistant Commissioner Derek Blair, or the anti-corruption tsar as the papers liked to describe him. As far as Frank could recall, Blair had been in the job for two or three years now and had spent the first couple of those focussed on the Met itself, embarking on a massive effort to weed out the bad apples. Strangely enough that had made him popular with the rank and file of the force, who for years had been suffering public opprobrium about their perceived uselessness.

Sitting at the small table was a woman of about his own age who he vaguely recognised, although at first he struggled to put a name to her. A politician, definitely. Aye, that was it. He'd seen her on *Question Time*, one of those put-upon junior ministers sent in to defend the latest indefensible government cock-up. And then it came to him. Caroline Connor, that was her name, he remembered her now. A Northern lass, in fact from Yorkshire like his Maggie, but cocky with it, liking very much the sound of her own voice. Mind you, that was kind of par for the course amongst the breed so he wouldn't hold it against her, and judging by her TV appearances, she even seemed to have a sense of humour too, which gave her a certain likeability that wasn't always present in her politician mates. But why was she here, that was the question, and with AC Blair too? No doubt he was about to find out.

He knocked on the door and strolled in. 'Afternoon ma'am, sir,' he said, then shot a welcoming smile in the direction of the politician. 'DI Frank Stewart, Department 12B. You won't have heard of us. We're a sort of backroom operation and they don't let us out very often.'

She laughed, then got up and proffered a hand. 'Caroline Connor, Junior Minister, Home Office.' There was something in her tone that said *I might have junior in my job title but I'm actually rather important.* But then, he supposed they all thought that about themselves, until the next reshuffle that was. But it was said with a discernible twinkle, if you could actually have a twinkle in your voice.

'Good to meet you too,' he said.

'Sit down Stewart and we'll get started,' Blair said. That made Frank smile to himself. He'd forgotten that the AC was one of these public school types who still addressed his underlings as if they were domestic staff at his grand country house.

'Thank you sir.' He gave his boss DCI Smart an enquiring look. 'So.....this is something about Scotland is it ma'am? That's what you said on the phone.'

'I'll leave it to the AC to explain Frank,' Jill said. 'Sir, if you're ok with that?'

'Yes sure Jill,' the AC replied. Aye, so that was how matters stood, Frank thought with some amusement. He was *Stewart* but she was *Jill*. Talk about knowing your place.

'The government as you know is deadly serious about weeding out corruption in public life,' the AC continued. 'It was the reason I was appointed to the Met and I think we have been reasonably successful in our activities in that regard.'

Frank nodded. 'Aye sir, it's been good and much appreciated by the decent officers on the force.'

Blair smiled. 'Thank you Stewart, that's nice of you to say so. But to cut a long story short, our efforts were duly noted upstairs and a year ago I was asked to extend my remit into other aspects of government and the civil service.' He said it without a hint of hubris although Frank did detect a certain pride in his tone which he thought was fair enough.

'Yes, so we asked Assistant Commissioner Blair to head up a government task force with me representing HMG.' It was Caroline Connor's first contribution and he wondered if she would be as modest as his big boss.

'I've worked *very* closely with the PM and the Home Secretary of course on this initiative,' she said, 'although I should say the *UWIPO* idea was mainly my own. It's something I have been very passionate about for a very long time and it was personally very gratifying to see it get off the ground.' *Question answered.*

'The *u-what*? Frank said.

'UWIPO. It stands for Unexplained Wealth in Public Office,' Connor said, laughing. 'I'm sorry, government is addicted to acronyms. In fact you're not actually allowed to start a project until you have one.'

Frank frowned, 'Well I *think* I kind of understand what that might be all about but to be honest it's not something I've seen or read anything about.'

'You won't have,' Blair said, 'because it's secret. *Top* secret.'

Connor nodded. 'That's right. We're flying this initiative under the state secrets mechanism rather than through the green and white paper provisos. Under the radar so to speak. So very few people are involved. Just a handful, and at the topmost level of government of course.'

'So what exactly does that mean?' Frank said, although he thought he could already guess.

'It means it doesn't go through the normal parliamentary process to become law. In fact, strictly speaking, it doesn't actually become a law of the land. Technically, we call it an executive order.'

'Sounds a bit dodgy to me,' Frank said, raising an eyebrow, 'but then, what do I know about what goes on at these exotic levels of government?' He saw Jill Smart wince and gave her an apologetic smile before adding, 'Sorry folks, I was only joking. But anyway, the thing is, where do I come into all of this?'

'Patience Frank, patience,' Blair said, smiling. What, a smile *and* use of the first-name now? Had he passed some secret test, like the freemasons or something?

'Okay sir. I'll await with my breath fully bated'.

'Very good Stewart. So, the UWIPO initiative is, well, I guess you could say it does what it says on the tin. We are looking for wealth for which the office holder does not have a credible explanation. Is that a fair description Caroline?'

She nodded. 'Exactly Derek. It's exactly that.' So he was *Derek* to her, was he? And there was no disguising the affection in her tone, which made Frank wonder exactly how close the AC and the junior minister had become over the course of this

UWIPO thingy. One thing was for sure, if these two were romantically entangled, *that* would take some explaining. She continued, 'And like so many government initiatives these days, this has been primarily an IT project.'

'Oh dear,' Frank grinned. 'You have my sympathies.'

She gave him a wry smile. 'This one, you will be pleased and perhaps surprised to hear, has actually proceeded to both time and budget. Although naturally I have had to keep a very close personal watch on it to ensure *that* outcome.' *Naturally.*

'Good to know.'

'Well, yes, we're delighted with the outcome,' Connor continued, 'but I guess I should give you some background on what it's all about. To cut a long story short, we're applying advanced cyber-scanning techniques to delve into the financial affairs of those who are the target of our investigations.'

He raised an eyebrow. 'You mean hacking? Isn't that illegal? The Computer Misuse Act 1990 if I'm not mistaken.'

'Naturally all appropriate measures will be taken to protect the human rights and privacy of the individual,' she said smoothly. Frank laughed to himself. That sounded exactly like the bollocks it was.

'We need to root out corruption in public office,' Blair said. 'It's vital to the health of our democracy, wouldn't you agree Frank? Otherwise the public loses trust.'

Aye, sure, but so is respecting the laws of the land was what he wanted to say, and more besides, but he didn't want to get his boss Jill Smart into any bother so made no comment other than a grudging *I guess so sir.* But he still hadn't heard what his role in the affair was to be, nor that of his homeland. Time to get to the point.

'So what exactly is it you want from me?' he said. 'Aye, and sorry for my impatience.'

'Okay if I take this one Derek?' Connor said. The AC nodded his assent. 'Okay Frank, so the initiative has passed Cabinet Committee stage and an overseeing body is being set up to ensure the provisions are enacted with proper regard to safeguarding procedures.' *More bollocks.* 'That means we're ready to go. And like all these major initiatives, it makes sense to start with a limited-scope pilot project. To prove the concept and test that the IT system is robust. All that kind of thing.'

Frank frowned. 'Okay...' Before she said another word, he guessed what was coming.

'So we...I mean the PM and Home Secretary and myself...we've decided that the pilot will be run in Scotland.'

'Are you bloody mental?' Frank exploded. 'Do you guys not remember that Poll Tax stuff back in the Margaret Thatcher years?' The blank looks he received in return gave him his answer. 'With the greatest of respect sir, it might be worth asking our government colleagues to do some basic research before pushing ahead with this. There'll be riots if this get out up there, you mark my words. We don't like being guinea-pigs for stuff like this, believe me.'

'On the contrary, we would expect the Scottish government to be one hundred percent supportive,' Connor said, 'given how desperately keen they are to call out corruption in the Westminster government. Or the English government, as they like to call us. But in fact, they will not get to know about any of this.'

'What, you've not spoken to them about this?' Frank said, surprised.

Connor gave him a look of amusement. 'Surely you can see that would defeat the whole purpose? As I said, no-one in public office must ever get to know that this surveillance capability even exists. Otherwise those with something to hide might take extra steps to avoid exposure.'

'This is pure politics isn't it?' he said. 'You guys hate the nationalists and Sheila McClelland in particular. You're looking to dig up dirt, aren't you?'

She smiled. 'As the Assistant Commissioner said, it is important that we root out corruption in public office. Actually for the record we don't expect that Scotland has any more or any less of it than any other part of the country, and so no, there's no political motivation in the decision. In fact Scotland was chosen quite randomly as the pilot location.'

'What, like in a raffle?' Frank said in a sardonic tone.

She smiled again. 'We used a rather more sophisticated algorithm, but yes Frank, essentially it was like drawing names from a hat.'

I don't believe that for a minute was what he wanted to say, but decided it might not go down too well with the AC. So he waited for her to continue.

'And just to reassure you, we are only targeting a limited sample of individuals and only a few of them will be connected with the Scottish government. In fact our main focus will be on serving police officers.'

'Oh no ma'am,' Frank said with alarm, turning to DCI Smart. 'You can't make me do this. Internal investigations are bloody toxic and I don't want to be involved. No way. I'm a detective, get me out of here.'

And it wasn't just the thought of being involved in some horrible internal shenanigans, he realised, as his brain struggled to process the full implications of what he had just heard. He wasn't an independence fanatic himself, not like some of his nutter countrymen, but that didn't mean he couldn't see the advantages of it either. In his view his homeland was a great wee country with a lot of very clever and hardworking people, and if they decided to go it alone, well they couldn't make any more of a mess of things than the UK government had done in recent years. He'd thought about it quite a bit in the last month or so, and had come to the view that if there was another referendum and he was eligible to vote, he would probably say *yes*. The fact was, there was a lot to be said for being in charge of your own destiny, for better or for worse. So if this thing he was being asked to do was to be a covert attack on the nationalists and the independence movement, he wasn't sure he wanted any part of it. In fact, he *definitely* didn't want any part of it.

'There's a promotion in it Frank,' Blair said, smiling. 'You'll immediately be made DCI and with some extra responsibility payments too, and of course we'll be covering all your living expenses whilst you're on the assignment up there. It's a great package and just so you know, I've already had it signed off by HR and the Commissioner. Your promotion letter's already typed and sitting on my desk.'

'What, do you think I can be bought sir?' The tone was quite a bit short of respectful and he immediately regretted saying it. 'Because if this is a political stunt, then I'm not sure I want to be involved. In fact, I'm not so sure it's something us cops should be involved in full stop.'

'It's not political,' Connor said sharply. 'Scotland was chosen randomly. I told you that.'

Frank gave her a sceptical look. 'Aye, well I'd like to believe that but I'm not sure I do. Anyway, I'm not doing the political stuff. No way.'

She shrugged. 'For the pilot, we already discussed at cabinet level whether or not we should include directly-elected individuals. We could quite easily exclude them for the first phase if that makes it more palatable.' The words came out smoothly, but her expression gave away what she really thought about having to grant this concession.

Frank was silent for a moment then said, 'Okay, but if any of this strays into anything that's in any way controversial, then I'll be slamming on the brakes. If you want to do anything of that nature, you'll need to find someone else.'

'I'd second that,' Jill Smart said quietly. 'It's your call of course sir,' she continued, looking at Blair, 'but it's a fundamental of policing in this country that we don't do politics. And this feels like politics to me.'

'I understand your concern, both of you,' Blair said, 'but you'll recognise that this is vitally important work and to get this sort of stuff done we need to ask our best officers to step up to the plate.'

Frank groaned. 'It's not just the politics sir. You see, I'm getting married soon, so moving to Scotland is just a big no-no for me and my wife-to-be. I mean, we're totally settled here in the metropolis. And she's got a wee boy at school and with all that lad's been through, he doesn't need any more disruption in his life.'

'It's only a six-month assignment, maximum,' Blair said. 'And Frank, you're one of our best, and I'm asking if you are prepared to put duty before any personal considerations, difficult though I know that will be. And the thing is, we need our best officers on the side of the good guys. If all the good guys said no, then where would we be?'

Frank shuffled uncomfortably in his seat. 'It's a tough call sir, it really is.'

Blair smiled. 'I appreciate that Frank. But I'd be really grateful if you would at least consider accepting this critical assignment. For the good of the country. In fact, for the defence of democracy itself. I think it's that important, I really do.'

Frank paused for a moment, sighed then shook his head. 'Bloody hell sir, and I say this with no absence of respect, but you're totally wasted in the police force.'

'How so, *DCI* Stewart?' Blair said, looking amused.

'You should have been a bloody double-glazing salesman,' Frank said, deadpan. 'Okay, I'll do it. But no bloody politics, okay?'

Chapter 4

Down the Old King's Head pub, the talk was, not surprisingly, of Scotland and nothing but Scotland.

'So you two have got a wee mission up there too?' Frank was enquiring whilst slurping on his pint. 'That's a bit of a coincidence, is it not?'

'Hey, less of the *wee* stuff brother,' Jimmy said, grinning. 'Ours is one of the biggest cases we've ever had, at least in terms of the profile of our client. Who, I think I'm allowed to say, is none other than our esteemed First Minister. Well, not *our* First Minister, us Stewarts living in England and all that. But you know what I mean.'

Frank gave a surprised look. 'What, the lovely Mrs McClelland? I won't have anything said against her, I think she's a very decent woman which is not something you can say about most politicians. But funnily enough, the aforementioned Sheila would be very interested to hear about *my* new wee job, and no mistake.'

'Why's that?' Maggie said.

'I'm sorry Maggie,' he said with mock seriousness. 'Despite me loving you more than the distance to the sun and back - and I'm using kilometres in my measurements, not miles - well, if I told you, I would have to kill you. And that wouldn't be much good with the wedding coming up. I definitely want you to be there, if it's okay with you.'

She laughed. 'Oh, so it's one of *those* cases is it? Okay, I won't press you. But when you phoned me earlier, with that mysterious *we might have to go to Scotland* stuff, were you serious? Because actually, I've been thinking about it, and it might be quite nice. Me and Jimmy's new assignment means we'll need to spend quite a bit of time north of the border too so it might actually be quite convenient to move up there for a while.' As she said it, she became conscious of Jimmy giving her a look that she took to be one of apprehension.

'I'm sorry Jimmy,' she said quietly. 'It's something we need to discuss because I haven't had a chance to ask you how you might feel about it.'

He shrugged. 'Might as well be up there as anywhere. Just stick me on a plane to Tenerife or somewhere on the weekend of the wedding. Not your wedding I mean,' he added hastily.

She placed a hand on his elbow. 'I know. Flora and Hugo. It will be difficult.' She gave Frank a sharp look as she sensed he was about to say something. It would be something well-intentioned and probably funny too, but not necessarily fully sensitive to his brother's feelings at this moment in time. Like recommending Jimmy recreate that scene in *The Graduate*, where Dustin Hoffman's character turns up at the church and runs away with the bride-to-be. That's the sort of thing Frank would definitely come up with, or something much worse besides. But as was often the case, he surprised her.

'Good idea Jimmy-boy,' he said softly. 'It's going to be a crap wedding anyway. I met that Hugo once and he's a complete arse. It'll be a bloody disaster, the whole thing, from start to finish.'

Jimmy was silent for a moment then said, 'But aye, I suppose there's worse things we could do than have a wee six-month stint up there. And Ollie would absolutely love it with the seaside and the hills and the lochs and everything. And I've got a few mates from the army up there so I could go hill-walking or mountain biking every weekend.'

Maggie smiled, pleased that Jimmy seemed to be trying to put a positive spin on the affair . 'Yes, well I loved my Yorkshire childhood and it's always been in the back of my mind that I want to do the same for Ollie. When I was a kid, my mum and dad took us up to the Dales nearly every weekend and I do miss the great outdoors. Although I know the scenery in Scotland is a whole lot grander.'

'Aye it is,' Jimmy said. 'It's the most beautiful country in the world, not that I'm biased or anything.'

'Bloody hell,' Frank laughed. 'You two sound like you're in an advert for the tourist board. Sheila McClelland might give you a job if you ask her nicely.'

'You've obviously not be listening,' Maggie said. 'As usual if I may say so. Because she's already given us a job, or have you forgotten already?'

'Oh aye, you're right,' he said, grinning. 'So anyway, is that a decision? About our Scotland move I mean? Can I tell Jill Smart that I'll take on her toxic career-wrecking wee project?'

Maggie's eyes narrowed. 'I thought you already had?'

He shuffled uncomfortably. 'Well, aye, in *principle*. But I told her it was subject to what you thought about it. She knows all about our wedding and everything of course.'

Jimmy laughed. 'Speaking of which, it's about time you two got that do organised, because I've already written my best man's speech. Oh and Maggie, I wouldn't leave it to Frankie-boy here. He couldn't organise the proverbial piss-up in a brewery.'

'Harsh mate,' Frank said, evidently without rancour. 'Actually, a piss-up in a brewery is the one thing I could organise, no problem. I've had lots of practice at *that*.'

'Don't worry,' Maggie said fondly. 'I've got it all planned in my head. It's going to be in the Dales of course, and my mum's found this lovely country house not far from Grassington that has a wedding licence and she's found a Friday that's available next May, which will be picture-postcard perfect, and there's twenty rooms for all the guests and she's even found a great band that is available too.'

'Wow,' Frank said, wide-eyed. 'So basically I don't need to do anything.'

She laughed. 'Well no, other than turning up, looking half-smart and saying *I do* when prompted by the vicar.'

'It's kilts for us,' Jimmy said, smiling at his brother. 'Got to be. And you've got the fat backside for it. You'll look perfect.'

'That I will take as a compliment brother. And aye, I do fancy the old highland dress if it's ok with you Maggie?'

'Of *course*,' she said. 'I can't wait to see you two in skirts. It'll be lovely.'

'So that's it then?' Jimmy said. 'A double decision? We're wearing kilts and we're moving to Scotland?'

He said it brightly, but it was as if he was trying too hard and for Maggie there was no disguising the undercurrent of trepidation in his voice. The last time he'd lived in Scotland, he'd been married to Flora, their little cottage in Lochmorehead a welcome sanctuary to which he could return from the hellish tours of duty out in Helmand. Their little love-nest he had called it, before everything had turned sour when he'd had that disastrous affair with the Swedish country singer Astrid Sorenson. Now she wondered how he would cope with being back in his homeland again.

One thing was for sure, she would have to make sure he didn't get within fifty miles of Ardmore and surroundings. Especially on Flora's wedding day.

***

The McClelland Tower - the search for the truth begins.

Yash Patel reached across his desk for his coffee, took a swig and read through the article for the second time. *His* article. For once, the sub-editors hadn't cocked about with his copy too much, something he had always hated. After all, it wasn't as if he just chucked these pieces together willy-nilly. On the contrary, everything he wrote was the result of considerable blood, sweat and tears, every word carefully considered for the effect it would have on the reader, and so there was nothing worse than when some spotty youth fresh from a journalism degree at some crappy third-rate uni decided he could improve on Yash's prose. *No way.* But no, this one had been left pretty much unadulterated, which was just the way he liked it and he had to admit it, he liked the headline too, which was rarely the case. The truth was though, the article was a bit fluffy, more of a travelogue really than a investigatory piece, majoring as it did on his visit to Loch Lomond and his under-the-radar landing on the island of Inchcailloch rather than revealing any facts about the tragedy itself. Having said that, his picture of that little cross, marking the grave of an anonymous victim, had really tugged at the heart-strings. But it was early days and that was the whole point of the article. A phishing piece you might say, designed to illicit information from the great British public. He'd had reasonable hopes of its success but he hadn't expected to hit the jackpot quite so soon.

Pleasingly, the article had led the front page in the Scottish edition, both print and on-line, the latter already generating a ton of reaction from the reader community, some of it virulently anti-

McClelland. Less expected but nonetheless welcome was the fact that it made the front pages of the UK edition too, albeit in cut-down form and stuck down in the right-hand -side corner. But that didn't matter to Yash, because less than four hours after its birth, the article had already began to pay dividends. An email had come in from someone identifying themselves as Professor Elizabeth Bates. And this Professor Bates wasn't serving out her tenure at some third-division academic outfit but at the top-drawer University of Cambridge no less. A professor of geotechnics too, whatever that was. He'd looked her biography up on the university's website and found that as well as her academic duties, she was also a director of a consultancy with the snappy name of *Cambridge Geotechnic Partners.* Very interesting, that. But not as interesting as what she had to say in her brief message, which was why he was just about to grab his coat and head for King's Cross for the forty-five minute journey up to the fine old University city.

Glancing out the window, he saw his editor Rod Clark pulling into his designated space in his big SUV. Which made Yash think back to that cold morning up in Loch Lomond, when he'd seen that solitary car parked up alongside the jetty and wondered whose it might be.

That car being the fancy Range Rover with the private plate *ALL 1Y.*

Chapter 5

He found Eleanor Campbell tucked away at her favoured location in a dark recess on the second floor, her chair pushed back against the wall as was her habit, as if to deter attack from the rear. Her head was barely visible above the bank of monitors that spread across the full width of the desk, but even from a fair distance away he could make out the ruffled brow, signifying that her mood that morning was not going to be sunny. Mind you, Frank thought, that meant nothing. Eleanor Campbell's mood was never sunny, although her recent marriage to the deadbeat Lloyd seemed to have softened her a bit, albeit it wouldn't have been at all obvious to the casual observer. But Frank wasn't a casual observer, having worked with the brilliant but out-of-the-box-cantankerous forensic officer for nearly three years now, their relationship having developed to such an extent that he had been honoured to be asked to give her away at her wedding. They weren't exactly mates, but over the period they had worked together they had developed what could best be described as an *understanding*. Much like a prisoner and his captor he'd often thought, although he wasn't sure who was who in the association.

But then, as he got closer, he noticed her desk had acquired a new ornament. One of these

Toblerone-shaped thingies that proclaimed your name and job title to the world, this one an expensive job fashioned from what looked like brass. *Eleanor Campbell. Senior IT Forensic Analyst.* He wondered what that was all about.

'Hey Mrs Senior IT Forensic Analyst woman, how's tricks? Married life suiting you?'

She glowered. 'What do you want Frank. I'm busy.'

He smiled. 'Aye, you always are. The Met gets its money's worth from you and no mistake.'

It had been meant as a throwaway remark but it evidently touched a nerve.

'Actually, they don't pay me anything like enough. Zak says I could get like twice or three times as much if I joined him properly. And so I'm thinking I might do that. He's saying he could stretch to six figures.'

So *that* was what the sign on the desk was all about. Eleanor was feeling under-valued, and knowing how good she was, that was a bloody dumb strategy on the part of her bosses over at Maida Vale labs. Then he gave her a puzzled look.

'Hang on. Zak, he's that super-hacker guy from MI5 or MI6 who's helped us out in the past? Am I right?'

'Except he's not with MI6 now. He's set up his own company and I *told* you that ages ago. But you *never* listen to me.'

That made him smile to himself, as he pictured the self-same remark being aimed, probably several times a day, at the hapless Lloyd.

'No, you're right, I don't. But aye, I remember now. He's set up that ethical hacking firm. You did tell me all about it right enough. They test the security of websites by trying to break in to them, am I correct?'

'It's like way more complicated than that,' she said, switching to her teacher-talking-to-dumb-five-year-old voice. 'But yes, their core business is cyber security. They've become one of the leading firms in the field in like no time at all.'

Frank nodded. He could imagine Zak whatever-his-name-was making a success of his new venture, even though he looked as if he was only fourteen years old, because he was one sharp cookie, no doubt about that. And if you believed what you heard in the media, there was no shortage of bad guys, usually Russian, trying to hack the systems of the country's big companies and organisations, for financial gain or out of sheer malice. This he suspected was a field where demand easily outstripped supply. But he wasn't here to discuss some spook's impressive career trajectory.

'Anyway, I've got some news,' he said.

She gave a seraphic smile. 'You're like moving to Scotland. To work on the UWIPO pilot. And it's secret.'

He looked at her, wide-eyed. 'Bloody hell Eleanor, how'd you know that? Have you been hacking my brain or something?'

She frowned. 'We haven't got that technology yet. But it was Zak's firm who developed the cyber-scanning software that they're using on UWIPO and I've been working on it too as the Home Office technical representative. It's been like way cool. And I knew they were planning to launch a pilot project.'

He nodded. 'Ah, so *that's* what's been keeping you so quiet these past six months. You've been on a big hacking spree. Right up your street I would say.'

She gave him a cold look. 'Yeah, as I said it's been a cool project but it's all perfectly ethical. It's just that it's being implemented under the state secrets mechanism because it's like super-sensitive.'

'They taught you that wee speech, didn't they?' he laughed. 'But I guess this is good news because maybe we'll still be working together after all.'

'That's good news?' she said, and not smiling.

'Took the words right out of my mouth,' he grinned. 'But maybe we'll even see you north of the border sometime soon. I hope your passport's up to date.'

'Yes it is. I got a new one for my honeymoon. But I didn't know you needed one for Scotland. Do you?'

He wasn't sure if she was serious or not. But her furrowed brow told him she was.

'No,' he laughed, 'you don't need a passport, not yet, but that might change if Sheila McClelland gets her way.'

Her puzzled look remained. Of course, she would never have heard of McClelland, current affairs being one of many subjects that failed to engage Eleanor's interest. He wondered in fact if she actually knew where Scotland was, given her famous uselessness at geography. She probably thought it was an island off the coast of Norway. Or part of Yorkshire.

Suddenly he became aware of a figure hovering behind him, its frame extensive enough for the office's old-school florescent lights to cast a shadow across Eleanor's desk.

'Hello Ronnie,' Frank said, swivelling to greet the corpulent shadow. 'What are you up to this fine morning?'

He saw that Detective Constable Ronnie French was wearing a concerned expression. 'Excuse me interrupting, but I've heard you're being moved up to jock-land and I was wondering if that means we'll be getting a new guv'nor.'

'Bloody hell,' Frank exclaimed. 'Bloody *hell*, is *nothing* a secret around here?' He gave Eleanor a sharp look as if to say *is this your doing*, her half-smile of unconvincing innocence immediately confirming that it was. 'Aye, well it's true, but as far as I'm aware, it's only a wee secondment and I'll still be running Department 12B remotely. Unless Jill Smart tells me otherwise.'

'I've heard you're being made DCI too guv. Congratulations. Nice work.'

Frank shook his head in mock disgust. 'Anything else you'd like to tell me about myself whilst you're at it? You might know stuff that I don't know myself.'

'Nah, that's everything I know guv, straight up,' French said, laughing. 'So when are you off? Soon I hear.'

'What, have you got your eyes on my desk or something Ronnie? But aye, it'll be soon. In fact me and my Maggie are heading up there at the weekend with her wee boy to look at houses.' He just loved the sound of that. *My Maggie*. He'd never get tired of saying that. So he said it again.

'Aye, me and my Maggie are hoping to find something nice out in the suburbs. Milngavie or Bearsden probably. Nice and handy to get out to Loch Lomond and the Trossachs and all these other beautiful places.'

He noted their blank faces and smiled to himself. They had no idea what they were missing. He for one was going to relish the opportunity to escape stifling London for a while and spend his weekends enjoying all that glorious fresh air with his Maggie and her brilliant wee son. And let's face it, he was going to need it. Because if one thing was a dead certainty, it was that the UWIPO pilot was guaranteed to stir up a ton of weapons-grade poo that would keep him fully occupied Monday to Friday, twenty-four-by-seven.

But even knowing that, he couldn't wait to get started.

The last six weeks had passed in a whirlwind of activity, with about a hundred items a day being added to Maggie's daunting to-do list. But relentlessly she had battered through it with Frank and Jimmy's help and now by some miracle they were almost settled. A nice little bungalow had been rented in a quiet street and Ollie was now enrolled in the local primary school and quickly becoming popular because of his size and his prowess at football. To her great amusement, her son had already managed to acquire a passable Glasgow accent, although fortunately of a posh variety, this being the up-market suburb of Milngavie. Yes, all and all the move had worked out pretty well, all things considered.

But now it was time to get to work.

'Are we going to be Bainbridge and Stewart, or Stewart and Bainbridge?' Maggie asked Jimmy as she lifted a pile of folders out of a packing case. 'I only ask because the sign-writer's going to be here in ten minutes.'

They had just moved into their new office, a modest one-room shop-front affair, but located on Byers Road in the heart of the city's Hillhead district and home of the revered fourteenth-century University. Her eyes had watered when the agent had told her how much the rent was, but they'd be able to take it on a short-term lease and give it up with just two months' notice so it wasn't much of a risk.

'Are you sure about this Maggie?' he said, as he dragged a small table over to one wall. 'The partnership I mean. Because I was perfectly happy when we were Bainbridge Associates and I was just an employee, honestly.'

She hadn't expected this and wondered if he perhaps was having second thoughts about their proposed new arrangement. 'I know you were. But now that we're up here and going to be practising law as well as doing our investigation work, it makes sense. You've got your LLB from Glasgow University and it will be good to have a locally-qualified lawyer on our team. Besides, you deserve it, after all you've done for me.'

And it was true. Quite simply, Captain Jimmy Stewart, ex-bomb squad hero and all-round amazing guy, had saved her life when she had been at her lowest ebb and looking like she was going to lose everything that was dear to her. And in return, she had mentally resolved to protect him against every sling and arrow of outrageous fortune that life might throw at him.

'Well, thank you,' he said, 'and of course I'm honoured, but really, it's not something I've ever really wanted.'

'Well you need to think about it pretty quickly,' she said, laughing. 'Before they paint the sign.'

'Okay then,' he said. 'If it's got to be anything then it's got to be Bainbridge and Stewart. And I do love the tagline by the way. *Bainbridge and Stewart. Wrongs Righted.* It's really good.'

'Yeah, if we were one of these fancy big law firms we would call it our mission statement. But it *is* my sort of vision for our firm. To be a place folks can come to when there's been a miscarriage of justice.'

He gave a wry smile. 'Or when there's been police cock-ups as in the Juliet McClelland case.'

She nodded. 'Exactly. Speaking of which, we're expecting her dad Willie Paterson any minute now. He works up at the University so he hasn't got far to come.'

'He's an academic then?'

She shook her head. 'I don't think so. Some sort of technician I think, looking after the buildings and stuff like that.'

On cue, they heard the ding of the bell above the door, signifying the arrival of a visitor, notable as being their first-ever to the new place. Willie Paterson walked in then paused for a moment as he surveyed the semi-chaotic scene. Maggie smiled at him and said, 'Sorry Willie, we've just moved in, but Jimmy's sorted a couple of chairs at the little desk over there. Come over and grab as seat. And I'm sorry we can't offer you a coffee or anything at the moment.'

'No bother,' he said, pulling out a chair. 'Glad you guys have finally got here.'

'We are as well,' Jimmy said pleasantly. 'So, if you don't mind Willie, we'll get straight down to business.'

Paterson nodded his assent.

'Okay,' Jimmy continued. 'Basically we need you to think about anything out of the ordinary that happened in the lead-up to Juliet's disappearance. Going back a week or two from when she was meant to be on shift at that hotel and didn't turn up. Or in fact as far back as you think is relevant.'

'Sure,' Paterson said. 'I saw her regularly, nearly every week in fact, ever since our reconciliation, if you want to call it that. And she was absolutely fine, really she was. She was enjoying her studies and she was on top of all the work she had to do as far as I could see. Although she said there was always a mountain to get through to be fair.'

'Just a little point before we go any further,' Maggie said. 'If you don't mind that is. You say your reconciliation. Perhaps you could explain a bit more about that?'

'Sure,' he said again. 'I was only eighteen when Juliet was born. I was doing my electrical apprenticeship here at the Uni and Sheila was a student. She was studying some dull History and Politics shite. She was unbelievable-looking back then, and well you know what it's like when lust takes over. But it turned out that she didn't see any future in me and I only saw her a couple of times before she dumped me. So I never knew she was expecting a baby, but after wee Juliet was born, she got in touch and told me it was mine, and for some stupid reason we decided to get together again for the sake of the wee girl.'

'But I'm guessing that didn't work out?' Maggie said.

'It wasn't my doing,' Paterson said, sounding defensive. 'Sheila was already bloody obsessed with politics and having me around was just like an anchor round her neck. And to tell the truth, I think she wished she hadn't had Juliet either.'

'And so the relationship broke down?'

Paterson gave Maggie a look of undisguised sadness. 'Aye it did, and I was so bloody gutted about that I can tell you. I don't mind admitting I went off the rails, with the drink and all that. I just couldn't bear not living with my wee girl so I tried to blank everything out of my mind with the bevvy. It was like that for years and years and I tell you now, I bitterly regret every second of that period.'

'But then you and Juliet made up I'm guessing?' Maggie said.

'That's right. About three years ago. She initiated it in actual fact and it was the happiest day of my life when I met up with her again. And we just took it from there. About once a week we'd have a wee coffee and a bacon roll down at the cafe and just chat about all sorts of stuff. It was nice, really nice.'

Jimmy nodded. 'And there was nothing out of the ordinary in the days or weeks leading up to her disappearance?'

Paterson seem to think about the question for a moment then said, 'Well not really, other than maybe just this one thing. You see, at the time she was sharing a student flat with a guy and another girl, you know, a couple of medics like her. But she'd found another place - just round the corner from here in fact, just off the Highburgh Road. It's a bit up-market round there and I think she was getting a fed up of living in student squalor. But I don't think the boy was that pleased about it because him and Juliet had been a bit of an item, although only on a casual basis like. But she wanted her own space, simple as that.'

'And who is this boy? I assume you know?' Maggie asked.

'Oh aye,' he said. 'Rob McNair. He's graduated now and works over at the Queen Elizabeth hospital on the south side. Doing that on-the-job training that these new medics have to go through. You know, with the twenty-hour shifts and all that.'

Maggie nodded. 'And was there some bad feeling between him and Juliet at the time? Because of her deciding to move out of their flat I mean?'

He shrugged. 'Nah, I wouldn't say bad feeling. I think he was a wee bit gutted but you know what these medical students are like. Full of themselves some of them are and I think Rob was one like that. Fancied himself rotten and I thought at the time he'd soon be fixed up with someone else. He's a good-looking guy and he knows it.'

Maggie smiled to herself. A bit like Jimmy, except he was a good-looking guy who seemed totally unaware of the fact.

'And did he? Get fixed up with someone else?'

Paterson shrugged again. 'I don't know. Actually I had a kind of a suspicion he might also have been having a bit of you-know-what with the other flat-mate. Rebecca something her name was. Pretty girl right enough but another one who was pretty full of herself. So I don't think Rob was left broken-hearted, let's put it that way. Although of course they were both pretty cut up by Juliet's disappearance, to give them their due.'

'Fair enough,' Jimmy said. 'So I guess we'll need to talk to the pair of them to see what their take on the affair is. But anyway, on the night of her disappearance, Juliet was due to work a shift at that big hotel up on Loch Lomond, that's right, isn't it?'

'Aye, that's right. The Auchterard, that's what it's called.'

'But it's quite a trek from here in the West End isn't it? What is it, at least twenty-five, maybe thirty miles? And that would make it nearly an hour's journey.'

'True enough. But the place is a bit up-market and they liked to have a better class of staff. So they'd rather taxi in a bunch of nice well-spoken middle-class students than employ some of the rough-arsed locals from Alexandria and the likes. And they paid good money so there was plenty of the Uni kids who were keen to get the work.'

'They taxied them up there then?' Maggie said, surprised. 'That sounds expensive.'

'Well most times they laid on a minibus and they'd take a few of the kids up and back. But aye, sometimes they'd lay on a taxi. '

'Like on the night in question,' Jimmy said, narrowing his eyes. 'Because I understand that evening a taxi had been sent to specifically collect Juliet, is that correct?'

Paterson nodded. 'Aye that's right. The agency would have organised all of that. The hotel seemed to have cocked up its staffing rotas big-time that night and needed some staff at the last moment. So the agency contacted Juliet at short notice and she said she was available.'

'And who's this agency?' Maggie asked.

'Cramond Staffing they're called. Got an office just down from here in Partick, on the Dumbarton Road. Quite a big outfit. Been going for years. A woman called Francis Cramond owns it and runs it.'

'Okay, we'll definitely need to talk to her as well,' Jimmy said. 'So as I understand it, the taxi turned up at Juliet's flat but she wasn't there. And sadly, she was never seen again. Have I got that right Willie?'

Paterson paused before replying, and when he spoke his voice was almost inaudible. 'Aye, you have. You have. And it's been killing me, absolutely killing me.'

Maggie gave him what she hoped was a sympathetic half-smile. 'Willie, I can't even start to imagine what you must have gone through. And you're still going through it of course. It must be awful.' She wondered what it must be like for Juliet's mother too, constantly in the public eye and having to put on a brave face for the media. That must be double hell, trying to hold it together.

'My whole life's dedicated now to finding out what happened,' he said. 'I think of bugger-all else to be honest.'

'We'll find out,' Jimmy said. 'Believe me, we will. But just getting back to when the taxi turned up at Juliet's flat. Were her flatmates in at the time? What are they called again? Aye, Rob and Rebecca. Were either of them in at the time?'

Paterson shook his head. 'Nah, they weren't. It was a Friday and they'd gone straight to the Students' Union for a drink after lectures. The last time they spoke to Juliet was about four o'clock when she told them she'd had a text from the agency and she would be working that night.'

'So this Rob and Rebecca were the last people to speak to her?' Maggie said.

He shrugged. 'Well there was a whole lecture theatre full of students so any one of them might have spoken to her. But aye, she definitely told Rob and Rebecca she was taking the shift at the Auchterard so wouldn't be going to the Union.'

'And then what? She walked back to her flat I presume?' Jimmy asked.

'Aye, well that's what we think,' Paterson said. 'Of course the police did an appeal at the time but nobody remembered seeing her. But you know what it's like, half-four on Friday night, everybody's going about their own business. They're all wrapped up in their own wee worlds, aren't they?'

'Yes, I guess so,' Maggie said, only half-listening as she tried to reconstruct the scene in her mind. Juliet tells her friends she can't come for a drink that night, then gathers up her lecture notes or laptop or whatever and walks the mile or so back to her flat. Probably she grabs something to eat then has a shower and changes into her work clothes and waits for her taxi to arrive. Except when it *did* arrive, she wasn't there. Meaning that none of the above might actually have happened, meaning she might have had some other plans altogether that she did not share with anyone else. But *what*?

She said, 'So Willie, unless there's anything else you can think of, I think we might be done.'

He shook his head, his face wearing a defeated expression. 'I've gone over it a thousand times in my mind. But no, there's nothing else I can think of. I wish there was, I really do.'

Afterwards they agreed the meeting had been a relative success, all things being considered. They knew quite a bit more about events leading up to Juliet's disappearance, and now they had three people to follow up on. Rob and Rebecca the medical students who had been the missing girl's flat-mates, the Rebecca one presumably now a doctor too, and then there was Francis Cramond, boss of the staffing firm that supplied the Auchterard place. Three people who with any luck might have something useful and interesting to say about the case.

But before that, Maggie fancied a spot of local familiarisation. She would round up Jimmy and together they would take a stroll down Byers Road and then on to that up-market street that Paterson had mentioned, the one that Juliet McClelland had planned to move to. A move that had been sadly dashed by fate.

Chapter 6

To say the atmosphere at New Gorbals police station was frosty would be like saying it gets a bit chilly on a January day in Alaska. Frank wasn't really that bothered about it, having spent most of his career ploughing a lone furrow, but there was no denying that a wee bit of sweetness and light made the working day a bit more appetizing. And the thing was, he couldn't exactly put his finger on what was the root cause of his Police Scotland colleagues - if that's what you would call them - giving him the cold shoulder. Was it maybe because he'd been allocated his own office, although admittedly a small and dingy one, because he was now a Detective *Chief* Inspector? Or maybe it was just because he had got that promotion. With a lot of the guys and gals in this cop shop having known him when he had been a mere Detective Sergeant, were they now simply resentful and jealous of his success? More likely was that they just didn't like fancy-dans from the Met swanning up the M74 and trampling all over their patch. Still, it wasn't a bad place to work, location-wise. He could catch a wee train from Milngavie at seven-thirty and be at his desk not long after half-past eight. Or, more accurately, be at a table in the canteen taking care of a steaming americano and a big bacon roll with brown sauce, the thousand-calorie intake offset in his mind by the one-and-a-half-mile walk from Queens Street station. All things considered, he was settling in nicely to life back in Scotland. But he should have known that as soon as you thought everything was going swimmingly, something would come along to upset the apple-cart. Or in this case, *someone*.

'So you're a DCI now Stewart eh? They must be bloody desperate down in the smoke if they're giving them away to the likes of you. What did you do, collect enough Nectar points or something?'

'Morning sir,' Frank said, ignoring the jibe. 'Good to see you again after all this time. Can I get you a wee cappuccino or something? My treat.'

Detective Chief Superintendent Peter Sweeney pulled out the chair beside Frank and lowered his powerful frame onto the cheap plastic structure. 'So what the hell are you doing here?' he said, his voice taking on a menacing air. 'That's what all the boys and girls in the station are asking themselves. Because nobody's bothered their arse to tell me what's going on, and I'm the top dog around these parts.'

Frank shrugged and took a sip of his coffee. 'Can't sir. It's a matter of national security so it's on a strictly need to know basis I'm afraid. That's my orders from above.'

Sweeney leaned forward until his face was just inches from Frank's, close enough to detect that the Super hadn't been too thorough with the toothpaste that morning.

'Well *I* need to know Frank. *I* need to know. You understand?'

'Perfectly sir. But I still can't tell you. You'll need to escalate it above my pay grade I'm afraid. AC Derek Blair's the man you want. He's a decent guy and his dad's from Glasgow. You'll find him at Kensington nick. He's got a nice big corner office down there.'

'I don't care if his office is in bloody Buckingham Palace next door to the King,' Sweeney grunted. 'He shouldn't be sending his *juniors* onto my patch without talking to me first.'

Of course, Frank thought, it should have been no more than he expected, because it was flipping obvious that the boys at New Gorbals nick would want to know why he was there. That's why he'd much rather have been based in some anonymous government building somewhere up in the town, but that wouldn't have worked either because government buildings up here were the fiefdom of the Edinburgh government and using one of them would have blown his cover. Besides which he needed to be in a cop-shop to get access to all the super-confidential police databases and other IT stuff, without which any investigations would be impossible. The fact was, there was nothing to do but grin and bear it. So he grinned at Sweeney and said,

'I'm sorry, didn't mean to be arsy sir. I'll maybe see if the Assistant Commissioner will give you a wee ring. It's only common courtesy after all.'

That seemed to partly mollify the Super who gave a grunt and levered himself off the plastic chair. As he made to leave he said, 'We'll be watching you Stewart. Just remember. We'll be watching you.'

'I appreciate that sir,' Frank said, trying to dial down the sarcasm but unsure if he was succeeding. 'Thank you for your help.' Immediately he wished he hadn't said it. It was going to be hard enough carrying out his task at this god-forsaken place without going out of the way to make enemies, especially a nasty piece of work like Sweeney. But at least his old mate DC Lexy McDonald was still based there and he was looking forward to catching up with her before too long. They'd actually arranged to meet today for breakfast but she had been called out on an urgent case. It seemed that the bereaved relatives of these poor folks who'd lost their lives in the McClelland Tower tragedy had got themselves organised and were up at Balmaha Bay, mob-handed and protesting against the decision to close off the island of Inchcailloch. Things were getting out of hand and the local plod at

Helensburgh had been forced to call in reinforcements from Glasgow.

Still, he had plenty to be getting on with, for today was going to be the day when the UWIPO case got properly up and running. He took a quick glance at the big clock that was mounted above the double entrance doors of the canteen. Aye, coming up to ten o'clock. Caroline Connor, Junior Minister at the Home Office would be here soon, with or without civil service entourage, he wasn't sure. He laughed as he thought about her mission. The government up here hated each and every one of these Westminster politicians and Sheila McClelland in particular would have an absolute fit if she knew that Connor was secretly stomping all over her territory. Especially if she ever found out the nature of the Junior Minister's trip north. That explained why Connor was travelling by government car rather than flying or taking the train, so that she wouldn't attract the attention and camera-phones of members of the public. It would have meant a four in the morning start or maybe earlier, but Frank suspected that wouldn't have concerned the ambitious minister one bit. It was rather as if she was some kind of enemy agent working behind the front line and he smiled to himself as he imagined her in camouflage gear with her face blacked up.

The only problem was, Connor just couldn't do incognito even if she'd wanted to. He hadn't really noticed before, so besotted was he with his Maggie, but it had occurred to him earlier that Caroline Connor was a notably attractive woman, and in an *in-your-face-look-at-me* way too, bursting with what fifty years ago would have been called sex appeal. There was no way she was going to be able to walk into this place without attracting the attention of the misogynist neanderthals that called New Gorbals their home. Still, that wasn't his problem. He was here to do a job.

Draining his cup and tossing it expertly into a bin, he got up and set out along the corridor that led to the entrance area. On arrival, he stabbed at the large button that operated the powered doors and stood back as they slowly swung towards him. As they opened, he could see that his visitors had arrived, three of them, Caroline Connor striking in a fitted navy business suit and tight-fitting white blouse, her skirt three inches above the knee, long slim legs accentuated by five-inch power heels. But it wasn't Connor who had caused him to stare open-mouthed with astonishment. It was one of the other two who had evidently accompanied her on the trip north.

'What the bloody hell are you doing here?' he said. 'You kept that bloody quiet, didn't you?'

'I've been like co-opted onto the programme,' Eleanor Campbell said, giving a seraphic smile. 'As *Principle* IT analyst.'

'Principle eh?' Frank said, laughing. 'Is that better than Senior? I guess it is. So am I to suppose they gave you that wee pay rise then to stop you legging it to Zak's firm? Six figures too I hope? Anyway, well done. But you should have told me you were coming up here, I'd have laid on the red carpet treatment. Even bought you a wee coffee.'

She glowered. 'You know I only drink decaf with oat milk, and I doubt if you have that *here*. And it's like *secret*. If I told you, I would have had to kill you.'

'Hey, that's my line,' he said, grinning. 'Anyway, welcome to Glasgow, all of you. Nice weather for this time of year.'

'It's good to be here Frank,' Connor said, with practiced smoothness. 'And this is Giles Harkness, from the Home Office. Giles is running the programme on a day-to-day basis. I'm just here to kick things off.'

Frank stretched out a hand. 'Nice to meet you Giles.' The man looked as if he had barely reached his twenties, and was so skinny that even the slim-cut suit he was wearing fell off his shoulders. One of these entitled fast-track guys no doubt, posh public school in the Home Counties then a PPE degree at Oxford or Cambridge, and here he was, just out of short trousers and in charge of one of the Government's most controversial schemes.

'Good to meet you too Chief Inspector, I'm looking forward to working with you,' Harkness said. In a broad Lancashire accent.

'I've got a wee room,' Frank said, chastened. 'Follow me folks.' He got them settled down then asked, 'So, what's the plan? How do we get started?'

'Well Giles will take you through the full details,' Connor said, 'but I wanted to come up *personally* to thank you again for taking on the project but also just to make sure - and forgive me if this sounds patronising - just to make sure you and your team are fully tuned-in to the highly-sensitive nature of the initiative, if I can put it that way.'

Aye you're right, it is bloody patronising was what he wanted to say but instead he said, 'There's no team right now Caroline. There's just me. And I can assure you I won't be leaking anything about this highly-sensitive initiative to myself. Not even in my sleep.'

To her credit, she laughed. 'No, I'm sure you won't do that Chief Inspector. But is this something you are going to be able to do on your own? Because we're seeing that the first pilot sweep has uncovered a number of potential lines of enquiry and we're worried you may end up with your hands full.'

'No worries,' he said, 'I think I can call in some of my Department 12B team if things get busy and we've also got some resources up here I can get some help from.' That help being in the shape he hoped of DC Lexy McDonald, although whether she would be available was still to be ascertained. 'But I'll be taking a quick look at anything that pops up first, just to make sure it's handled sensitively, just like you've requested.'

'Very good,' she nodded. 'So Giles, perhaps you can bring us up to speed with where we are.'

He smiled. 'Yeah, sure Caroline. So as you know Chief Inspector....'

'Let me stop you there,' Frank said. 'Call me Frank. Please. Both of you. It takes less time, now that you've got to put that *chief* in front of my title.'

'Ok Frank, Giles said, laughing. 'So as you know, we're using this as a pilot project, effectively to test the IT technology, make sure it hangs together when we get to use it in earnest.' He stopped as he caught sight of Eleanor's expression of disapproval . '...Not that we expect any problems in that regard of course.'

'It's how it plays out politically, that's what you're really interested in, isn't it?' Frank said. 'Whether it gets the support of the public or whether they see it as a big-brother intrusion on folks' rights, even if the folks in question are the despised politicians and big-wigs.'

Connor smiled. 'I suspect it will depend on who gets caught in the spotlight and what naughty things they have been doing. But yes, there's an element of that. But we think the public sentiment is strongly anti-corruption right now given the scandals of recent years. Now we'll get to find out if that belief is true.'

He wondered exactly what scandals she was referring to. There was that recent one in her own governing party of course, where the Minister for Overseas Aid had been caught helping himself to some cash aid of his own, but up here in Scotland he couldn't think of anything quite so high-profile. Unless that was if you believed the rumours swirling around the McClelland Tower business, with talk of cash changing hands in brown envelopes and officials enjoying wee holidays out in Dubai, rumours he very much hoped weren't true. Now of course it was the terrible aftermath of the tragedy that was centre-stage, with the relatives of the loved ones getting organised and beginning to speak out, but even with that, the rumours of corrupt practices were still circulating. It would be interesting if anything connected with that business came out of the pilot, that was for sure.

'I suppose we will,' he said. 'So Giles, give us the details.'

'Okay,' he said. 'We've chosen one hundred individuals for the initial pilot sweep and though they are from occupational groups we have specifically identified, the individuals themselves have been chosen at random. Approximately half of them are senior police officers and the other half are senior civil servants in the Scottish government. We've also selected a small handful of elected representatives too. One or two from the parliament and one or two from the big city councils.'

'Look, I thought we had agreed to keep the politicians out of it this time around?' Frank said, not hiding his annoyance. 'That's what we said.'

Connor smiled. 'Yes, but this is just one or two across the political spectrum. For fairness.'

Frank shook his head in disgust. 'What you mean is, in case it all comes out? So that you can pretend to be even-handed? Everyone in this together?'

'Well, it's you that wanted the politicians excluded,' she said, looking smug. 'You can't have it all ways.'

'Aye, I suppose so,' he said grudgingly. 'But I wouldn't mind seeing which of them are on that list.'

'Don't worry, they're all nobodies,' Harkness said, 'if that doesn't sound too cruel. Nobody that anyone would have heard of, here or anywhere else. It's a tick-box exercise.'

Frank shrugged. 'Well I hope you're right. But as far as the guys who *are* on it are concerned, am I right in thinking we've been sweeping all over cyberspace to track down any dodgy cash that may have come their way? Is that it in a nutshell?'

'Like *cyberspace*? Eleanor said, giving him a sarcastic look. 'You don't even know what cyberspace is, do you? Like *obviously*. And anyway, we don't have that anymore.'

Frank laughed. 'But I *do* know what it is as it happens. It's wires. Lots of wires, all joined together, many of them under the sea. But if we don't have cyberspace anymore, what do we have? Come on then Miss Clever-Dick, tell us.'

She shrugged. 'It's the metaverse. Everybody knows that.'

'I'll write that down,' he said. 'So getting back to the point, we sweep this new metaverse thingy looking for bad stuff and then what?'

'We've done a spreadsheet,' Giles said. 'We started with the simple top-level sweep. It looks at their salaries and makes an estimate of their outgoings and compares it with their assets. Specifically bank accounts, homes and cars. It then red-flags if there's an obvious mismatch or yellow flags if it might be worth digging a little further.'

'That's the *simple* sweep is it?' Frank said, impressed.

Giles nodded. 'In the top-level sweep we're just looking at UK financial institutions. The deep sweep goes international and seeks out deliberately-hidden assets. That's stage two and we've not run that yet for this group of individuals. With that technology, we've got access to the dark web too, although Eleanor can explain the ins and outs of all of that much better than me.'

Having been on the end of one too many of Miss Campbell's technical elucidations, Frank was prepared to dispute that assertion. But luckily, she took the matter into her own hands with what he took to be a précis.

'The dark web is like way too complicated to explain to *ordinary* people,' she said, without a trace of irony. 'It's mainly virtual, sitting on megaservers on the metaverse infrastructure core. It's like it doesn't actually exist in the real world.'

'Good to know,' Frank said, furrowing his brow. 'Megaservers eh? Can't go wrong with them.'

She glowered at him but said nothing. 'Anyway,' Frank continued. 'I think I'm right in my understanding that you guys have recently done this first-pass or top-level sweep or whatever you call it.'

'That's right,' Giles said, nodding 'And remember, we're looking at UK-held bank accounts and assets only. Property, cars, stuff like that. And lifestyle indicators are on our radar too.'

'Lifestyle indicators?' What are they?'

Giles smiled. 'Expensive holidays, memberships to expensive leisure clubs, trips to major sporting and cultural events and so on.'

'Right, got all of that. So the sixty-four thousand dollar question is, did you find anything? Any red flags as you call them?'

'I think we can say yes to that,' Caroline Connor said, with just a hint of self-satisfaction. 'Three, maybe four persons of interest. Persons who I think would be worthy of an initial investigation, let's put it that way.'

Frank smiled. 'Aye well that's why I'm here. So this spreadsheet....'

Giles reached into his leather attaché case, pulled out a slim notebook computer, laid it on the desk and opened it up.

'Have you not got a wee print-out?' Frank said. 'And I suppose it *would* be a wee one if there's only three or four names on it.'

'This is like the twenty-first century and this material is *secret* as well,' Eleanor said, in another of her voices that was familiar to Frank, this one known to behavioural psychologists as the scolding parent. 'You can't just leave bits of paper lying about for *anyone* to pick up.'

Connor laughed. 'That's you told. But Eleanor does make a fair point. We need to be extremely careful about confidentiality.'

He gave a rueful smile. 'Aye, you're right of course. So come on Giles, spin round the wee computer so I can take a look.'

The civil servant complied, saying, 'You'll see there are four red-flagged names in the top page of the spreadsheet Frank. And as it happens two of them are actually policemen. We wondered in fact if you might know any of them.'

Frank screwed up his eyes to focus on the document, and then let out a grunt prompted by a mixture of surprise and amusement.

'Well I was bloody *talking* to one of them not more than half an hour ago. Would you believe it! This guy here,' he said, pointing to a row of the document. This was a turn up for the books right enough, although he wasn't sure it was one to be applauded. So the Detective Chief Superintendent was on the take was he? If it was true, this was going to have to be handled with more than an ounce of savvy, because Sweeney was a guy to be feared, and now it seemed there might be some unsavoury underworld associates to be considered too. This was one he wasn't going to rush into for sure. Or in fact, rush into at all.

'And what about the other policeman?' Connor said. 'Do you know her too?'

He gave the screen another careful look. 'Aye, Belinda Cresswell. I know *of* her right enough. She was at the Met, one of these fast-track types. She's an assistant Chief Constable up here now isn't she? So what's she supposed to have done then?'

Giles spun the laptop round and peered at the screen for a moment or two, then nodded. 'Ah yeah, the software's flagged an expenditure mismatch. Two Caribbean cruises and a trip to an England rugby match in South Africa.'

Frank laughed. 'Maybe she's got a sugar-daddy.'

Connor gave him a sharp look. 'It is possible for women to be financially successful and independent in this day and age you know.'

He held up his hands in apology. 'I know, honestly it was just a stupid joke. But if it was all legit, I don't suppose her name would be on your wee spreadsheet.'

'True,' she conceded. 'But no doubt the rights and wrongs will emerge in your investigation. This isn't a witch-hunt you know. We'd be delighted if all of these turn out to be nothing at all.'

He gave her a doubtful look. 'Aye, sure you would. So is there anybody else we should be looking at? What I actually mean is, is there anybody a bit easier?'

'There is one person we are particularly interested in,' Giles said. 'Although one that may be a little *controversial*, let's just say.' He spun the laptop back round to face Frank, then jabbed a finger at the screen. 'This fellow here.'

Frank recognised the name immediately. A fellow whom he knew to be a very senior official in the Procurator's office, a fellow powerful enough to decide which criminal cases came to court and which ones were quietly dropped, and a fellow with the ear of the highest echelons of government.

That being the fellow who was presently married to first minister Sheila McClelland.

Chapter 7

By luck the next train out of King's Cross was the fast one and in less than an hour Yash was striding purposefully out through the elegant arched entrance of Cambridge railway station in search of a cab that would take him onwards to his meeting place. But of course that was him all over, he reflected. *Purposeful*. Yash Patel, a man on a mission to make a name for himself, by uncovering the biggest and most lurid stories in the land. And as for this one, well he could smell it in his blood. This was going to be bloody huge, a scandal that would rock the Scottish government to its core. The trouble was, that was all he had at the moment, a basic hunch that something about the whole affair stank to high heaven. No real facts yet, at least not any that would pass the scrutiny of the paper's super-sensitive legal team. But hopefully this Professor Bates woman would have something to give him that would lead to the breakthrough he'd been searching for.

'Bullard Labs mate,' he shouted as he jumped into the back of the first taxi on the rank. 'I've got the postcode if you don't know where it is.'

The driver grunted an indistinct reply, punched a couple of buttons on his display screen then flicked the indicator stalk as he made to pull out. Fine, Yash thought, I can't be arsed with these chatty ones anyway, the ones that think they're entitled to an opinion on anything even if they know sod-all about the subject. He relaxed back in his seat, took out his phone and swiped down to his address book. Right, he'd give the Scottish guy one more try and if he didn't hear from him later that day, then the job was going to someone else.

He listened as the call connected and then rang. And rang and rang. No answer, again. *Hello, this is Ally, if you leave your number and a wee message I'll get back to you soon as I can. Cheerio.* Well sod it, Yash thought, there must be a thousand guys with boats on that loch that would take him and his photographer to Inchcailloch. Because that was the plan, to sneak back onto the islet and take some photographs for the Sunday magazine. *Exclusive: The Pictures They Don't Want You to See.* The editor was excited about the feature and had already reserved a twelve-page slot for next month. And of course the name and mug-shot of Yash Patel was going to be all over it. *Dippy-dippy-do.* That would be something to look forward to, big-time.

'We're here,' the driver said, pulling up outside an nondescript two-storey office block. 'That'll be fourteen quid.'

Yash took out his wallet and removed two notes. 'Here's fifteen mate. Keep the change.'

Elizabeth Bates turned out to be nothing like he'd imagined her, his expectation framed by the movie stereotype of professors as being old with mad hair. Professor Bates was neither old nor especially hirsute. Probably late thirties he guessed and if truth be told, rather unremarkable in the looks department. Glancing at her wedding finger, he noted too the absence of a ring. Not surprising really, given her distinct plainness. He suspected she might be one of these sad academics who were married to their work in the absence of anything more exciting going on in their lives. Cruel, yeah, but probably true. But then he remembered about Cambridge Geotechnic Partners, the firm of which she was a director, and it turned out, the founder too. The other day he'd looked up their details on one of these companies' websites and found out that last year they'd had a turnover approaching two million pounds, which was not at all shabby, and caused him to reflect that perhaps his unconsidered assessment of her life might need some rapid revision. You could do a lot with two million quid a year, and for a moment he found himself wondering how Professor Bates spent the impressive mountain of cash she must have raked in.

'We'll go to our refectory and grab a coffee if that's okay,' Bates said pleasantly. 'My office here is tiny and I've only got one chair.'

'Sounds great.'

'I was wondering why you decided to come to meet me in person,' she said as she led him along the corridor that evidently led to the eating-place, 'because what I know about the McClelland Tower business is all pretty sketchy. I don't think it will take more than five or ten minutes to cover it.'

'It's just what I do,' Yash said. 'A story only comes to life for me when I've seen the locations and met the actors in the flesh.' And it was true. His best stories had always came to him fully-formed like movies in his mind, imagining them in three dimensions, as if he was a director of a Hollywood block-buster. And Cambridge University was an iconic institution, known and respected all round the world. It was only right that it should be awarded a starring role in this story.

'So I'm one of your actors?' she said in an amused tone. 'Should I be honoured?'

He laughed. 'Sorry, I know it sounds vaguely insulting, but it's not meant to be. As I said, it's just the way I see things in my head. It's odd I admit , but I've always worked this way.'

She directed him to a table near the door then went off to fetch their drinks, returning a minute or so later with a tray and two mugs.

'Cheers,' Yash said. 'So obviously, I was excited by your e-mail, although much of the detail I confess was a bit technical for me.'

'Yes, I'm sorry,' she said, smiling, 'but us geeks find it difficult to speak in plain English.'

'No problem. So maybe you could give me a quick run-through, and as fast as you like. I'm conscious that I don't want to take up too much of your valuable time.'

She laughed. 'You've made all that effort to come so I'm sure I can stretch it to half an hour at least. Anyway, let me start by asking if you've heard of Oresund Civil Engineering?'

He shook his head. 'Afraid not.'

'That's not surprising, it's a rather specialist field. But they're one of Europe's largest Civil Engineering consultancies, really big in their field. The firm was spun out of several Scandinavian university departments about twenty years ago, when Sweden and Denmark were building the Oresund link between Malmo and Copenhagen. It was one of the most impressive feats of civil engineering in the world when it was built, and still is in my opinion. It's sixteen kilometres long and they had to build a bridge, a tunnel and create an artificial island in the process. It was a massive undertaking. Quite stunning. And they had a *lot* of geophysical complexity to be dealt with.'

'Oh yeah, I remember that TV programme, *The Bridge* wasn't it? Somebody was murdered halfway across it as I recall. Great programme.'

'That's right. But the point is, Oresund are probably the leading firm in the world when it comes to construction projects that involve challenging geophysical environments. It's their speciality.'

'Okay,' he said slowly. 'And so they had some involvement in the tower project did they?'

She nodded. 'The scheme was conceived by the Scottish government when the UK was still in the EU, you know, pre-Brexit and all that. And under EU rules, projects of that type involving significant expenditure of public money had to go out to general tender. So with Oresund's track-record and experience, it was a no-brainer that they should be one of the contenders. But obviously it costs a huge amount of money to put together a bid for this size of project so they always like to do some desk-based feasibility work before they start deploying expensive resources on-site.'

He nodded. 'Which, I'm guessing, is where you come in.'

'Indeed,' she said. 'My little firm has worked with Oresund for quite a number of years now on lots of projects. We provide them with detailed reports of the geophysical environment of a proposed site, so that they can assess the complexity and feasibility of any proposed project. Basically, it informs them whether it is worth bidding on a scheme or not.'

'I can see the value in that, at least I think I can,' he said, furrowing his brow. 'So they asked your firm to take a look at this one?'

'They did and it was a very interesting job. Yash, I'm guessing you won't have heard of the Highland Boundary Fault.'

He laughed. 'You guessed right. What is it?'

'I'll show you.' She unfolded a sheet of paper she had been carrying and laid it on the table facing him. 'You'll at least recognise the map of Scotland I assume? So you see that diagonal line running across it? That's the geological boundary between what are usually described as the Lowlands and the Highlands.'

He scrutinised the map for a moment then said, 'Okay... and that means that there are different rocks on either side of the line then does it? That's what I'm guessing.'

She nodded. 'Actually, that's not a bad way of putting it. But look here,' she said, pointing, 'do you see where it runs?'

'Bloody hell,' he exclaimed. 'It goes right across Loch Lomond, doesn't it?'

'Not just that. If you look closely, you'll see it runs right through the middle of the island of Inchcailloch. Right through it.'

He paused for a moment as he tried to process the implications of what she was telling him.

'So, that means what? That it's dangerous to build a tower or something like it right on top of this fault?'

She shook her head. 'Well not necessarily dangerous. The Boundary fault isn't like the ones you find in New Zealand for example which are dangerously unstable and cause these terrible earthquakes. But it does lead to very challenging geological conditions on the ground. I won't go into the boring technical details but in layman's terms it means you can have a complex and inconsistent mix of very soft rocks and very hard rocks in just a few cubic metres of ground.'

'And so I'm guessing all of this would have been covered in the work you did for these Oresund guys?'

'Exactly', she said. 'My work explained how difficult and costly it would be to engineer the foundations for such a heavy structure as the tower. My report in fact questioned the feasibility of it being able to be done at all.'

He gave her a puzzled look. 'How do you mean?'

She shrugged. 'Again, I don't want to be over-technical, but to support a structure like this would need extensive piling. And the problem is, with so many hard rocks in the geological mix, it might in fact prove impossible to do at all. There are some rocks there that are just practically impossible to drill through. But you might not find that out until you'd drilled down a couple of hundred metres and already spent a few million pounds in the process.'

'And all of this was covered in your report?'

'It was. And I'm immodest enough to think my summary was instrumental in their decision not to proceed with a bid.'

Yash could feel his excitement growing as his mind raced ahead, already composing the devastating paragraphs that would send the Edinburgh government into a tailspin.

'And this summary of yours, what did it say? If you don't mind me asking?'

She laughed. 'I'm sorry Yash, it was rather full of complicated engineering jargon as usual I'm afraid. But for once it's quite straightforward to put it in layman's terms and that's exactly what I did for them too.'

She paused for a moment then said, 'Basically, I told them not to touch it with a barge-pole. Not in a million years.'

'But yet the Scottish government still went ahead with the project. So how did that come about do you know?'

She gave a wry smile. 'They found their own expert. Dougal McCrae is his name. He's a *professor* at the University of Glasgow. The way she phrased it made it clear what she thought about this Professor McCrae. 'Quite convenient, don't you think?'

'So this guy said it would be okay did he?'

'That guy didn't know what he was talking about,' she said acerbically. 'But yes, he said it would be okay.'

Yash smiled. 'I bet he wished he hadn't said that now.'

She shrugged. 'I wouldn't be so sure of that. Everyone involved is in denial. I think *act of God* is now the official explanation. Which is very useful as a cover-up mechanism.'

'So you think that's what going on? A cover up?'

'Don't you? It was a terrible storm that New Year's Eve, but as many commentators have pointed out, no other buildings in Scotland fell over that night. So if it was an act of God, he was very specific and very cruel in his target.'

'And have they asked you or Oresund to present at this public enquiry that's about to start?' Patel asked.

'Of course not,' she said, giving a cynical smile. 'But they have naturally invited Professor McCrae.'

'Bloody hell,' he said, his mind leaping ahead once again to his next submission of copy to his annoying editor Rod Clark.

For this was a story that just kept giving and giving.

Chapter 8

There was no doubt about it, with the move and everything that went with it they'd got a bit behind schedule on the Juliet McClelland investigation, which is why Maggie had decided they should divide and separate in the follow-ups to the meeting with Juliet's father Willie Paterson. Maggie would head across the river to interview the two medical students, now doctors, who had shared a flat with Juliet, and Jimmy would wander the few hundred yards down the road to speak to the agency boss Francis Cramond.

Mentally, she did the calculation. Ten weeks, that's how long they'd been in Glasgow now, and already it felt as if her previous life barely existed. Of course the change had been momentous, and not just in a geographical sense either. Because now she was actually *living* with Frank Stewart, sharing a bed and an en-suite bathroom and a kitchen and a television remote control, things she hadn't had to do for over two years, ever since her first marriage fell apart. The bed bit she liked, very much indeed. The kitchen, less so, since Frank had turned out to be borderline-obsessive in his need to wash up and tidy away after they had prepared even the simplest of dishes. And as for the TV, he, probably quite understandably given his day-job, refused to watch a single crime drama, a genre that she loved. But all-in-all, they weren't the hardest of adjustments to make, she knew that, in what she saw as a dress-rehearsal for the blissful married life that was just around the corner, and the most important thing was that little Ollie had settled into his new school and his new life with no obvious problems. Still, just *once* she would have liked to have caught a bloody episode of *Vera*.

It was no more than a twenty-minute drive through the tunnel, the traffic slow but steady at this busy time of the morning, and she easily found a parking space in the multi-storey that adjoined the main hospital building. It was a two-minute walk to reach the entrance atrium, a huge and imposing space that seemed to reach all the way up through the centre of the massive eleven-or-twelve storey structure. She'd read somewhere that this newish hospital, built a few years earlier on the site of an old Victorian infirmary, had not been without its problems, something to do with pigeon poo infesting the air-conditioning system she seemed to recall, but now it couldn't help but impress with its shininess and scale. A mezzanine, suspended fifty feet or so above the ground level, hosted the cafe facility where she had arranged to meet the two young doctors. Doctor Rob McNair had helpfully sent a picture of himself when they had made the arrangements, but this morning the place was a sea of medical staff in their uniforms and scrubs and as a result it wasn't easy to pick out any one individual. But after scanning the room for a while she finally spotted them, sitting at a table more or less in the middle of the cafe.

'Hello,' she said, smiling as she approached their table. 'I'm Maggie Bainbridge, but you've probably guessed that already.'

'Hi Maggie,' McNair said, getting to his feet. 'I'm Rob and this is Doctor Rebecca Johnson.'

'Becky,' the woman said.

They were an attractive pair, Maggie thought, this Rob and Becky, he tall with a mop of tight dark curls, she a slight and slim blonde with seductive saucer eyes, a tiny turned-up nose and a full mouth. What were they, twenty-five, twenty-six? Everyone was attractive at that age, and here they were with the world at their feet, embarking on a career that although challenging was also meaningful, an occupation that made a difference to people's lives. Not like being a bloody lawyer she thought with some bitterness, where you made a difference to people's lives all right, but not in a good way. But attractive though they undoubtedly were, they also looked pretty knackered, a consequence she assumed of their current assignment to the A&E department.

'Thank you for agreeing to see me,' Maggie said. 'I know it must have been very difficult for you both to fit me in.'

'We've just come off shift,' Becky said. 'Twelve hours and it's non-stop. But hey, that's what we signed up for.'

'I couldn't do it,' Maggie said. 'It would kill me after a couple of days, I know it would.'

McNair gave a rueful smile. 'We're meant to say you get used to it, but you really don't. But anyway, you're here to talk about Juliet, not the hardships of junior hospital doctors.'

Maggie nodded. 'And I apologise in advance because I know it must be a very painful subject for you both. As I said in my phone-call, her father, mother and step-father have commissioned my firm to take another look into what happened, and I'm hoping you might be able to help us.'

'I don't see how,' Becky said, quite sharply. 'She just disappeared that night. We saw her at lectures in the afternoon, and that was the last anyone saw of her. We went over it all with the police at the time. About a dozen times at least.'

'I appreciate that, but I think what I was hoping for was perhaps some insight into her state of mind at the time of her disappearance. You know, was she maybe worried about something, perhaps her studies, or maybe something else. Like a relationship for example.'

She had chosen the words quite deliberately, given Willie Paterson's belief that Juliet and McNair may have been something more than just flatmates. And looking at their suddenly anxious expressions she knew she had struck a raw nerve. *Not bad after just a couple of minutes.*

'What have you heard?' Becky said, her tone suddenly a mixture of aggression and concern. 'Who have you been talking to?'

'Nobody, other than her parents and step-father.' Maggie paused for a moment as she considered what to say next. Originally she had been disappointed that she wasn't going to be able to speak to the pair individually, but now she could see the advantage in seeing them together. If they had something to hide, the chances are they would have conspired to make sure their stories were consistent, but in Maggie's experience you could always spot that fakery a mile off. There was always something just too *off-pat* about that sort of thing, something you could always see through. But McNair's response surprised her.

'Yeah sure, Juliet and me had been quite close I suppose, at one time,' he said. 'But it was nothing *serious*. You know, just one of these casual student things.'

Maggie smiled. 'I'm afraid it's been quite a while since I was at Uni.' She was silent for a second then said, 'So forgive my bluntness, but does that mean you were sleeping together?'

If McNair was offended, he didn't show it. 'Yes we were as it happens, but *everybody* does that, don't they?' he said smoothly. 'That's what being a student is all about, wouldn't you say? Sex, drugs and rock and roll. It doesn't mean anything, it's just what you do at that point in your life.'

'And at the time of Juliet's disappearance, were you still in that relationship?'

He laughed, a condescending sneer that Maggie found particularly grating. 'It wasn't a *relationship* as you call it, it was just *sex*. But no, we hadn't had a *shag* for quite some time if that's what you are asking. Folks move on, don't they? That's what happens. It's natural. Pastures new and all that.'

It had only taken Maggie two minutes to decide she didn't like this arrogant arsehole one bit. She was tempted to say something which showed it but managed to bite her lip. Instead she said,

'And was it you who had moved on to pastures new, as you put it, or was it Juliet?'

'Do you mean, did she dump me? No, that didn't happen, no way. As if.' He laughed again, and Maggie couldn't help notice the look he exchanged with Becky Johnson. 'It just came to a sort of natural end,' he continued. 'A sort of mutual decision, without anything actually being said, if you know what I mean.'

'And this fizzling out, if I can call it that. When exactly was it?'

McNair shrugged. 'I don't know. Four or five months before she disappeared, something like that.'

'So I'm guessing that might have been about the time she decided to move out of the flat.' Without waiting for an answer, she said, 'Do you think the ending of your relationship was what motivated her decision? Because I guess it would have been very difficult for her to continue living at the flat when it had come to its natural end, as you describe it.'

'Juliet was a big girl,' Becky said, quite coldly. 'These things happen in life and you need to be able to deal with them, don't you? I mean, people are breaking up all the time.'

What a horrible young woman, Maggie thought, so smug and callous and dripping with self-satisfaction. She was pretty sure now what had been going on in that household, the minxy Becky Johnson setting her sights on her tall handsome flatmate, and no doubt getting extra pleasure from the devastation of her supposed friend Juliet when her conquest had turned out successfully. But perhaps she was being unfair. Maybe the McNair-Juliet thing had genuinely come to its natural end as he'd said and he'd then felt free to take up with their mutual flatmate. It was a bit lacking in class perhaps, but it wasn't against the law.

'So why *do* you think she decided to move out?' Maggie asked. 'If it wasn't to do with the break-up?'

Becky shrugged. 'I'm sure I don't know. Maybe she was fed up living in our scruffy hovel. To be honest, it was going to be a bit of a relief for Rob and me. I hated the police coming round every week, sniffing about the place.'

Maggie looked surprised. 'And why was that? Why were the police visiting you every week?'

'Security of course,' McNair said. 'Juliet's mummy is not *universally* popular in Scotland, despite what her propagandists will try to tell you. And there's a lot of bam-pots out there believe me who might want to do the McClellands harm. So yeah, they sent a thick copper round once a week to check the locks and stuff like that, make sure we didn't go out and leave the front door on the latch. Obvious stuff.'

It was something that Maggie hadn't thought of before, but on reflection it was quite obvious. Although Juliet's mother divided opinion, she was still First Minister, and as McNair had said, there was probably no shortage of inadequates seeking their fifteen minutes of fame.

'And had there been actual threats?' she asked. 'I mean in the period leading up to Juliet's disappearance?'

'I don't think so,' McNair said. 'And I'm sure she would have said if there had been.'

'So anything else?' Maggie said, sensing the interview was approaching its natural conclusion. 'Anything else that might explain what happened to her that night?'

McNair shook his head. 'I've gone over it again and again, but no, I can't think of anything. Really I can't. And I've tried, believe me.' And just in that moment, Maggie saw a glimmer of sadness in his eyes. Maybe, just maybe, his relationship with Juliet hadn't been as casual as he was trying to make out. Maybe it had been her that had ended it, leaving him hurt and even angry at the slight to his precious ego. But had he been angry enough to do something crazy, and been prepared to wait four or five months to do it? However much she disliked the guy, it didn't seem likely.

'Well thank you both,' she said, getting to her feet. 'You've got my contact details. If you think of anything else, please let me know.'

As she walked to her car, she reflected on what she had just heard and what she had previously found out about the police investigation from reading Asvina's case-notes. Because the one thing that hadn't been mentioned in anything she'd seen or read about the case was what she now saw as the obvious conclusion. Which was that Juliet, inwardly devastated by her break-up with McNair and struggling to hold it together, had that day suddenly cracked and decided without any premeditation to take her own life. Maggie had looked at the map of the West End only yesterday and realised that the University was about five minutes walk to the River Kelvin and not much more than ten to the Clyde itself. Surely that was the most likely scenario, a sudden mental breakdown and a short walk to the riverbank before Juliet McClelland threw herself in to the freezing water, her lungs quickly filling up and extinguishing the life from her, the current sweeping her body downstream and onward to the cold Irish Sea.

And then suddenly a wave of dread swept through her as she thought of Jimmy. He'd been through so much in recent years, particularly the terrible loss of that young sergeant out in Belfast, a loss he continued to blame himself for and which she knew he still had nightmares about. Then there was the break-up of his marriage to Flora, culminating with the recent news that she was to re-marry. That sort of stuff would be hard enough for anyone to take, but like all these ex-army guys, he was good at holding it all in so that nobody knew what was really going on inside his head. But *she* knew, and now, quite out of the blue she feared for him. She would need to sit him down, talk to him, find out how he was really feeling.

And she had to do it *right now*.

***

The rain had settled to a light drizzle as Jimmy weaved his way down Byers Road, the busy pavement an obstacle course of students with umbrellas, which to him seemed an unnecessary encumbrance on what was pretty much a dry day by Glasgow standards. In five minutes time he'd be meeting with the agency woman, and he was very much looking forward to it. It was great that the Juliet McClelland investigation was now finally up and running, because God how he needed something to focus on, something to distract his mind, something to stop him feeling so utterly awful inside.

He'd seen it time and time again with shed-loads of his army mates, when one day and completely out of the blue it suddenly all became too much to take. Some turned to drink, some to violence, some walked away from everything they loved, but way too few turned to anyone for help. You were a soldier, honed on the battlefield, a rough tough guy who'd experienced stuff that the ordinary bloke in the street just couldn't imagine. So what were you going to do, phone some stupid do-gooder on a helpline and say *I'm feeling shit*? No way, that was never going to happen, not in a month of Sundays. And now here he was, in pretty much the same boat as the rest of them, desperately trying to shake off the feelings of despair but not exactly succeeding. He knew what he should do of course was to talk to Frank or Maggie about it, but that would have been stupidly selfish, in particular after all Maggie had been through. Now finally she was in a great place and looking forward to marrying his daft brother. What right did he have to upset their sweet little apple-cart? *None whatsoever.*

The offices of Cramond Staffing occupied a double shop-front premises on the Dumbarton Road, not entirely unlike their own embryonic establishment, although a lot bigger and a whole lot more swish too. The open-plan ground floor hosted seven or eight desks, occupied by staff wearing polo-shirts bearing the company's logo, chattering away on their headsets. A spiral staircase in one corner suggested the presence of further worker-bees on the first floor. Running along the full length of the back wall was a glass-fronted private office, which Jimmy assumed would be that of the boss Francis Cramond. Just as he was about to make enquiries, a woman descended the staircase and made her way towards him, hand outstretched in greeting.

'Mr Stewart I presume? Jimmy, isn't it?'

He smiled. 'That's right. Mrs Cramond?'

'Francis,' she said. 'And it's Miss. I used to be Mrs McBride but I dumped the name and the husband that went with it a while back. Anyway, follow me into my lair. I've got a coffee machine, it brews quite nice stuff and more importantly it's not too complicated for me to work.'

'Sounds great,' he said, glad that he evidently wasn't expected to make any comment about her marital status. He guessed she was about fifty, and she was quite nice looking too, although a bit over-made-up for his taste. She wore a navy dress with an elegant string of pearls which although no expert, he guessed were of the expensive variety, like the ones he'd often seen Maggie's friend Asvina Rani wearing.

'Take a seat,' she said, as she slid a mug under the nozzle of the drinks dispenser. 'Coffee, tea?'

'Coffee, white no sugar please. Francis, it's very good of you to see me, I think I explained on the phone what it was all about.'

He had indeed explained on the phone, and the truth was it hadn't been that easy to persuade her to accept the meeting, it being her opinion that there was nothing she could add to what she had already told the police. But there had been something in the tone of her voice that made him wonder if there was more to it than that, which made him rather more persistent than he might ordinarily have been. He'd tried to explain how much the grieving parents were still suffering and how this investigation was perhaps their last opportunity to find some sort of peace, and eventually he had overcome her reluctance. But today, she seemed perfectly calm and relaxed. Perhaps she had just been busy.

'Juliet was on your books, if that's the right terminology,' Jimmy said. 'And she often got work up at the Auchterard hotel? Is that right?'

Cramond nodded. 'Yes, it's a very good contract for us and it works really well for them too. I don't know if you know the place Jimmy, but it's seriously up-market. It's super-swish and they have their championship-standard golf course right on the lochside, and all that makes it a huge attraction for wealthy American and Japanese golf fans in particular. And so obviously having top-quality staff is critical to the whole experience. We're lucky that we have a fantastic pool of nicely-spoken well-educated young people right here on our doorstep so it's a win-win. The young people get double the hourly rate they would get for ordinary bar-work here in the city and the tips are pretty amazing too. So we have no shortage of applicants and we can pick the very best.'

'And Juliet was one of the best?' Jimmy asked. 'I assume so.'

'She was. She was a stunning-looking girl but with a lovely way about her too. One in a million really. Such a tragedy.'

Jimmy nodded. 'Aye it was, which is why we're involved. Do you mind if I ask you, what was Juliet's mood in the weeks leading up to her disappearance?'

Her reply took him a little by surprise. 'I've absolutely no idea. I only ever met her once you see, when I conducted the initial interview for her job at the Auchterard. The client insists on it, that I vet all their candidates personally. But after we take them on, my staff manage the day-to-day business. Most communication will actually be electronic, you know, texts and the like. We don't tend to have to speak to our staff very often at all. Only if there's a complication with a roster perhaps. But generally it all goes pretty smoothly.

It's a horrible thing to say, but once we take them on, they're just a name on a spreadsheet.'

'And Juliet hadn't caused you any problems, meaning you or one of your team have had cause to speak with her?'

Cramond shook her head. 'No, not that I'm aware of. She was a generally reliable girl and seldom gave us any problems at all.' She gave him a sympathetic look. 'As I said on the phone Jimmy, I can't really see how I can help you.'

For a moment he was silent as he struggled with where to go next with the interview. Then he said, 'So when did you first hear about the situation? Her disappearance I mean. Because presumably there was some come-back to the agency from the hotel when she didn't turn up for her shift?'

She smiled. 'We have a management duty roster that covers twenty-four-seven, but I'm not on it myself of course. I do know the hotel phoned the member of staff who was on duty that night to report it but unfortunately there was nothing we could do at such short notice. We phoned around trying to get a last-minute replacement but no-one was available. So in answer to your question, I didn't hear about it until nearly four days later, when the police called me to ask some questions.'

'Okay,' Jimmy said, thinking furiously. 'So what about some of the other staff you place at the hotel? Were any of them particularly close to Juliet do you know? Because I'd like to ask them about her state of mind around the time of her disappearance.'

She shrugged. 'I wouldn't know that and I doubt even if any of my staff would know either. But you could ask Phoebe Wilson, she's the member of our team who has most dealings with the Auchterard. She's not in today but I'll text you her number.'

'Aye, that would be great,' he said. 'And what about the people up at the hotel, like the managers? Did they ever talk to you about it afterwards?'

She shook her head. 'They did offer their condolences of course, but no they didn't say anything specific about Juliet. As I said, there were never really any issues with her. She was generally reliable and everything just went pretty seamlessly from our point of view.'

He'd only been here for less than ten minutes but already he was beginning to think that the visit had been a bit of a waste of time, given that Francis Cramond seemed to be unable to add any meaningful insight into Juliet McClelland's state of mind or what might have happened to her. Maybe he would have to take a trip up to the Auchterard himself and see if any of the folks up there had anything to add. But right now, it seemed there wasn't much more he could do here.

'Aye, well thanks for your time Francis,' he said, getting up from his chair. 'I appreciate it.'

She smiled. 'I hope I was some help.' She hadn't been, but he wasn't going to say that. Instead he gave a thumbs-up and made for the door saying, 'And I'll give you a wee buzz if I think of anything else.'

As he passed through the front office, he became aware there was some sort of a hullabaloo going on. One of the desks along the side wall had one of these big shiny helium balloons attached to it, advertising that the occupant had evidently just turned thirty years of age. On cue, a raucous but notably tuneless rendition of *happy birthday to you* started up, and he smiled as the recipient of the accolade got to her feet and made an embarrassed bow. The performance was reaching its conclusion just as he opened the front door to step into the street, and he paused for a moment to listen to the final line of the song.

Happy birthday dear Phoebe, happy birthday to you.

He looked at the birthday girl closely, making sure he would recognise her the next time he saw her. Because there *definitely* was going to be a next time.

Chapter 9

Maggie's relocation northwards hadn't been without its challenges of course, that was only to be expected given the enormity of the change, but one thing at least had gone spectacularly well. Much to her great pleasure, her little gang had found a new Thursday-evening pub to replace Shoreditch's iconic Old King's Head, this one a traditional Glasgow corner bar on the Great Western Road just a couple of streets up from the office. The Horseshoe Bar it was named, and it made up in relaxed conviviality what it lacked in luxurious appointments. Frank had explained that in its heavy-industry heyday, the city had a bar on just about every corner, where on a Friday night the working man, set free after five days of back-breaking toil, would happily squander his wee wage-packet drowning in a sea of alcoholic beverage. Back then experienced wives would be waiting at the gate of the shipyard or locomotive works to extract the week's housekeeping money, a habit it didn't take long for newly-weds to adopt once the early rose-tinted days of marriage had inevitably evaporated. But nowadays, there really was no such thing as the working man, and nobody got their wages in little brown envelopes anymore, although she conceded there was plenty of work that even today was rewarded by a wad of banknotes stuffed into a back pocket. The plumbers, joiners, electricians, the legions of skilled self-employed tradesmen who serviced the nation's householders, not many of them would turn down a lucrative cash-in-hand job if it was offered to them. She supposed that it was this group who were today's equivalent, and this evening as she surveyed the bar-room she saw plenty of them in evidence, muscular guys in jeans and sweatshirts, most still wearing their work-boots, clutching pints and laughing with their mates.

Evidently Frank had caught her looking and gave her a wry smile.

'See anything you fancy, do you? Although to be fair, they all look a wee bit young for you.'

She laughed. 'Bloody cheek. And a lot of young guys fancy the more mature woman, that's what I've read in my magazines. So you just watch your step Frank Stewart.'

He leant over and kissed her on the cheek. 'So looks like it's back to the gym for me then. If I'm going to be in competition with these chunky fellas.'

Jimmy gave him a playful thump on the shoulder. 'What do you mean, *back* to the gym? You don't even have the strength to open their front door.'

'Nor the inclination bruv, believe me,' Frank said, laughing. 'And anyway, there's no need, looking the way I do. But come on, it looks like these glasses are emptying fast. Time you got to the bar Jimmy-boy and topped us up.'

Maggie smiled to herself, listening to his brother's ritual protests as he made for the bar. Once again she considered how fortunate she had been that Captain Jimmy Stewart had turned up out of the blue at that recruitment fair nearly three years ago. Three years during which everything had changed, most of it for the better, and now next spring there was to be a wedding at which incredibly, she would be the bride. Yes, for her everything was fixed up nicely, and now she had to do everything in her power to fix Jimmy too.

'A chardonnay and two wee beers,' Jimmy said on his return, setting the drinks down on the nearby table.

'Cheers mate,' Frank said, grabbing his pint and holding it aloft. 'Oh and I meant to say, my pal Lexy McDonald is going to be joining us later tonight. But I'll sort out her drink when she gets here.'

'That's nice,' Maggie said. 'So how's it all going then? Your secret mission I mean.'

'Very secretly, although there have been developments, that's all I can reveal. But what's not a secret is that somehow Eleanor Campbell's got herself involved. She was up here the other day with that Caroline Connor woman.'

'Sounds like an old rock band getting back together,' Jimmy said, smiling. 'A good band mind you. With quite a few hits to their credit.'

'Hey, less of the old,' Frank said in mock protest. 'I don't think either of *them* have reached thirty and me myself, I'm barely pushing forty.'

'You're forty-four, like me,' Maggie said, laughing. 'You need to embrace it instead of fighting it. Go with the flow. Celebrate the wrinkles.'

'Plenty of them to celebrate,' Frank said. 'Anyway, how's your wee job going? And oh by the way, I'm jealous because yours is the kind of affair that normally ends up with our boys and girls in Department 12B. We specialise in police cock-ups as you're very well aware and I thought we had cornered the market for them.'

'We're a lot cheaper,' Jimmy said, tongue-in-cheek, 'and a wee bit of competition is always healthy. But actually, something interesting happened today at that agency. I've not had a chance to update you yet Maggie, but I wasn't exactly sure that Francis Cramond was telling the whole truth and nothing but the truth. Let's just say I'm going to have an interesting conversation with a wee lassie called Phoebe.'

'I had quite a similar experience with my two doctors,' Maggie said, 'although I think in their case they were telling *some* of the truth but definitely not the whole truth.'

'Sounds interesting,' Jimmy said. 'So it sounds as if we have plenty to follow up on. And on that subject, I think we'll need to take a trip up to Loch Lomond and talk to some of the folks at the Auchterard hotel, see if they can shed any light on Juliet's mood in the days and weeks before she died. Because as far as Cramond was concerned, she wasn't worried about anything at all.'

Frank laughed. 'So you two are going to have a nice day out are you? Just make sure you can get it on expenses because I've heard they charge about ten quid for a coffee and it's another fiver if you want a wee bit of shortbread to go with it. But then again, I don't suppose business is all that great up there at the moment, given what's been kicking off.'

'What's that then?' Maggie asked.

He frowned. 'It's that McClelland Tower business. The relatives of all these poor folks who died have moved their protest to outside the front door of the Auchterard because some numpty put a post on their website suggesting the hotel would be a great place to stay if you want to gawk at the ruins of the tower. You can see it from the front of the place of course, it's only a few hundred yards across the water.'

'That's sick,' Jimmy said. 'Idiots.'

'Aye, they took it down pretty sharpish and blamed it on some spotty lad in their marketing department. But the damage was done. That's why Lexy's been up there, even though she's a DC now. It's all got a bit nasty and it's been a case of all hands to the pump.'

'I notice our old friend Yash Patel has got his teeth into the Tower story now too,' Maggie said. 'They were talking about it this morning on the breakfast news.'

'Aye, did you see that picture a couple of weeks ago of the wee cross standing all on its own?' Frank said. 'That really broke my heart.'

'Yes that was tragic,' Maggie said. 'But now Yash seems to have come up with some other sensation, something about big revelations to come although nothing specific. But what was interesting was that the Scottish government provided a statement from Sheila McClelland saying that her government were aware of the rumours circulating around and that there was no truth in any of them.'

'So what rumours are these?' Frank asked.

Maggie shrugged. 'No idea. But I'm guessing our client Mrs McClelland is sufficiently worried that she saw the need to pre-empt Yash's story. So I'm thinking we'll be hearing a lot more of this in the days and weeks to come.'

'Or even in the next five minutes,' Frank said, laughing as he nodded his head in the direction of the front door. 'Because here's our Lexy, looking remarkably fresh-faced after a day on the barricades.'

'Hello everyone,' Lexy McDonald said brightly, slipping her bag off her shoulder and placing it on the table. 'Sorry I'm a bit late, but I was pretty jammy to get away in the circumstances.' She looked at Frank with a pleading expression. 'And by the way sir, I'm absolutely dying for a drink.'

'My brother will do the business instantly,' he said. 'Pint is it, or a large white wine?'

'Pint please.'

Maggie had only met Lexy a couple of times before although she heard plenty about her from Frank. A freckly red-head who hailed from one of the far-flung islands if she recalled correctly, although she couldn't remember which one and even if she could it wouldn't have meant anything to her given her sketchiness about the geography of these parts. What she did know, courtesy of Frank, was that the twenty-seven-year-old DC McDonald was destined for great things, being blessed with a keen intelligence and a steely determination to go with it, but with an easy personality that made people instantly warm to her. It was a rare combination Maggie thought, so rare that she couldn't recall bumping into a single person who had it in all her twenty years as a not-very-successful barrister. But that wasn't such a surprise she reflected, given her former profession's propensity to attract braying public-school idiots to its ranks. The fact was, most of the sad cases she'd been defending were more likeable than the majority of her former colleagues.

'I don't condone the disruption of course,' Frank said, taking the glass from Jimmy and handing it to Lexy, 'but you've got to feel sympathy for these protestors. The government just wants to sweep the whole thing under the carpet and pretend it never happened, and never mind about the grieving relatives.'

'They were all very nice and polite actually,' Lexy said, taking a generous swig of her beer.

'More sad than angry really. But that's not why I was late. You see, a body's been found. Just a mile or so up the loch, near that Milarrochy visitor centre.'

'What, a *murder*?' Frank said, surprised.

'No doubt about it sir. The guy's been stabbed to death. And with about half-a-dozen deep wounds, from what the SOCOs are telling me. Pretty grizzly altogether, that's what they said.'

'Poor guy. So any idea who the victim is?'

Lexy nodded. 'They've not done the formal identification yet. But a local cop who was at the scene said it was a bloke he vaguely knew. Some guy who owned two or three boats, the kind that take folks on pleasure cruises and the like. He's got them moored up at Ardlui according to the PC.' She took out her phone and swiped down to where she had evidently recorded the name of the victim. 'Yeah, here it is. An Alasdair Russell, known as Ally. In his early fifties or thereabouts they think. They were only just loading up the body to take it to Glasgow when I left.'

'So any idea who's going to be heading up the investigation?' Frank said. 'I expect it's a bit early to say.'

Lexy grimaced. 'The jungle drums are saying DCS Sweeney is going to run with it. So I'm going to try and swerve it if I can. No disrespect to the Super of course sir. But you know what he's like.'

Maggie looked on with amusement as Frank gave a knowing smile, one of relief more than anything she suspected. She didn't know this Sweeney guy, but she did know that Frank badly wanted Lexy McDonald on his team for his mysterious mission, whatever *that* was.

'Well, I'll find plenty for you to do on my investigation,' he said. 'Don't you worry about that. So these protesters, what is they're after?'

Lexy shrugged. 'They're calling for justice, but I'm not sure they know exactly what that means. But with the public enquiry starting in the next couple of weeks, they just want to make their voices heard. And I don't blame them for that.'

'I think that's what Yash's investigation is all about,' Maggie said. 'To stop there being a cover up. Because the narrative being put out by the Scottish government is that it was a terrible accident caused by a freak storm. Which of course, they say, was almost certainly a result of global climate change.'

'Aye, very convenient,' Frank said. 'I just hope for the sake of the victim's families our boy Yash gets to the bottom of it. Because in my opinion it was more than the bloody Scottish weather that caused it.'

Jimmy smiled. 'If he doesn't then it won't be for the want of trying. Because we know what he's like when he gets his teeth into something. Relentless, that's the word isn't it?'

Maggie nodded then glanced at her watch. 'Oops, time for us to go Frank. Ollie's with the babysitter and she'll be wanting double time if we don't get back by half-seven.'

He gave her a thumbs up then proceeded to down his pint in one long swallow, burping unceremoniously as he laid the empty glass on the table.

'Beg your pardon' he said, smiling. 'Ready when you are Maggie. Same place, same time next week, what do you all say?'

There were, quite naturally, no dissenters.

Chapter 10

Junior minister Caroline Connor and her sidekick Giles had naturally supplied Frank with a copy of the spreadsheet spewed out by the debut sweep of the UK government's fancy new *UWIPO* software system, and now there it lay, taking centre-stage on his new desk at New Gorbals nick. In fact it had lain there for nearly two days now, he doing nothing much more than staring at it mournfully as he tried to figure out what to do next. Such was the disturbing and frankly incendiary nature of its revelations that he expected it to burst into flames at any minute. Actually he would have given quite a lot for it to just disappear, but no, as he shot it another rueful glance, it was still there, taunting him. He reflected that the most attractive option at the moment was to stick it at the bottom of a pile marked *too difficult* and tell Jill Smart that he wanted bugger-all to do with the whole thing. But he knew that would get short shrift, with no prospect of a negotiated settlement either. Much as it pained him, he knew there was nothing for it but to grin and bloody bear it.

Still, it wasn't all doom and gloom, because if the slippery Sweeney really had been up to no good, it would be a great pleasure to bring him to book and make no mistake. The trouble was, that particular course of action came with a pretty huge risk of causing unpleasant collateral damage to himself and any other officer who might get in the way of the inevitable backlash. So if he was going to pursue the Super- as was his clear duty, there was no doubt about *that* - it would have to be undertaken with the greatest of care and no little cunning too. And if that wasn't difficult enough, there was the question of what to do with Mr Andrew McClelland, or the *first husband* as the papers up here had dubbed him. He was one powerful fella in his own right before you even considered who he was married to. *Bloody hell*.

One thing had been puzzling him though, and that was why McClelland was on the list in the first place. With Sweeney, it was fairly obvious. The spreadsheet listed things like his salary - nearly seventy grand per annum, about ten times what he was worth in Frank's sour opinion- , his assets - a house in the posh suburb of Newton Mearns worth about four hundred thousand but with a three-hundred-and-fifty grand mortgage on it. So the Chief Super was pretty well-off by most standards but not outside the means of a forty-nine-year-old who'd enjoyed a steady rise to the top of his profession, however unmerited that rise might have been. No, the reason he was on the list seemed to be down to the cars. It appeared his driveway was graced with three vehicles worth more than a hundred and fifty thousand quid between them- a big executive SUV, a sleek one-hundred-and-eighty-mile-an-hour sports job and a top-of the-range Tesla electric car. Evidently the Super was a car enthusiast, but the question was how could he afford them on his salary? Perhaps there was a legitimate explanation as to how he had acquired the vehicles, but if there was, it was an explanation that Frank would be interested to hear. Although whether it was a conversation he would look forward to was an entirely different matter.

With McClelland however, it was a different story, in fact quite the opposite. What seemed to have shoved him into the red category was a large dollop of cash going *out* of his account, to the tune of nearly six grand a month, leaving as regular as clockwork on the twenty-eighth. That accounted for more than three-quarters of his take-home salary, which according to the spreadsheet was seven-thousand-six-hundred quid a month, that after-tax amount stacking up with the whacking one-hundred-and-forty grand a year he earned from his top job in the Procurator service. Looking at the history, these payments appeared to have been going on all through the preceding two-year period that was in the scope of this initial UWIPO sweep, and got Frank wondering how McClelland could actually afford them, because it certainly didn't leave him with much spare cash to do anything else. Very interesting yes, but it still didn't explain why McClelland was on the list. With some trepidation, he picked up his phone and swiped across to his *favourites*. Aye, that was a misnomer if there ever was one.

She answered first ring with a terse '*Yes?*'

'Oh hi Eleanor, it's Frank here.'

'*Like yeah, it says so on my phone. What do you want? I'm busy.*'

He laughed. 'Aye, always great to speak to you too. Listen, I'll be quick but I've got a question for you, about the UWIPO stuff.'

'*What do you want to know?*'

He smiled to himself. This was a bit more of a positive reaction than he'd been expecting. He said,

'It's about the folks that end up in the red category when they're paying *out* money, not getting it in. But loads of people have to pay out money, you know for the old alimony or big bank loans or that sort of stuff. So what exactly is this all about? Why are they flagged up?'

There was silence at the end of the phone and he wasn't sure if she was thinking or just being awkward.

'*I just write the code,*' she said finally. He waited for her to continue but she didn't.

'Okay....,' he said, not quite sure where to take this next. 'So is that a *don't know*?' Or, he thought, more likely it's a *I do know but I can't be arsed to tell you*. But then he felt a tingling of remorse as he realised he had misjudged her, at the same time relieved that he hadn't let out the sarcastic comment that had been on the tip of his tongue.

'Yeah, I'm just looking at the requirements spec now to see what is says... yeah, I kind of remember now...yeah, that's it.'

'Brilliant,' he said in anticipation. 'So what's the story then?'

'The software should identify any payments over one thousand pounds to bank accounts within jurisdictions that practice non-disclosure of holder's identity.'

'Sorry Eleanor,' he said, 'but what exactly does that mean?'

'I'm just reading what it says in the requirements,' she said testily. *'But what I think it means is the software should flag it up if they're making payments to or receiving payments from an account in places where you can't find out who's account it is.'*

He nodded. 'Okay, that make sense. So I guess we're talking about places like Switzerland and the Cayman Islands. But I thought this first sweep was for the targets' UK stuff only, or did I misunderstand?'

'Nope you're right, it's just their UK income and assets. But the software does track receipts and payments to and from these hidden kind of accounts. It just doesn't dig any deeper in the phase one pass.'

'But I'm guessing it could do? You and Zak and the guys have the capability to do that?'

'Like yeah. But that's not been authorised for use yet. That's not until phase two.'

He nodded. 'Fair enough. And thanks for that Eleanor, that's helped my understanding no end. I'll hang up and let you get on with your real work. I'd imagine that something interesting and important?'

He heard her sigh. *'I guess it's important, but it's not like interesting.'*

'So what is it, if you don't mind me asking?'

She sighed again. *'It's phase two. But it's only a few hundred lines of code. Total dullsville.'*

***

The call had been enlightening but it hadn't really solved Frank's problem as to what he should do next. The clear priority ought to be Chief

Superintendent Sweeney rather than Belinda Cresswell's dodgy holidays, but the more he thought about that, the less he fancied it. Luckily, there was the opportunity to delay the decision for a wee while yet because Lexy had earlier tipped him off by text that Sweeney was already up at the Ally Russell murder scene and would be doing a statement to the media, timed to coincide with the lunchtime news bulletins. He picked up his phone and opened the BBC's media player, something he wouldn't have been able to do even six weeks ago. But since moving into their comfortable rental property, Maggie's wee boy Ollie had taken him under his wing and was dragging him into the twenty-first century when it came to technology. Sweeney was standing with his back to the loch, the location no doubt chosen deliberately by the producer so that the cameras could pick out the ghostly silhouette of the ruined tower in the far distance. He didn't like the bloke of course, and few people did, but there was no doubting that he was a smooth operator. *We've identified the victim as Mr Alasdair Russell, a local man who owned a small fleet of pleasure craft here on Loch Lomond. Our scene-of-crime officers are completing their sweep of the murder scene and Mr Russell's body has been taken to Glasgow for post-mortem. We're appealing to anyone who may have seen anything or anyone in the Milarrochy area in the hours between approximately four o clock in the morning to eight am the next day to come forward. Thank you for your time ladies and gentlemen and we'll of course update you if we have anything else to report.* It was short and sweet and exactly to the point, Sweeney sounding effortlessly commanding and in control. That was the problem with this whole bloody thing. The Chief Super might be a horrible human being but up until now Frank had always seen him as a competent and honest cop. And of course he had been the guy who'd caught the serial killer Denis Northcote, which hadn't done his career any harm at all. But now it seemed he might not be quite as honest as he appeared.

Gloomily Frank played the confrontation scene out in his head. *Can I just have a word sir, if you've got a minute? Aye, it's about these nice cars of yours sir, nearly a hundred and fifty grand's worth if I've got my sums right. Can you explain how you can possibly afford them on your salary?'*

No, he didn't fancy this one little bit, and what if he was wrong? What if there was a perfectly plausible explanation, however improbable that was? There would be an almighty stink, and he, newly-promoted DCI Frank Stewart, would be right at the epicentre of it. It wasn't likely to turn out well, and he imagined his DCI going up in smoke with him ending up at sergeant level or even worse, wearing a bloody uniform. And then, quite out of the blue, an idea came to him, an idea that caused an immediate and marked uplift in his mood.

He picked up his phone again and swiped. This call wasn't answered instantly, but Frank didn't expect it would be. After about two dozen rings, the recipient finally picked up.

'ello?'

'Well hello yourself Frenchie,' Frank said, failing to suppress a smirk. 'Tell me, how do you fancy a nice wee holiday in Scotland?'

Chapter 11

The Phoebe Wilson plan had been formulated as a result of a surveillance mission that Maggie had personally carried out on the two proceeding days. At least when she said surveillance, it was more like hanging about with intent. On reflection, it would probably have been easier to get Jimmy to do it, given he had actually seen the girl in the flesh, but instead he had provided a self-consciously apologetic description. *She looks a bit like a prop forward if that means anything to you.* He wouldn't meant to have been cruel, she knew that, it not being in his nature, but the description had proved accurate enough for the subsequent identification to be unequivocal. Maggie had stationed herself across the street from the offices of Cramond Staffing at about twelve-fifteen, hoping that the girl's lunch break would be at twelve-thirty or thereabouts and praying it wasn't nearer one o'clock or that she took lunch at her desk. Because it was now late November, and although unseasonably warm, the penetrating drizzle and stiff breeze was perfectly in season for the West of Scotland, the wind making the employment of an umbrella inadvisable if not impossible. Periodically she had to wipe drips of precipitation from her nose, whilst cursing under her breath as she imagined what her hair must look like as the rain slowly transformed it into a lank damp mess. But she comforted herself with the fact that this at least felt like proper detective work, as if she was a female Humphrey Bogart although minus the gabardine mac with a turned-up collar. At twenty-past, a steady flow of Cramond's staff began to step into the street, mostly in pairs but some solo performers too. Most, she observed, turned left as they exited the premises, and as Maggie scanned along the pavement in that direction, she spotted a probable destination, a branch of a well-known provider of sandwiches, savouries and bakes. And cakes of course, a part of their product range with which Maggie was all too familiar. Annoyingly she had to wait a further ten minutes in the rain before finally their target appeared. Phoebe Wilson emerged wearing a commodious beige parka, with the fur-lined hood up as a sensible response to the weather, the garment only serving to amplify her generous proportions. Like the others, she too made a sharp left on exit and it seemed odds-on that she was heading towards the sandwich shop. Maggie took advantage of a gap in the traffic to dart across the road in pursuit, and was rewarded a few seconds later by seeing Miss Wilson indeed step into the premises. Impulsively she followed her in and saw that the girl was in the process of removing her parka, evidently to reserve one of the few small tables that lined one wall of the shop. She placed the dripping garment over a chair then joined the short queue waiting at the serving counter. Maggie hesitated for a moment then joined the line immediately behind her, being not quite sure exactly what she was hoping to achieve, but reasoning that if nothing else she would come out of the encounter with a nice cake. Ahead of her, the girl was now being served, ordering a cheese sandwich, a steak pasty, a caramel-iced bun and a large full-fat-milk latte. Fourteen hundred calories minimum, Maggie thought, totting it up, maybe more, then admonished herself for being so judgemental. It wasn't as if she wasn't carrying a few extra pounds herself, a fact which had been preying on her mind for quite some time as she contemplated what she would wear at her wedding. She had set her sights on something sleek and shimmering, but recognised that right now she was as far from sleek as she ever wanted to be. And at that moment she made a decision. This next cake, whichever one she chose -and it might as well be a big one, the biggest they have -would be the last to pass her lips until the big day.

The next day, pleasingly dry, she had repeated the surveillance exercise and was gratified to find that Phoebe Wilson's routine was near-identical to the day before. This time Maggie had not entered the shop itself, being content to linger around the entrance as if she was a potential customer deciding whether to succumb to its temptations or not. After a thirty-second argument with her conscience, she had made her choice. *Damn*. But so what, she had thought, tomorrow Jimmy would be with her and he would undoubtedly stiffen her resolve. And now tomorrow had come. Sitting at the desk in her office, she glanced at her watch which was showing twelve-twenty. *Perfect*. She closed down her laptop and stood up, smiled at Jimmy then nodded towards the door.

'Right then, are we all set for our upcoming exciting encounter with Miss Wilson?' she said, picking up her handbag and slinging it across her shoulder.

'Absolutely boss,' he said, ' although I'm not sure how exciting it will be. So the plan is we're going to follow her into that wee sandwich shop and intercept her just as she's getting stuck into her cream doughnut and grande latte?'

She laughed. 'Never mind the *boss* stuff, I'm your partner now, or have you forgotten already? But yeah, fortunately she does seem to be a lady of habit as far as her lunchtime routine is concerned, so that is indeed the plan if you can call it that. So come on, we'd better get a move on.'

Locking the office door behind them, they wandered down Byers Road, chatting amiably about this and that, and soon they had reached the busy junction with Dumbarton Road. Two hundred yards further on and the premises of Cramond Staffing were in sight.

'She'll be out in a minute or two and then a short stroll to the shop,' she said to Jimmy as they approached the offices, 'if she follows her routine from the last two days. And then we'll just shimmy up behind her and have a little chat.'

He smiled and gave her a thumbs-up. 'She might recognise me but I don't suppose that matters too much.'

On cue, they saw Phoebe Wilson leaving her place of employment on what was now clearly established as her daily mission. This time she wore a navy fleece, one hand buried in a pocket, the other holding her phone in front of her for what exact purpose they could not say. But on reaching the sandwich shop, her routine was the same. Outerwear removed and placed over a chair to reserve her place, then sandwich, bake, cake and latte ordered.

'We'd better order something too I guess,' Jimmy whispered, 'but that's no hardship because I'm bloody starving anyway.'

'Okay,' Maggie nodded. 'But no cakes for me please. I'm on my best behaviour.'

'You can have half of mine,' he said, grinning. 'There's no calories in somebody else's.'

It took a few minutes for their order to be prepared, and as they waited, Maggie glanced over to Wilson and gave a half-smile. To her amusement but not to her surprise, she saw that the girl's eyes had been fixed on Jimmy. He really was such a ridiculously good-looking guy she reflected for about the hundredth time, and once again it seemed his good looks might come in very useful in an investigation. The teenager behind the counter handed over their order and beamed him a smile, she too evidently having succumbed to his charms.

'Mind if we join you?' Jimmy said, nodding at the two empty seats on the opposite side of Wilson's table. They sat down without waiting for an answer.

Maggie smiled again. 'It's Phoebe isn't it? You work for Miss Cramond at the agency. Jimmy saw them singing happy birthday to you the other day. Many happy returns by the way.'

Wilson looked at her, suddenly suspicious. 'Aye, that's right, I work there.'

'We're private investigators and we're working for the family of Juliet McClelland,' Jimmy said pleasantly. 'I'm Jimmy and this is Maggie. We'd like to ask you a couple of questions if you don't mind. It's purely routine, nothing to worry about.'

'I'm no' allowed to,' the girl said. 'You need to talk to Miss Cramond if you want to know anything.'

Jimmy nodded. 'I spoke to her a couple of days ago and she told me you were the member of staff who dealt with Juliet on a day-to-day basis. Is that right?'

'But she told me I wasn't to say anything,' Phoebe protested again. 'It's against company policy.'

So Jimmy was correct, Maggie thought. Francis Cramond had lied about Phoebe being out on the day of Jimmy's original visit, presumably because she wanted to get to the girl before Bainbridge & Stewart had a chance to talk to her. Maybe Cramond was just a control freak and there was nothing in it, but it was damned suspicious nonetheless.

'We obviously don't want to get you into any trouble,' she said soothingly, 'but Juliet's poor family has suffered so much and I'm sure you would want to do anything you can to help them. Because can you imagine how your loved ones would feel if you went missing and they didn't know what had happened to you?'

The girl gave them a sad look. 'Aye, my maw would be pure devastated if that happened.'

'And all we want to know is how Juliet was feeling in the days before her disappearance,' Jimmy said. 'We wondered if you had perhaps talked to her around that time.'

She shrugged. 'I usually spoke to her a couple of times a week. Just to make arrangements and to see when she was available, that kind of thing. She was nice. We always had a wee chat about this and that.'

Maggie nodded. 'And would you say she was feeling okay the last time you spoke to her?'

'Yeah, really she was. I think she was well over everything by then and she was looking forward to getting into her new flat.'

Jimmy gave her a puzzled look. 'What do you mean, she was well over everything?'

'Man trouble. Well, we all have that don't we?' she said, her voice taking on a conspiratorial whisper. 'But in this case it was more like woman trouble. You see, she'd found out a few months earlier her boyfriend was shagging her so-called friend, and they were flat-mates too. An awful situation. But then you can never trust them can you? Never in a million years.'

Maggie wasn't sure whether Phoebe was referring to men in general or woman friends in particular. But thinking back to her own now sadly-distant school days, there were more than a few of her friends who thought anything in trousers was fair game, whether he was someone else's boyfriend or not.

'No, I agree,' she said. 'But you thought she was over it?'

The girl nodded. 'Defo. I mean Juliet was absolutely beautiful, off the scale. *She* didn't have any trouble attracting men, in fact the opposite. Guys were always trying it on with her.' She gave Jimmy a wistful look. 'I mean, that's what they *do*, isn't it? They're always trying to get into our knickers.'

He shot Maggie a look then, suppressing a laugh, said, 'Aye some of us, but not *all* of us to be fair. But if I can ask, when was the last time you spoke to Juliet, and can you remember exactly what you talked about?'

She nodded again. 'Well actually, it was her that phoned me, I remember that.' Abruptly she stopped, as if realising she was about to say something she shouldn't. *Or wasn't allowed to.*

'Go on,' Maggie said gently. 'What did you talk about on that last occasion?'

The girl shuffled uncomfortably, looking as if she might burst into tears at any moment.

She reached over and put her hand on the girl's. 'You need to tell us Phoebe. Think of the poor family and how much they're suffering. They won't get another moment's peace in their lives if they don't find out what happened to her.'

'She was asking for more shifts on the gourmet cruises. They paid really amazing and I think she needed the money for her new flat.'

'Gourmet cruises?' Jimmy asked, puzzled. 'What are they? Is this something the hotel was running?'

She shook her head. 'A guy had a wee cruise boat and they had some famous chef who worked at a big hotel in Glasgow. A bunch of rich guys were in a kind of dining club and they met up on the boat every couple of months for a big fancy meal and drunk loads of hundred-pound-a-bottle wines.'

'Okay,' Maggie said, pausing for a moment as she digested this new information. 'So do I take it that Cramond Staffing were supplying the waiting staff? And that Juliet sometimes worked on the boat?'

'Aye, that's right,' the girl mumbled. 'That's right. But I wasn't supposed to tell you that.'

'Don't worry,' Maggie said, giving her a warm smile. 'We're very discreet, it's the nature of the job. It won't go any further.'

'You see, it's all done in cash,' Phoebe continued, unprompted. 'Nobody wants to pay too much tax these days and the government just wastes it anyway. That's what I think anyway.'

Or what Francis Cramond told you to say more like, Maggie thought, smiling to herself. So was this some grubby little side-scam, a few rich guys recycling probably ill-gotten wads of cash whilst a look-the-other-way boat guy and an agency owner enjoyed some of the collateral benefit? No doubt the famous chef would have been paid cash-in-hand too, like these loadsamoney tradesmen she'd seen the other night at the Horseshoe Bar. The black economy, that's what they called it, and from what Maggie could see, it was booming.

'But that's not where Juliet was working the night she disappeared was it?' she said. 'She was meant to be doing a shift at the Auchterard Hotel as I understand it.'

Phoebe nodded. 'No that's right. There wasn't another cruise scheduled for a couple of weeks so I got her a slot at the hotel. She was okay with that.'

'And would it have been you they phoned first when she didn't turn up?' Jimmy asked.

The girl hesitated for a moment, then said defensively, 'Aye, but it was a Friday and I was out with a bunch of friends in the pub. It was noisy and I didn't see the missed call message until it was too late to find them someone else.'

'But I think you were supposed to be on duty?' he said. 'At least on some kind of standby?'

She shuffled uncomfortably in her seat. 'Aye I was. But it happens sometimes. I mean you can't answer every call twenty-four-by-seven can you?'

'No you can't,' Maggie said in what she hoped was a sympathetic tone. Sensing she wouldn't get much more from the girl today, she made to bring the meeting to a close.

'Well look, you've been *so* helpful Phoebe, but maybe you could just give us the details of the cruise firm and then we'll leave you in peace.'

The girl shook her head, looking alarmed. 'No way. I've told you way too much already. Miss Cramond will kill me if she finds out. And anyway, I didn't know who they were.'

'That's okay,' Maggie said, deciding it was best not to push it. 'It's probably not that important anyway. But we'll be off now, and just to confirm, this has just been between the three of us, trust us on that.' Jimmy gave her a questioning look, the question almost certainly being *what, aren't we going to bring this up with Francis Cramond*?

'Aye, thanks for all of that,' he said, getting to his feet. 'It's been a big help and the family will be really grateful. So we'll shoot off now and let you enjoy your lunch.'

***

Back in the Byers Road office, they reflected on what they had learned. One thing for certain was that Maggie's jump-into-the-Clyde suicide theory had now been totally shot down in flames. She pretty much knew already that Juliet McClelland had been cheated on by her medical student boyfriend and her scheming flatmate, and now those suspicions had been confirmed. But it seemed that rather than driving her to the depths of despair, the beautiful young woman had been able to shrug off the betrayal and was moving on with her life, her day-to-day focussed on earning enough to fund her swish new flat. The problem was it still left the big unanswered question, which was where they hell *had* she gone that Friday after her lectures were over if not to end her life? Could have gone *anywhere* was the answer to that one, which didn't help at all.

As for the revelation of the gourmet cruises, well that was an interesting development although neither Maggie nor Jimmy were sure where it took them if anywhere. Sooner or later they would have to bring the matter up with Francis Cramond, despite their promise to Phoebe Wilson, but the first stage would be to take a run up to Loch Lomond, visit the Auchterard hotel and at the same time see what they could find out about the outfit that ran these trips. Jimmy had told her there were quite a few little firms who ran that kind of thing, some even giving you the opportunity to catch your own fish and have it cooked fresh on-board. Someone was bound to be able to point them to this top-of-the-range firm, and then maybe they could give a different perspective on Juliet's mood leading up to the disappearance, although since they only seemed to run a few times a year that might be a long shot. She suspected they were more likely to find some joy at the hotel where she often did one or two shifts a week. That was still a long shot too of course but until they thought of anything better, it would have to do for now. But then suddenly another thought had come to her. Juliet seemed to have been laser-focussed on earning enough to fund her swish new flat. Maggie remembered she and Jimmy had taken a stroll up to Highburgh Road a week or two ago and pressed their noses against the windows of a couple of estate agents' windows, noting that you needed to find fifteen hundred a month minimum to rent anything even half-decent in that neck of the woods. You would need to take on a *ton* of bar-work to earn that sort of money, even if your seriously up-market employer was paying double the market rate.

So yeah, quite a productive day all-in-all and for once she was feeling reasonably up-beat about the case. But there was one thing that was serving to dampen the spirits, something that Jimmy had said earlier, almost casually in passing. *Given your wee mission statement, I think it would work for you too.* His choice of words had both jarred and sent a shiver of concern down her spine. He hadn't said *our* mission statement, he hadn't said it would work for *us* too.

And now she started to worry what might be going through his mind.

Chapter 12

The review meeting with his editor Rod Clark had been a bit tetchy to say the least, but of course that was Clark all over, a nit-picking corporate robot if ever there was one. *We need to run this one past the lawyers. We're talking about a live murder enquiry here and the paper could be prosecuted for perverting the course of justice. This story is nothing but another pile of Patel conspiracy theories.* God, the guy was such a *total* old woman and *so* out of tune with the current zeitgeist. Conspiracy theories? Didn't he know the whole world now *ran* on conspiracy theories? They were the ultimate click-bait, acting like cat-nip to the army of nutcase online commentators who polished their fragile egos by seeing their equally crackpot opinions in print. And Clark should know by now that conspiracy theories sold papers too, particularly when wrapped in the respectable veneer of a quality newspaper like the *Chronicle* and penned by a crack award-winning journalist like Yash Patel. And if he didn't know, the paper's owners would soon put him right on that score, or replace him with someone who did.

So his boat guy Russell had been murdered, which explained why he hadn't been returning his calls. The guy's body had been dumped in plain sight just a mile up the loch from where the new but now-closed bridge took you over to

Inchcailloch and the McClelland Tower. The Scottish government didn't want any visitors to the place, and Russell had been running covert excursions from the marina at Ardlui. Now, very conveniently for the government, Ally Russell was dead, knifed to death by the loch-side, a graphic warning to any other wee boat guys on the loch who might fancy taking up the vacancy. Yeah, of course it was nuts to think that was why Russell had been killed, but he made a mental note to look a bit more closely at the guy's life-story. Because there was one thing that had been bugging him from the time Russell had taken him over to Inchcailloch. Which was, how could a little boatman afford a hundred-grand Range Rover?

On Sunday, half of the colour supplement would be dedicated to the wider story, under an expanded headline that he'd written himself after rejecting a ton of pathetic efforts from the paper's useless sub-editors. *The McClelland Tower - the Pictures They Don't Want You to See and the Stories They Don't Want you to Hear.*

Yes, *stories plural* not *story singular*. It had been of course nothing but a stroke of luck that Russell's murder should coincide with the upcoming publication of his blockbuster article. As conspiracy theories went, linking Russell's death to the lockdown of Inchcailloch was off-the-scale perfection, even if Yash knew it to be complete bollocks. Nonetheless he'd even been able to find some low-level gossiping numpty at the Edinburgh parliament to talk to him about it, that numpty becoming that great love of the newspaper reporter, the unnamed source. *An unnamed source told me there had been discussions at the highest level of government about taking serious action against the organisers of the illegal boat trips.* It was perfect, absolutely perfect. Drop the hints, make the improbable connections, give it a good stir. A simple recipe that never failed to deliver the goods.

But that, much to his satisfaction, was only the half of it. First of all, he'd had confirmation from Professor Elizabeth Bates of Cambridge University that Oresund Civil Engineering had submitted a detailed paper to the Scottish government explaining their reasons for not bidding on the Lomond Tower project, spelling out the problematic geology along the Highland Boundary Fault. *So they knew.* That wasn't a conspiracy theory, that was a rock-solid, verifiable fact. *Consumed with an arrogant nationalistic hubris, the Edinburgh government chose to ignore the warnings given by Europe's most eminent and respected civil engineering consultancy.* The paragraphs almost wrote themselves.

Secondly, he'd been doing some digging into the background of the company who *did* win the project, a Glasgow-based outfit called Premier Construction. What was interesting to Yash was that three months before they were awarded the contract, the company had changed its name from Cramond Construction & Engineering. That, it turned out, was the same Cramond Construction & Engineering that had screwed up the building of a new bridge over the river estuary up at Inverness and had been two years late with a multi-million-pound extension to the big general hospital in Dundee. But somehow that dubious track-record hadn't bothered the government when they were handing out the contract for the Tower. That wasn't a conspiracy theory either, that was another *fact*. Wow, this was turning out to be some article, he thought, maybe even the best in what already had been a pretty amazing career, even if he did say so himself.

And to top it all off, the pictures were great too, he having had no problem finding another guy with a boat to take him and his photographer on to the islet, and this time he was only charged a hundred quid for the privilege. But it wasn't the pictures of the wrecked tower and that little forlorn cross that were going to cause the sensation around the Sunday-morning breakfast tables. No, it was the photograph that Rod Clark had reluctantly agreed to put on the front page of the supplement, the one taken at an Edinburgh drinks reception just three months before the contract for the Lomond Tower was awarded.

That being the photograph of Davie Cramond, Executive Chairman of newly-named Premier Construction, sharing a nice glass of wine with smiling First Minister Sheila McClelland.

Chapter 13

It was a crisp winter's morning, the rising sun beaming in over her right shoulder as she threaded the old Golf up the A809 towards Drymen. Even here, just four or five miles north of her new home in Milngavie, the landscape was lovely, reminding her a little of her home county of Yorkshire and making her wonder if she could ever live in London again. Beside her sat Jimmy, staring morosely out of the window, having barely spoken a word since they'd set out. In thirty minutes or so they'd be at the hotel and sitting down with one Mary-Anne Pearson, who rejoiced under the title of *Vice-President Resourcing, Bar & Restaurant* according to the confirmatory e-mail she had sent them the previous day, and who would hopefully provide useful insight into Juliet McClelland's state of mind in the days and weeks leading up to her disappearance. So now Maggie had to make a decision. Should she enjoy the quiet but unsettling silence that presently prevailed and wait until the drive home before bringing up the subject that had been causing her such worry, or should she bite the bullet and do it now? She glanced over at Jimmy and gave him a half-smile.

'Jimmy, I hope you don't mind, but I've been wanting to talk to you for a while,' she began quietly. 'It's about something that's been really worrying me. About you actually.'

He shrugged. 'I'm alright. You don't have to worry about me. Honestly you don't.'

'I know I don't *have* to, but I do nonetheless. We care about you a lot, Frank and me. But I know what you men are like, it's not something you ever want to talk about. But I wondered if you might want to talk about it with me. And don't worry, according to the sat-nav there's only twenty-six minutes until we get there. So the agony won't be prolonged too much.'

He laughed. 'Aye, well that's good to know.' He was silent for a moment then said, 'But you know what it is. It's the divorce and now Flora getting remarried and all that stuff. I've tried but I just can't get it out of my head. And I'm hardly sleeping and when I do sleep I get these horrible crazy nightmares, all mixed up with Flora and Astrid and Naomi, and they're all in terrible danger and I don't get to save any of them. And then when I'm awake, it's as if I'm not actually in the here and now. I'm here physically but mentally my mind is all over the place. That's what screwed up my relationship with Terezka. She said she couldn't be with me until I let it all go. But how the hell can I let it all go? How the hell can I?'

Maggie gave him a sad look as she carefully weighed up what she should say next. She knew all about Sergeant Naomi Harris, the young army colleague who had lost her life in a terrorist attack in Belfast, and for whose death he blamed himself, and Astrid Sorenson, the beautiful Swedish country singer with whom he'd had an affair, causing the break-up of his marriage. But then Terezka Berger had come along and she thought he'd finally found the happiness he deserved. But it was not to be and now it seemed that break-up had been the straw that broke the camel's back.

She reached over and squeezed his hand. 'You can talk to me anytime of course and I'll always listen. But I'm just a friend and that's what has been really worrying me.' She paused. 'Look, I don't know how to say this, but I think it might be really helpful if perhaps you spoke to a professional. A mental health professional I mean.'

'What, you mean go and see a bloody shrink? No way. I'll work it out, I just need some time, that's all.'

His reaction was as she had feared, but with some satisfaction she realised it had only served to stiffen her resolve. As a true friend, she knew what she must do. She wouldn't be helping him one bit by trying to sweeten the bitter pill.

'Well I'm sorry Jimmy, but you've been bloody trying that for two years now and it hasn't exactly been a success to be fair.' She paused for a moment. 'No offence, but for such a big tough guy you've been pretty hopeless.' It was meant as a joke, and she hoped he would see it that way.

He gave a half-smile. 'I know, I know. It's just making that first phone-call, isn't it? *Hello, I'm Captain Jimmy Stewart and I'm not doing too good.* And then you get some stupid wee lassie who just fires a lot of bollocks platitudes at you.'

Maggie laughed. 'Well if you like *I'll* give you all the bollocks platitudes you can handle, but I'm not sure that's what you need right now. The fact is you need to make that phone-call, and if you won't do it for yourself, then do it for me and Frank. I know it's selfish of me, but I just can't be happy when you're not. And I've got my wedding coming up and I don't want the best man to be a miserable git.' She wondered if she should just go ahead and say what she'd really been thinking at that moment. *And I don't want the best man not to be there because he did something really stupid like killing himself.* But of course he wouldn't do that she thought, slightly shame-faced for it even to have crossed her mind. *Not Jimmy.* Then she remembered about all the cases she had read about, the terrible act of suicide leaving a trail of shattered and bewildered mothers, fathers, brothers, sisters, lovers and friends, not a single one having any idea that things had got so bleak, or even that there was a problem at all. The fact was, you weren't doing anybody any favours by not facing up to the huge elephant in the room, and facing up to it squarely and honestly. But maybe she would leave that one for the trip home. She said,

'Anyway, I've said my piece and it's only because I care about you. We both do, me and Frank. A lot.'

Glancing over, she was relieved to see him smile. He said, 'And I appreciate it, I really do. But there's just one thing I need to tell you right now. Something important.'

'What's that?' she said, her heart all of a sudden missing a beat.

He grinned. 'You've just sailed past the turn-off for the Loch. I've no idea how you could have missed the tourist sign 'cos it's the size of a flippin' house.'

***

The winter sun was now almost due south of them, beaming a dappled purple light that bounced off the shimmering surface of the loch and illuminated the soaring mountains that closed in on either side. Their viewpoint as they drove up the gravelled drive of the hotel was pretty much that which would have been enjoyed from the Lomond Tower, though without the advantage accrued by being five hundred feet up. It was a glorious sight, with Ben Lomond rising majestically to the east, reaching over three thousand feet in height which she knew from Jimmy was the threshold at which it could be classified as a Monro. She remembered being told the last time they'd been in these parts that there were over two hundred of these Monros in Scotland and that conquering them all was the number one challenge for hill-walking enthusiasts. As they turned into the car-park, a huge sign spelt out its welcome. *The Auchterard - proud member of the Kitchner of Chicago Hotel Group.* The building was an impressively ornate sandstone structure, originally built as a private home by a rich Glasgow ship-owner in Victorian times before becoming a hotel sometime during the twentieth century. In latter years according to Frank it had become pretty run-down until it was acquired about ten years ago by a US conglomerate who had pumped serious money into the place and built the championship golf course alongside the loch. Now it was thriving by all accounts, proving there were plenty of people in this world who didn't baulk at paying five hundred pounds a night for a room, even if it did have a view to die for.

'What a place eh?' Jimmy said admiringly as they parked up. 'It's just a pity that me and Frank are so rubbish at golf or I'd get him up here for a wee thrash round. Although I doubt if we could afford the green fees. And we'd probably lose about fifty balls on the way round too.'

Maggie laughed. 'Yeah, it is pretty fancy. I'm feeling I should park as far away from the door as I can so my scruffy little car doesn't lower the tone of the place.'

Mary-Anne Pearson met them in reception and led them through to a large comfortable lounge, expensively furnished with soft leather armchairs and sofas, sitting on a plush purple tartan carpet.

'Take a seat please and welcome to the Auchterard,' she said, the American accent unmistakeable. Maggie hadn't expected that, though in retrospect it shouldn't have been a surprise given the ownership of the hotel. Pearson looked about fifty, slim and immaculately coiffered, her sober dark navy pinafore dress and crisp white blouse with rolled-up sleeves somehow reminding Maggie of a nineteen-seventies air hostess.

'I guess you're not from around these parts,' Jimmy said, smiling.

'How *did* you guess?' Pearson said, returning the smile. 'No, my home State is Illinois. I came here to help set up the provisioning and catering operation when Kitchner Group took over the hotel and I loved it so much that I stayed on.'

'Even with our wonderful Scottish weather?'

'You've obviously never experienced a Chicago winter,' she laughed. 'Believe me, it's positively tropical here by comparison. We've got a big lake too, but the arctic wind roars in across ours at about twenty below zero in your Celsius degrees.'

'Sounds seriously shivery,' Maggie said, giving a mock grimace. 'But thanks so much for seeing us, I know you must be terribly busy.'

Pearson nodded. 'Well it's a little bit quieter right now, but it's the lull before the storm. It goes crazy here over Christmas as you might imagine. But spring through summer is our busiest period of course, when we can make full use of our lochside frontage and our beautiful golf course.'

'It is an amazing location,' Jimmy said. 'So as we said on the phone, we wanted to talk to you about Juliet McClelland. We're working for the family, hoping to find out what happened to her.'

Pearson nodded. 'Sure, and such a terrible business. Everyone here was devastated as you might imagine.'

'How long did she work here?' Maggie asked.

'About two years or so,' Pearson said. 'When we began to employ students from the Universities, she was one of the first.'

'Aye, that interests me,' Jimmy said. 'Because it seems a pretty expensive exercise to ship kids in from Glasgow.'

'Well it's not just Glasgow, we get quite a few from Stirling too which is a little nearer,' she said. 'And yes it is quite expensive but we had quite a time trying to find the right quality of people locally, and of course our guests expect to be served by quality staff. The arrangement works very well for us, because it gives us access to well-trained servers for our busy summer period.'

Maggie nodded. 'Yes, I hadn't thought of that. So do lots of your staff go on to work for you during the summer recess then?'

'Yes they do,' Pearson said. 'That's what we plan for. It's a very efficient method of resourcing our needs. And we have very comfortable staff accommodation here on site so it works very well for all parties.'

'And Juliet? Did she ever work here in the summer?'

'Yes, she did for the first year she was with us. But not the last year. I think that time she accompanied her mother on a speaking tour of

Canada and the US. It was a free vacation for her I guess.'

'And how well did you get to know her whilst she worked here?' Maggie asked.

'Pretty well,' Pearson said. 'I don't manage the day-to-day of course, but I'm always walking the floor and I make it my business to get to know our waiting staff. She was a very nice girl, bright and intelligent and of course very beautiful too, which is always such an advantage in life, don't you think? Although *that's* purely down to the genes you are lucky enough to inherit I suppose.' Maggie gave a wry smile as she noticed Mary-Anne shooting Jimmy an admiring look. He surely was the exception that proved the rule, she thought, because it was her colleague's attractiveness that had made him the target of that Swedish temptress, and look where that had got him.

'And what was her mood like in the few weeks before she disappeared?' Jimmy said. 'Did you get a chance to assess that?'

Pearson shrugged. 'Okay, I think. She'd been through quite a time but seemed to have emerged pretty unscathed from what I could tell.'

'By quite a time, do you mean her break-up with her boyfriend?' Maggie said, interested.

'Yes that,' Pearson said, 'but I think her family background was rather dysfunctional too. She had been estranged from her real father and her mother was too obsessed with her career to give her much time. I think in fact that's why she went on that North American trip, to try and bond with her mum.'

'But her real father was back in her life wasn't he?' Jimmy said. 'About a year before her disappearance if I've got that right.'

She nodded. 'Yes, and I think she was very happy about that.'

'So there was nothing that stood out,' Maggie said, struggling to mask her disappointment at how bland the meeting at been thus far. 'Nothing that would point to why she might simply disappear I mean?'

'Not really,' Pearson said, furrowing her brow. 'Although it wasn't the first time she had missed a shift. I put it down to it being her period.' She gave Jimmy an apologetic look. 'We call it the curse for good reason. You see I'd noticed she'd missed three earlier Friday shifts and when I checked the dates I saw they were four weeks apart.'

Maggie said, 'So when she didn't turn up on the evening she disappeared, is that what you thought it must be? Her period?'

She paused for a moment before replying. 'Yes I did, and I must admit I wasn't feeling very sympathetic.' She gave Maggie a knowing smile. 'I mean we all have to put up with it, don't we? The fact was I was quite annoyed and it did briefly cross my mind that I would call the agency in the morning and tell them we couldn't use her again.' She sighed. 'And then of course we found out that she had disappeared. I'm just so glad I didn't make that call.'

'You couldn't have known,' Jimmy said in a kindly tone. 'There's just one other thing though if you don't mind. A girl at the Cramond agency told us Juliet sometimes got work on a cruise boat, some outfit that ran gourmet or cordon-bleu evenings, that kind of thing. Do you know anything about them, can I ask?'

She shrugged. 'There's a few of them operate on the loch but none of them are anything to do with the hotel. In any case I doubt if any of them would be up to the standard our guests expect.' It was said as if it were an obvious statement of fact, rather than with any animosity. 'But if you're looking for any one of them in particular you could ask our Sandy McDuff. He's head of concierge and a genius at sourcing anything our guests may request, no matter how obscure. He's in this morning, I'll give him a call when we're done.'

She paused again then gave them a sharp look. 'Just as long as you're not wanting to visit Inchcailloch of course. Because we've made it clear to all our staff that's off-limits. '

'No of course not,' Maggie said. 'But as a matter of fact we had wondered whether the tower had affected your business. Because it is pretty close, isn't it?'

By her expression, it seemed Pearson didn't welcome this line of questioning. 'It's very difficult for us. We were very supportive of the project originally because for many of our guests it added to the attractions of our location. Not *all* of course, but us North Americans have what could almost be described as a tradition of erecting towers in beauty spots. Niagara Falls of course being a case in point. But now, we have to tread very carefully. We don't mention it in any of our marketing, but we are obliged to say that a small handful of our rooms to the north have a view of the wreckage. And the sad truth is there are some guests to which this is an added attraction.'

Jimmy nodded. 'Aye, I can see the difficulty. I guess you need to tread pretty delicately.'

'Exactly,' Pearson said. 'It's our corporate view that they should tear the thing down so that the tragedy gradually and respectfully fades out of the public consciousness. But that's not the government's view and we have no choice but to make the best of that decision. But I digress. I just wanted to make it clear that visits to the island are strictly off-limits.'

'No, we understand that of course,' Maggie said. 'So just to wrap up, can we just confirm that Juliet didn't say anything to you that might have given any pointers as to why she disappeared?'

Pearson gave her a sad look. 'No, nothing. But you're talking as if you think it was Juliet's own decision to walk out of her life.' She paused. 'But that's not what happened, is it? Someone took her didn't they? Abducted her. And then probably murdered her. Otherwise she would have turned up by now, surely?'

Maggie sighed. 'We don't know that for sure. All anybody knows was she wasn't there when your taxi came to pick her up. That's all anybody knows.'

And it was true, she reflected, no-one did know anything else. Except that was for the person or persons who had taken Juliet McClelland's life.

**

Head of Concierge Sandy McDuff turned out to be central casting's archetypal Highlander, a huge man in his fifties with flowing ginger locks and a matching goatee beard. He could quite easily be a clan chief, Maggie thought, or perhaps one of these strongmen who tossed those chopped-down telegraph poles at a Highland Games. He wore a kilt and a smart black jacket with a collar and tie, with matching black brogues polished to a mirror-like sheen. Even the name seemed a caricature, causing Maggie to wonder whether it was actually his own or had he been christened something less impressive, like Jim Smith. Or Colin Crapper, an unfortunate boy she had been at school with. Real name or not, it was evident McDuff had a personality as large as his physique, greeting them with a loud and effusive *great to meet you guys, welcome to Loch Lomond and the Auchterard.*

'Thanks for coming over to talk to us Sandy,' Maggie said. 'We appreciate it.'

'That's my job,' he said, laughing. 'So what can I do for you folks?'

'We were wondering if you knew of anyone who ran dining cruises on the loch,' she said. 'Specifically gourmet ones, you know with fancy food and equally fancy wines. Mary-Anne thought you might.'

He shrugged. 'There's a few lads out of Balloch who run these kind of things, but it's more a big bevvy session for the boys. You know, a wee fish supper from the chip-shop and a couple of cases of Tennant's lager, then throw a line over the side of the boat and see if you can catch anything. Usually they just catch a cold.'

Jimmy laughed. 'Aye, I've been on a few of these myself in my time. But we were thinking of something a bit more up-market.'

McDuff furrowed his brow as if to stimulate his thought processes. He paused and then said, 'Not sure if I do, to be honest. But I've got a vague recollection now that a couple of our corporate membership guys are into that sort of thing.'

'Corporate membership?' Maggie said. 'What do you mean by that?'

'Our golf course is one of the best in the whole country, and I mean the UK, not just Scotland. It's mainly for our hotel guests, but we do have a small local membership.' He lowered his voice to a whisper, as if he was about to share some great confidence. 'Very exclusive of course, and *very* expensive. There's just a hundred members.'

'How expensive is *very* expensive?' Jimmy asked. 'If you don't mind me asking?'

McDuff gave a knowing smile. 'How much do you think? Take a guess.'

Jimmy shrugged. 'No idea. Maybe two or three thousand a year, something like that?'

He laughed. 'Twenty five grand a year. And they need to spend five grand in the bar and restaurant too.'

'Phew, that *is* bloody expensive,' Jimmy said.

'Aye, but it's all charged to their companies. I bet they don't even notice and it's probably tax-deductable too.' It was said with admiration rather than resentment, making Maggie wonder if Sandy McDuff might be a regular beneficiary of the executive members' generosity. She knew the type from her barrister days, another caricature, this one being the golf-club bore. More than a few of her rich and middle-aged colleagues at Drake Chambers had played the game, and were capable of boring for England on the subject of the risible pastime. She'd also noticed that the same type often liked to brag about the price of the bottles in their personal wine cellars and about how much they'd paid for dinner in the latest fashionable eating place.

'That's interesting,' Maggie said. 'So do you have a name for one of these gentlemen, so that we can ask a couple of questions?'

McDuff paused for a moment then gave a slow shake of the head. 'I cannae do that, not really. Not with the data protection stuff and all that. Not without speaking to management first.'

Maggie had anticipated the response, not really expecting much more. 'Yes, I can fully understand that Sandy,' she said, 'and don't worry, we wouldn't dream of approaching any of the gentlemen in question until you had confirmed they were happy to speak to us. So we'd be really grateful if you checked with your management then let us know.'

Jimmy nodded. 'And to be honest, it would be really handy if you could do it now, whilst we're here. We've got a wee feedback meeting with Juliet's family in a day or two and it would be great if we had *something* to report to them. Even if it's not really relevant to the case. They just like to see progress you see.'

McDuff nodded. 'Aye, well I wouldn't want Juliet's poor family to be suffering any more than they are.' He paused again then said, his voice reduced to a whisper. 'Look..there's probably a way we can speed all this up if you want. You know, oil the wheels a bit, if you know what I'm saying.'

Maggie shot Jimmy a wry look then said to McDuff, 'Actually I'm not sure that I do know. What exactly are you suggesting?'

'I'm suggesting the sum of fifty pounds,' he said. 'Let's just call it a wee consultancy fee if you will.' There wasn't a hint of shame in his tone,

Maggie noted, but then again, she supposed this was a routine *modus operandi* in his line of work. Theatre tickets for sell-out shows, the best tables in the most fashionable restaurants in Glasgow, favourable tee-off times on the Championship course, that would be all part of the job description for an up-market *concierge* like Sandy McDuff. It was hardly surprising that he should extend his activities to a spot of private enterprise, but that didn't mean it didn't leave a sour taste in her mouth.

Jimmy had already removed his wallet from his pocket and was slipping out the required banknotes. 'There you go,' he said, handing the cash to McDuff. 'I don't suppose I'll be getting a receipt.'

McDuff took the money without looking at it and quickly stuffed it into a pocket. 'Cheers guys,' he said. 'Appreciated. So the gentlemen you should speak to is Mr Cramond, Mr Davie Cramond. He's one of our first members and he was our first men's captain too. He has a regular four-ball nearly every Friday morning and him and his pals generally have a wee lunch afterwards so you could probably catch him then. And I'll tell you what, you wouldn't believe the size of their bar bill.'

'I can well imagine,' Maggie said, nodding. 'Well I must say you've been extremely helpful

Sandy. We'll obviously try and get in touch with this Mr Cramond and see if he is able to help us, but for now we'll leave you in peace.'

'And just to be clear,' McDuff said with a sudden look of concern, 'you won't tell him it was me who gave you his name? Because that wouldn't be good for me.'

Jimmy laughed. 'No worries Sandy, I'm sure there's a way that can be arranged. Shall we say, oh I don't know, maybe fifty quid?'

***

On the drive back there was plenty to talk about of course, like whether this Davie Cramond guy was any relation to Francis Cramond of the eponymous staffing agency, and what to make of the fact that Juliet McClelland's attendance record at the hotel had not been unblemished. But it wasn't any of that which was preoccupying Maggie's thoughts as she piloted the Golf southwards. The question was, would she have the courage to say what needed saying, to actually say it out loud? On the way up she'd told him how much she was worried about him, and now he couldn't possibly have any doubt about the depth of her concern. But still she knew she had to say it, to say the actual words, stripped of disguise or obfuscation, no matter how stupid and ridiculous it sounded. *Jimmy, have you ever had thoughts of self-harming?*

With just five minutes until they arrived back at their office, she still hadn't said it.

Chapter 14

The reaction had been everything he'd been hoping for and a whole lot more besides. Unbeknown to Yash, his editor Rod Clark had decided to run with the story on the front page of the paper, not just in the colour supplement. *McClelland Tower scandal: Government Ignored Top Consultants' Advice.* Out in media-land it was the report from Oresund Consultants that was currently attracting top billing, meaning that dynamite photograph of Sheila McClelland with construction boss Davie Cramond seemed to have passed virtually unnoticed. Not to worry, Yash thought, there was plenty of time for *that* to come to prominence, and in the meantime he was going to milk every last second of the attention he was getting. He'd already been on two of the Sunday-morning political shows to talk about it, and after one of them, a producer had taken him to one side and asked if he'd every considered switching his career to television. *Considered it*? Getting on the telly was his burning ambition, and now it seemed it might be within touching distance. According to the producer, it had been a while since the networks had run a *proper* news-investigation programme, and a smart and telegenic guy like Yash Patel, who had the added advantage of ticking all the required diversity boxes, might be exactly what they were looking for right now. No promises of course, but god, wasn't it exciting?

He'd always known he was good-looking of course - I mean, you only had to look in the mirror - and *way* good-looking enough to be on the box. Not only that, he was a whole lot cleverer than any of the morons who were doing it now, and now here was validation. *Bring it on.*

Yep, things were looking very sweet in the world of Yash Patel. But the ridiculous and incredible thing was that life just seemed to be getting better and better. Because only that morning he'd received a tip-off from one of his contacts, this guy a Home Office insider with a long-running grudge against the government. And this was a tip-off that put him on the scent of a story that might easily turn out to be even bigger than the McClelland Tower one. According to his loose-lipped source, the government was secretly employing deep cyber-sweeping technologies to spy on its own people. Not only that, but right now it seemed they were engaged in a little practice run.

In Scotland.

Chapter 15

It turned out it was going to take a few days before Ronnie French could free himself of his existing commitments and make the trek north, so in the meantime Frank was left with nothing much to do but a bit of desk-based legwork, the kind of stuff that he loathed with a passion. Especially as the natives of New Gorbals police station were unlikely to prove cooperative with what he needed to do. The original plan had been to co-opt his mate DC Lexy McDonald, but it looked as if he would be fighting a losing battle to get her on his team, now that another body had apparently been discovered on the shores of Loch Lomond. The murder squad was already short-staffed before this latest one turned up, and now it would be a case of drafting in anyone who wasn't already assigned to a major investigation. Unfortunately for Frank, that was likely to include wee Lexy. Fortunately, as far as he knew anyway, DCS Sweeney hadn't yet commandeered her for his murder team. *Yet*.

'So, what do you know about this latest killing Lexy?' he was asking her as they enjoyed americanos and breakfast rolls and sausage down in the canteen. 'Are we assuming the two of them are related, you know, this one and the Ally Russell murder?'

She took a sip of her coffee and furrowed her brow. 'We don't know sir, but the feeling is perhaps not. Russell was killed by multiple stab wounds, and this victim suffered the same fate too, but the difference is the face of this poor guy has been totally disfigured too. Like something from a horror movie, that's what one of the SOCOs told me, totally unrecognisable. And the body was found miles away on the other side of the water from Russell. Just a few hundred yards south from the big Ardlui marina if you know it.'

'Vaguely,' Frank said, grimacing as he pictured the evidently disturbing scene, 'but I suppose that was probably the point of the guy being so badly disfigured, to make identification that much harder. Have they any ideas who it is yet?'

She shook her head. 'Not a clue. They're going to be putting an appeal out in the media in the next day or two, but obviously they won't be able to use a photograph given the state of him.'

He nodded. 'Well I guess someone will come forward eventually, when whoever it is gets reported missing. So I'm assuming they're not going to make any connection to the Russell case during this big media shindig?'

'No, I don't think so sir. They've not identified the second victim yet and I as said, the MOs are a bit different.'

Frank shrugged. 'Aye, but not *that* different. And besides, that's two guys who've been whacked and then their bodies dumped at the side of the loch in the space of just three weeks. I mean, if that's not a connection, what is? When was the last time anything like that happened up there I ask you? Probably in about eighteen-twenty.'

'Well since you mention it sir, there's some buzz on social media saying the Lomond Tower disaster should be treated as murder too,' she said. 'After what that Patel guy wrote in his article in the Chronicle the other day.'

He laughed. 'Aye, I know all about Yash Patel from bitter experience. He's like a wee terrier with a rubber bone when he gets a hold of a story.'

'He's saying the government knew it wasn't safe to build on Inchcailloch but they went ahead anyway.'

'Aye, that's what Patel says right enough, but what about innocent until proven guilty? And to be honest, it's got nowt to do with us.'

'*Nowt* sir?' she said, laughing.

'It's Yorkshire, at any rate cartoon Yorkshire. My Maggie uses it all the time and I've just picked it up. But anyway Lexy, any news about whether they're putting you on the case or not?'

She smiled apologetically. 'Yeah, I'm moving over next week sir, just as soon as they get all the IT set up in the big investigation room. Sorry, but it's all hands to the pump.'

He gave a resigned shrug. 'Aye, well I kind of guessed that would be the case. But does that mean you're at a loose end for the next day or two?'

'Well not exactly sir,' she said, shooting him a look of mild suspicion. 'For a start I've got the Fiscal's paperwork to do on a robbery I've been on and that's not a five-minute job as you well know. But yeah, I might have a few hours to spare if you've got something you need me to do for you.'

He smiled. 'As it happens, I do have something. It's not too complicated, but it might be a wee bit sensitive.'

She gave him a curious look. 'What do you mean sir?'

Just as he was about to answer, he became aware of a figure approaching their table at pace. Shit, this was the last person he wanted to see right now. Or at any time, come to think of it.

'Morning sir, how goes it?' he said, giving the DCS a distrustful look.

Sweeney looked straight at Lexy and gestured towards the door with his head. 'Make yourself scarce McDonald. Pronto. And don't come back.'

He watched as she stood up, pointing to the exit as if to reinforce his command, then languidly lowered himself into the seat she had just vacated.

'So Stewart, I spoke to your *Assistant Commissioner* Blair like you suggested.' He gave a sneering laugh. 'Anti-corruption tsar they call him. I mean, what's that all about? And he's a right smooth bastard isn't he? Too smooth to be a copper if you ask me.'

Frank shrugged. 'I don't really move in such elevated circles sir, so I couldn't really say whether he is or whether he isn't.'

'He is, take it from me,' Sweeney said. 'So it turned out the AC wasn't too keen to share with me, which I told him was a diabolical liberty given the *generous* hand of hospitality we had extended to yourself up here. But in the end, he saw it my way.'

'Well that's good,' Frank said uncertainly, at the same time wondering where exactly this conversation was going to end up. Presumably the AC had told Sweeney about UWIPO and the fact that the pilot study was being run in Scotland. But Blair hadn't been involved in any of the detail of the actual pilot sweep, so was probably unaware that Sweeney had been caught in its net. Because if the DCS did know *that*, this conversation was going to get even more awkward than it already was.

'So Stewart, I know what's going on here,' he said, his voice dripping with malice, 'and I don't like it one little bit. What do you think you're doing, you *English* bastards coming up here and poking your noses into our private business?'

Frank gave a sardonic smile. 'In case you've not noticed sir, I'm from Glasgow.'

'Not to me Stewart. To me, you're a bloody traitor. And so is that little smart-arse McDonald as far as I'm concerned. I've seen you two, all pally-wally, sharing sneaky wee cups of coffee. Don't think I haven't noticed. Everybody has, believe you me. And I'll tell you something else. We don't like it.'

'She's got nothing to do with it,' Frank said, suddenly alarmed. 'Nothing at all.'

'Aye, you're *telling* me that,' Sweeney said malevolently. 'But the thing is, I don't believe you. So let me tell *you* something, just so you know.'

Frank looked at him suspiciously but said nothing. He was pretty sure what was coming next, and he didn't think he would like it. And then Sweeney spoke, confirming his worst fears.

'Keep your bloody nose out of our business, okay? Because if you don't, your wee mate DC Lexy McDonald can say bye-bye to her promising career. And actually when I think about it, it's a very dangerous job being a policeman, and there's a lot of really bad people out there. You know what can happen in the line of duty, don't you? Wrong place, wrong time and bang!' He leered as he slammed his fist down on the table. 'And all you have to show for years of dedicated service is a poxy wee medal and your nearest and dearest weeping at your funeral and saying how proud they were of you. Pathetic really.'

Frank could feel his anger rising as he struggled to maintain a measure of calm. *And then he lost the struggle.* He stood up, pushing his face up to within an inch of Sweeney's.

'If anything happens to her *sir*,' he said, spelling out the words to leave no doubt how he felt, 'then I'll make it my life's mission to come after you with everything I've got. Just so you know.' The DCS didn't move an inch, returning Frank's stare with interest and giving a slow laugh.

'You're playing *away* out of you league Stewart, but it's entirely up to you. Your choice. Nothing *stopping* you carrying on of course, but if you want my advice, I'd get your things, take a wee stroll up to the Central Station and bugger off back to London. And don't come back.' He stood up and pushed his chair away, causing it to clatter onto its back. 'Bye bye.'

**

It wasn't until about an hour afterwards that it began to sink in just how problematic the situation had now become. The right thing to do of course was to pursue the truth irrespective of Sweeney's crude threats, but if doing the right thing meant putting Lexy McDonald's career or even her life in danger, well that was a step too far. And anyway, so what if the Chief Super was a bent copper? He wouldn't be the first and he certainly wouldn't be the last, and what were they talking about in any case? So he was swanning about in some fancy motors at someone else's expense. *So what?* The whole thing just wasn't worth the hassle, that was his opinion. And then he pulled himself up short. If everybody just turned a blind eye to corruption, no matter how small-scale, then what sort of state would the country end up in? Maybe AC Blair hadn't been exaggerating when he said the threat was to democracy itself.

In that moment, Frank had made up his mind. He wasn't going to let Sweeney win, no way. But on the other hand, he recognised if he was going to succeed, it was going to need a pretty radical change of tactics. What was it Jimmy had said, something his brother had learned from his time in the army? *Regrouping is not retreating.* Obviously It would be magnitudes more difficult in terms of day-to-day operation if he had to move base-camp from New Gorbals nick, no question about that, not least because he wouldn't have instant access to the Police National Computer and a lot more besides. But with a wee mate like Eleanor Campbell, he was sure that particular technical obstacle could be overcome, and then really all he needed was a new headquarters, and all *that* would need was a desk and convenient access to coffee and chocolate. Suddenly a smile crossed his face as the perfect location came to mind. *Byers Road.* A nice spot up in the West End with a cosy wee coffee place just two doors down. He was sure Maggie and Jimmy wouldn't mind shoving up and making a space for him. Oh aye, and one for Ronnie French too, that would be handy.

But when he thought about it some more, he realised that it wasn't really such a smart idea. The exact opposite in fact, because as dumb ideas went, this one was off the scale in terms of dumbness. Sure, Eleanor Campbell was an IT wizard, unarguably, but she was also as far away from being a rule-breaking maverick as anyone in the Metropolitan Police. The thought of having Frank Stewart holed up in some rickety shop-front office with his laptop sitting, unsecured, on an equally rickety desk, with that same laptop equipped with access to super-sensitive databases? That would give her a herd of kittens, to mangle the popular cliché. He could still work at Maggie and Jimmy's place of course, but with no access to any of the support you got in a cop-shop, it would be like working with your hands tied behind your back. And it wasn't just that, because if he was truthful with himself, he wasn't sure how he and Maggie would get on if they shared an office, even if in theory they were working on completely different things. There had already been adjustments to their relationship in the few weeks they had been living together, none so far affecting the great affection they shared for one another. But of course, that was the thing, wasn't it? None of Maggie's few foibles - like insisting on a clean cup for every cup of tea yet re-using the same teabag three times - had bothered him in the slightest, and in fact, each seemed to add to her wonderful attractiveness in his eyes. But what about her? How was *she* feeling after five or six weeks sharing that nice wee bungalow with *him*? She hadn't made any complaints yet, not even mild ones as far as he could remember, but maybe if they were together twenty-four-by-seven that might change. Aye, sharing an office was a risk, a definite case of chancing fate and pushing his luck too far. He wasn't going there, no way.

So that was it then, decided, although not without some serious misgivings. He would have to stick it out at New Gorbals despite the corrosive atmosphere, and he wasn't going to abandon the pursuit of Sweeney either. But he didn't need to be in the station day-in, day out. He could do a bit of this fashionable working-from-home stuff for a start, and from time to time he could slope off to a cafe or even a pub with his wee notebook. Whatever the location, he recognised the operation was going to need some fair dollops of both stealth and cunning if he was going to make any progress. Luckily a germ of an idea had just appeared centre-stage in that decaying lump of grey matter he called his brain. What it needed was some sort of diversionary tactic, perhaps a false trail that made it clear to Sweeney that he had nothing to worry about.

It was a stupid plan, yes, but was it stupid enough such that it might just about work?

Chapter 16

One of the things Maggie and Jimmy had agreed they'd missed since their move up north was their frequent case conferences at the jam-packed Starbucks on Fleet Street. Somehow the combination of strong coffee and a change of scenery stimulated the old grey cells, to such an extent that some of their most significant breakthroughs had been made in that unprepossessing establishment. Which is why, on a dull and damp Thursday morning, they had decamped three doors down from their Byers Road office to the newly-opened *Bikini Baristas Cafe*. She'd laughed when she'd spotted the sign going up over the door a couple of days earlier, mixed with an amused curiosity as to whether the place would be staffed by young women - and she had half-hoped, young men too - in skimpy designer swimwear. But no, the proprietor, a tattooed and impressively-muscled fifty-something guy called Stevie, wore just a simple black T-shirt bearing the legend *Bikinis*, a uniform shared by the rest of his staff. One day she resolved to ask him about the origin of the name, but for the time being it would have to remain a mystery.

'Nice wee place this,' Jimmy was saying as a waitress inexpertly placed their drinks on the table, in the process filling his saucer with a small pool of treacle-brown liquid. 'So let's hope the coffee's just as nice. Mind you, it should be, given the prices.'

'It's proper excellent,' the waitress interjected in a broad Glasgow accent, ignoring the spillage. 'You'll love it. Defo. We use only the best beans so we do.'

Maggie laughed. 'Well that's good to hear, thank you.'

'Nae problem,' she said, 'I'm Lori by the way. Hope to see youse again.' Tucking her tray under her arm, she sashayed back to the serving counter.

Jimmy shot Maggie an amused look. 'Well at least the lassie's got the customer-interaction bit spot on,' he whispered. 'Fair play to the boy Stevie for that. Now she just needs to figure out how to work a tray.'

'And it *is* excellent coffee,' Maggie said, taking a sip from her cup. 'Quite nutty and flavoursome if that doesn't sound too pretentious.'

'It does sound just a *wee* bit pretentious,' he said, laughing. 'But aye, it's good stuff right enough.'

She grinned. 'Well I'm glad you agree with my *obviously* expert opinion. Anyway, I think this place will do nicely for us, so let's get down to work, because don't forget we're meeting with our client in an hour's time. I'll begin by asking you what you make of what we've found out so far.'

He was silent for a moment then said, 'Aye, well it's all quite interesting, isn't it? So for a start, are we ruling out the two doctors as suspects? Even though their behaviour was pretty deplorable.'

She nodded. 'It was, definitely. But on the evening Juliet disappeared, the two of them went straight to the Union for a drink and there were about a hundred witnesses to say they stayed there all night. So, yes, I'm afraid we need to rule them out, just like the police did in the original investigation. Although what they did to her was a definite catalyst for what happened afterwards, wasn't it?'

'Aye it definitely set off the chain of events,' Jimmy said. 'I think that after the betrayal Juliet adopted a *screw you* attitude, even though she must still have been really hurting inside. So she decides to move out, but not to just any old dump but to that lovely flat up on the Highburgh Road. I think that was an in-your-face show of her moving on to bigger and better things.'

'Exactly,' Maggie said. 'And for that she needs money. So she takes as many shifts as she can get at the Auchterard and she also works as a waitress on this gourmet cruise thing.'

Jimmy nodded. 'Which we are assuming was particularly lucrative, given how keen she was to bag the shifts on it.'

'Yes, which reminds me that we need to follow that up with Francis Cramond at the agency, see what she's got to say about it all.'

'Although remember we promised Phoebe Wilson we wouldn't betray her confidence, which makes that a bit problematic. Especially as it seems to involve some cash-in-hand tax-dodging scam.'

Maggie sighed. 'Yes we did promise her that, didn't we? No matter, if we manage to find out a bit more about these cruises we can probably approach Mrs Cramond from a different angle, without having to implicate our donut-loving Phoebe.'

'It's Miss Cramond by the way, something she was terribly keen to remind me of. She used to be Mrs McBride apparently.'

'Yeah, it's got to be more than a coincidence don't you think?' she said, wrinkling her nose in contemplation. 'As we said on the way back from the hotel, wouldn't it be weird if Francis actually turns out to be related to this Davie Cramond character?'

He nodded. 'Who, by the way, we now know to be the boss-man of the firm that built the Lomond Tower. I don't think that's something you'd want on your CV is it?'

'No, you wouldn't. And if you believe the Chronicle, Mr Cramond is an acquaintance if not a pal of Sheila McClelland.'

'Aye, it's mental how it all seems to be getting tangled up,' Jimmy said, wide-eyed. 'And like you say, if she turns out to be related to him...anyroads, I'm sure we'll find out soon enough when we have our wee chat with him. The concierge guy said he always has a round with some mates on a Friday morning so maybe we can take a trip up there tomorrow. The forecast's not too bad so I guess their golf game will probably go ahead as normal.'

She nodded. 'Good idea. So there's just a couple of other things that we need to think about before we meet with the client. The first one is that thing Mary-Anne Pearson said about Juliet missing a few shifts because of her period.'

'Aye that was interesting, because somehow I imagined Juliet as Miss Reliable. But I think it was you who said they don't call it the curse for nothing. You could ask either of her despicable ex-flat mates if she suffered from bad period pains, because they would be bound to know. And notice what I did there,' he added, grinning. 'I said *you* could ask them.'

'Of course,' Maggie said, thinking out loud, 'but actually it would be easier to just ask her mother. She would know, and she would probably know her dates too.'

He nodded. 'Aye, good call. And what was the other thing you were thinking of?'

'I think we need another public appeal. Because Juliet didn't just evaporate that night. *Someone* must have seen something.'

***

They hadn't expected First Minister McClelland to be at the meeting given her busy schedule but nor were they expecting her husband, so they were surprised to find Andrew McClelland waiting for them outside when they got back to their office. Not that he had any choice but to wait outside, given they'd locked up when they'd sloped off for their coffee break.

'I've been standing here for nearly ten minutes,' he said, not hiding his displeasure. 'In the rain.'

'Sorry,' Maggie said, glancing at her watch and feeling slightly flustered, 'but the meeting wasn't scheduled to start for another fifteen minutes. But you're right, we need to get a receptionist.' She fumbled in her handbag for the key. 'Sorry,' she repeated as she turned it in the lock. 'Please, come on in.'

'Actually we didn't know you were coming,' Jimmy said, pulling him out a chair. 'We thought it was just Willie.'

McClelland gave a dismissive snort. 'I don't think we can leave it in the hands of *him*, can we? Given his shambolic lifestyle, I expect he'll even be late for this meeting.'

She smiled. 'Well we're still a bit early as I said. Look, can we get you a coffee Andrew, whilst we're waiting for Willie? We've discovered a great wee place just a couple of doors down and they do takeaways.'

'No thank you,' he said stiffly. 'I'm not expecting the meeting to take long.'

'We've got quite a lot to get through actually,' Maggie said, slightly defensively. 'We've made some progress I think.'

'I'll be the judge of that,' McClelland said sharply. 'We're paying you plenty, so there'd *better* be some progress.'

She was about to respond then bit her lip. The fee structure of Bainbridge and Stewart was totally transparent and they'd given their client a pretty detailed estimate up-front of how much they expected to spend on the matter. The fact was, Andrew McClelland hadn't wanted them appointed in the first place so it wasn't surprising that his default position would be to find fault with everything they did. Luckily, they were spared further awkwardness by the arrival of Willie Paterson, a full eight minutes early.

'Have you started?' he said anxiously, removing his parka and tossing it carelessly over a chair. As he took his seat, he shot McClelland a look of obvious disapproval then said, 'I wasn't expecting *you*. I thought it was me that was supposed to liaise with these guys.'

'Sheila was anxious that I should attend,' McClelland said. 'Naturally it's extremely important that she gets an accurate update on what little progress there has been.'

Maggie recognised the subtle barb but once again didn't take the bait. Instead she said, 'In answer to your question Willie, no we haven't started yet. Do you want a coffee before we get going?'

Paterson shook his head. 'No, let's get straight into it. Please.'

She nodded. 'Of course.' Then as succinctly as she could, she ran through everything they had done since the inaugural meeting. Unfortunately, hearing it said out loud made her think they hadn't really achieved very much at all. Plenty of background, yes, but as for anything of substance, well that was still lacking. But fortunately, what little they had seemed enough for Juliet's father.

'That's magic so it is,' he said. 'So are you thinking this cruise business might have something to do with her disappearance?'

Maggie shook her head. 'We don't think so but we don't actually know just yet. Really it's just another missing piece in the jigsaw, something we want to try to slot into place.'

'A waste of time if you ask me,' Andrew McClelland said, 'like everything else you seem to be doing.'

Jimmy gave him a benign smile. 'It's not like it is on the telly Andrew,' he said. 'We don't rush about in fast motors with our guns pointing out the window shooting baddies. It's like a wee mosaic. We build up a picture from a thousand tiny pieces until suddenly you can see exactly what it is. That's what we're doing at the moment. Collecting the wee tiles to stick on our mosaic until the picture reveals itself.'

'Very poetic,' McClelland said. 'But just another way of saying you're burning through our money and getting nowhere fast.'

This needs to be nipped in the bud, Maggie thought, or we *will* be getting nowhere.

'The thing is Andrew, the *police* got nowhere with the original investigation and they threw every resource they had at it, and a lot more besides. We can't match that of course, but we can be smarter than them and we can take a few short-cuts too, which is a big advantage for us. But as you know, our contract lets you shut us down at anytime with no quibble.' She paused for a moment and looked him straight in the eye. 'If that's what you want, we can stop right now, no problem. We'll shake hands and that will be it. No hard feelings.' *And then you'll have to go home and tell your wife what you've done.* That was a conversation she would like to be a fly on the wall for, Maggie thought. But one it seemed that was never going to happen, as McClelland first shuffled uncomfortably then said, 'Well, I'll be expecting some proper progress at the next review. A lot more than *this* crap for definite.'

'Of course,' Maggie said calmly. 'And to that end, there's some information I need to get from your wife. But before that, I want to ask you both something.' She paused for a second. 'My question is, would you support another public appeal for information?'

'What, do you mean sticking up posters and that sort of stuff?' Paterson said eagerly. *'Did you see this woman*, that kind of thing? I would, definitely. Of course I would.'

'Yes Willie, but I was thinking a bit more than just posters.' She looked at McClelland and said, 'We wondered if the First Minister might do another personal appeal. I know she did one at the time of Juliet's disappearance, but now that we're looking at the case again, it might be time for another one. It would be very powerful, and it might jog some memories.'

He gave her a withering look. 'So this is what we're paying you for is it? Clutching at straws doesn't even half describe it.'

'People don't just disappear into thin air,' Jimmy said. 'We know that. We also know she wasn't at home when the taxi guy called for her. So after her lecture, she must have gone somewhere else. Where, that's the bloody question we need to answer. Where did she go? And was she with someone, or was she going to meet someone? And if she was doing any of that, someone must have seen her. *Must have*.'

'No way are we doing that,' McClelland said. 'With my wife's profile, we'd be flushing out every nut-case within fifty miles of Hillhead, just trying to get their fifteen minutes of fame. So you can forget that right now.'

'It's not just your decision,' Paterson said sharply. 'Me, I think it sounds like a good idea. As Jimmy said, someone must have seen her that night.'

Maggie paused for a moment then said, 'Look Andrew, I *can* see the point you're making, but it's like Jimmy said. It's all about sifting through a pile of tiny clues and separating the wheat from the chaff so to speak. If a personal appeal from the First Minister generated a lot of chaff, then that is something we would just have to deal with. In the hope that somewhere amongst it all was that vital clue that we are all looking for.'

McClelland gave a dismissive grunt. 'I won't support that, and of course I'll recommend to my wife that she doesn't do it. If anyone had seen anything that night, they would have come forward by now. All this will do is generate more pain for us as a family. So you and your *associate* here ' - he nodded at Jimmy, making no attempt to hide his contempt - 'need to come up with something a lot better than that otherwise we *will* be terminating our professional relationship.'

'It's not just your decision,' Paterson repeated, this time not concealing his anger. 'Juliet is my daughter and we need to do everything we can to find her. And if you and Sheila won't help, then I'll be talking to the media and telling them that. And I'll do it, believe me I will.'

Maggie saw Jimmy shoot her a look that said *what the hell do we do now?* She remembered that the threat to go to the media was one that Willie Paterson had used before, and it would be a story that the hacks would definitely salivate over. She could just imagine the headlines. *Family splits over Juliet search as First Minister refuses appeal.* In some ways it might help, because it would certainly put Juliet's disappearance back in the public eye. But no, they needed a specific appeal for witnesses on that specific night, rather than having the general public gorging on a pile of salacious gossip.

'Okay,' she said, hoping to choose her words carefully so as to steer a middle ground that would appease the warring parties, 'what if we go with a low-key campaign to start with? A few posters around Hillhead and the West End and some posts on a bunch of University social media groups. We know it's a transient population around here with students coming and going so the chances of success are slim, but I don't think it can do any harm.'

'I would agree,' Jimmy said. 'That would be pretty easy to set up and you never know, we might just hit the jackpot.'

'Do it,' Paterson said. 'Right away, please.'

'What about you Andrew?' Maggie asked. 'Are you okay with that?'

He gave her another dismissive look. 'I thought I made my opinion plain. But yes, if you want to waste your time, go ahead.'

Maggie nodded. 'Good, that's settled then. So we'll get that underway and then meet up again in around eight or ten days time to see how it's gone. Everyone happy with that?'

It was pretty evident that McClelland wasn't happy at all, but Maggie was glad that he had at least decided against exercising his veto. Now finally there was some semblance of a plan although afterwards, chatting it through with Jimmy, there was one thing they just couldn't get straight in their mind.

Why was Andrew McClelland so fervently set against a public appeal by his wife?

Chapter 17

It had come highly recommended, this Bikini Cafe place, and it was ideally located for what Frank had in mind for the morning. Lexy McDonald wasn't due on shift until midday, so she could join him for the video call, and with it being well away from New Gorbals nick there was little chance of any nosey-parkers spotting their clandestine assignation. And of course it was pretty handy that it was just a couple of doors down from Maggie and Jimmy's new place. After the meeting he planned to pop in there and with any luck he might bag another kiss, even though it was barely ninety minutes since he'd enjoyed the last one, a pleasingly lingering affair that was only interrupted by wee Ollie appearing on the scene and making a comically-exaggerated fingers-down-the-throat gesture.

He laid down the menu as he saw a young waitress approach his table.

'Hiya, I'm Lori and I'm going to be your server today. What can I get for you?'

Frank smiled. 'I'll be having a large americano with hot milk and a couple of these iced doughnut thingies as well. But I'm just waiting for my colleague to arrive. She'll only be a minute or two.'

'Aye nae bother sir.' He gave her a mildly quizzical look, gathering she was not planning to withdraw. After a moment's hesitation she said, 'Actually you look dead like a guy who was in here the other day. Dead good-looking he was.'

He gave her a wry smile. 'Aye, that would be my wee brother Jimmy. Good looks run in our family you see. It's a bit of a curse actually. We never get a moment's peace from women, me especially.'

'So you're his brother?' she said eagerly, his attempt at humour evidently passing her by. 'Will you give me his number then?'

He laughed. 'Well Lori, I admire your directness but no I don't think I'd better do that, not without his say-so.'

She looked momentarily crestfallen. 'Aye, well I suppose he's already got a girlfriend, has he?'

'Hundreds of them,' Frank said, deadpan. 'He has to keep a special wee diary in alphabetical order to keep track of them. So he doesn't get them all mixed up. But actually, I don't think he's got a Lori yet.'

'Very funny,' she said, a bit less amiably. She nodded towards the door. 'But I think this might be your pal arriving now.'

'Morning sir,' Lexy said, slipping her bag off her shoulder and placing it on the table. 'Nice wee place this. And dead easy for the subway.'

'Aye it is,' he said, smiling. 'This is Lori by the way, she's going to be our server today.'

'Hi Lori,' she said, pulling out the chair. 'Just a cappuccino for me please.'

'Nae bother,' the waitress said, scribbling the order on her pad as she scuttled off. 'Back in a minute or two.'

'Thanks for coming over Lexy,' Frank said. 'I just wanted to give you a heads-up on my plan with regard to Detective Chief Superintendent Sweeney and also to make sure you understand that I can't have you involved in this in any way. And then we'll give Ronnie and Eleanor a call.'

'But I've snuck over here this morning sir,' she said, smiling. 'So I *am* involved already.'

He nodded. 'What I mean is, I don't want you doing anything that can be traced back to you. And I'm being serious. No private enterprise on this one, understand?'

'So why am I here sir?' she said. That was the thing about Lexy, he thought with some amusement. She was a persistent little bugger.

'I just want you to keep your ears open for any canteen gossip about the Chief Super. Because everyone will know about these fancy motors of his and will no doubt have an opinion on how he came by them.'

She looked disappointed. 'Is that all sir? Just that?'

'Aye, just that and no more. Anyway, let's see if we can get the Glimmer Twins now. We're using Facetime today.'

She raised an eyebrow. 'Ooh sir, have you been on a course? That's very leading-edge for you.'

'Remember I'm a Chief Inspector now, DC McDonald. Any more of that and I'll have you on traffic duty.'

She laughed. 'We've not done traffic duty for about forty years now sir. Just in case you haven't noticed.'

'Aye okay smarty-pants. Anyway let's see if we can get our pair on the line.'

Eleanor Campbell answered on the first ring with a sharp 'hello'. She was evidently at her favoured desk in Atlee House, tucked away against a wall on the second floor where it struggled to be illuminated by the ancient strip lighting, giving her face a ghostly pallor. Alongside her sat DC Ronnie French, he similarly afflicted pallor-wise, although Frenchie looked the same in the brightest of summer sunshine, the consequence of a life misspent in the salubrious pubs and snooker halls of his native Essex.

'Hello yourself,' Frank said. 'So the place hasn't burnt down in my absence then?'

'We're missing you guv,' French said, grimacing. 'DCI Smart's here nearly every day and driving us nuts. No offence of course, but she's doing my head in. She keeps asking me for updates on my cases. I'm run off my feet.'

Frank laughed. 'Well it might surprise you Frenchie, but the Met does actually pay you to do a wee bit of actual work from time to time. In fact thinking about it, maybe you two both need that wee bit of discipline. Maybe I let the place go soft.' Catching Eleanor's withering look he decided to curtail that particular line of conversation. 'So anyway, to business,' he said hurriedly. 'To UWIPO, and in particular, to a couple of its victims, starting with one DCS Peter Archibald Sweeney.'

'The car guy,' French said.

'Exactly. So what I want to know Eleanor is how your fancy software picked up on these flash motors and if there's any trail that tells us where the money came from to pay for them. Because I think I'm right in saying that there's no record of any movements of funds either in or out of his bank account that would explain it?'

'We do a wide sweep,' she said. 'We do like *obviously* look at bank accounts as a first pass but that doesn't normally work because you would have to be pretty dumb to pay any dishonest cash into your regular current account. So we look at the DVLA and insurance company databases to see if there are any expensive vehicles taxed or insured in their name. That's how we found Sweeney actually. There was nothing at the Licensing Agency but we found a multi-car insurance policy on the three vehicles in his name. With Arista Insurance.'

Frank paused for a moment as he tried to make sense of what she'd told him, then said, 'So that means what, that he doesn't actually *own* these cars? If his name didn't show up against them at the DVLA I mean.'

'Maybe it means he's just got the use of them guv,' Frenchie said. 'Somebody's doing him a huge favour though, letting him loose on a hundred and fifty grand's-worth of motor. And it's still unexplained loot, no matter how you look at it.'

'But we know the registration numbers so the actual owner will be on the DVLA database I suppose?' Lexy asked.

French shrugged. 'Yeah, but it'll probably be a company. With about ten layers of ownership to confuse the arse off of anyone who comes looking.'

'Which means the Super could still be the ultimate owner I suppose?' Lexy said.

'Aye, you're right Lexy, I hadn't thought of that,' Frank said. 'Anyway Eleanor and Ronnie, that's your first wee bit of homework. Do some digging and see if you can unravel that trail for me.'

'Sure guv,' French said laconically. 'That should be easy enough for Eleanor.' The forensic officer shot him a contemptuous look but said nothing.

'Good,' Frank said, 'so that's the first part of the exercise sorted. The second part is, I want us to go back over the last two or three years and see if there were any cases that Sweeney was involved in where he might have had the opportunity to make some personal profit. We'll be looking at drugs busts primarily I'd guess, or more specifically drugs investigations that somehow didn't make it to court. Where he might have been paid to look the other way, that kind of thing.'

'They keep a book actually, at New Gorbals,' Lexy said, smirking. 'They use it to manage who works on what and it goes back for years. And when I say book, I mean *books*. There's loads of them, going way back.'

Frank looked surprised. 'What, an *actual* book? But haven't we've got that gazillion-million-quid system that's supposed to do all that? They implemented it nationwide about four years ago, in every force. I remember going on the training course. Fell asleep but they did a lovely lunch.'

Lexy laughed. 'And do *you* use it sir?'

'No way. It's crap.'

She laughed again. 'So I rest my case. I bet every force in the country actually uses some kind of wee book, even if they pretend to use the new computer system. *Our* top brass sit down once a week to do the staff planning and one of them writes it all up and sticks the book in his drawer. So you see, I couldn't get a hold of it even if I wanted to. '

'Well I wouldn't want you trying, don't worry about that. But how then do we find out what he was up to two years ago if we can't see the magic book?'

Ronnie French shrugged. 'We could look at the court schedules guv. We can get them online and it usually tells you the names of the cops involved in the prosecution.'

'Good thinking Frenchie,' Frank said approvingly, being made aware once again how easy it was to underestimate the corpulent DC. 'So Ronnie, add that to your wee list will you?'

'But guv,' French protested, 'I *told* you I'm run off my feet.'

'Aye, but I'm sure you'll manage to squeeze it in somehow. Just for me. So that brings me to the last thing on my list.'

Eleanor piped up, 'I'm like busy too,' evidently detecting that the next task was likely to be coming her way.

'I don't think this will take you long,' Frank said soothingly. 'In fact I distinctly remember you telling me it was only a few lines of code, and with you being such an ace coder, that's only five minutes' work. I'm sure that's what you said.'

She glared at him, leaning forward such that her nose was almost touching the screen of her phone. 'I said it's a few *hundred* lines of code. That's not the same thing.'

'Good to know,' he said, smiling. 'But knowing you, I'm guessing you'll have already done it. Am I right?'

She gave him a sheepish look. 'You're right. You see, it was like a *mega*-interesting project. I had to do seventeen SQL joins across six virtual domains and two military-grade firewalls, and there was a ton of in-browser recursive code too.'

'Pretty straightforward then,' he smirked, unable to resist the joke, but then instantly regretting it. 'So does that mean we can now find out where our guy Andrew McClelland's six grand a month is going?'

'*Which* guy?' she said sourly.

He heard Ronnie French laughing off-camera. 'I think you might have to buy her flowers guv. She's just about to storm off-set.'

Involuntarily Frank laughed too, which he recognised as not the smartest reaction in the circumstances. But then Eleanor said something that took him totally by surprise.

'So I know where his money goes. Like *already*.'

I thought you didn't even know which guy we're talking about was what he was about to say, but he checked himself just in time. Instead he said, 'Really? Well that's bloody amazing Eleanor, it really is.' And he wasn't joking either, this *was* bloody amazing. 'But how come?'

'I needed a test case for my code, and like *obviously* it had to be real because you can't simulate such complexity in my development environment.' Her irritation had evaporated almost as soon as it had arrived, being replaced by a modest self-satisfaction.

'So you used Andrew McClelland as a test case? That's absolutely brilliant. So, what's the answer then? Where does this money end up? Who's getting it I mean?'

She shrugged. 'A woman.'

'That's right guv,' French said. 'It goes on a convoluted route but ends up back in a current account here in the UK in the name of some bird called Miranda Temple.'

'And who's she? Do we know?'

'No, not yet. But I've been...'

Frank laughed. 'I know, you've been run off your feet. But I bet you know what I'm going to say, don't you?'

'Yeah I bloody do guv,' he said gloomily. '*Add it to your list*.'

'Quite correct. So troops, I think we might be getting somewhere now. We've got a wee plan for DCS Sweeney and we've got a mystery woman to track down, who might be able to tell us what our Mr McClelland's been up to. You know what Lexy, maybe we should celebrate with another couple of these doughnuts.'

She laughed. 'Sounds a good idea sir. A nice wee doughnut then back to my gruesome murder enquiry.'

'Well you know what they say about all work and no play. Okay guys, we'll hang up now, but Ronnie, I'll be expecting you and Eleanor to get back to me with good news in the next couple of days. Over and out.'

'So that's probably it then as far as your involvement goes,' Frank said to Lexy after he had hung up. 'But I guess you'll have your hands full on your murder job anyway. Talking of which, is there any progress on finding out who your victim is yet?'

She shrugged. 'No sir. They're running another appeal on the evening news tonight in the hope that someone will come forward, but no, he's a real mystery man.'

'Aye, well it's a bit tricky to run a murder enquiry when you don't know who the victim is that's for sure. And they're still not connecting your case with that earlier one, the Ally Russell guy?'

'No sir,' she said through a mouthful of doughnut. 'The Chief Super says there's no obvious connection other than they were both found on the shores of the Loch. Although he did say that might change if they ever find out who the second victim is.'

'And no progress on the Russell case either? No speculation on the motive, or any suspects?'

She gave a wry smile. 'Nothing other than that bollocks the journalist guy wrote in the Chronicle.'

He laughed. 'That the government had him killed because he was sneaking tourists onto Inchcailloch?'

'That's the one sir. As I said, pure bollocks, if you'll pardon the expression.' She stood up, grabbing her bag and slinging it over her shoulder. 'Anyway sir, must get back. And I'll keep my ear to the ground like you asked.'

'And Lexy, what else *mustn't* you do?'

'Anything sir. I mustn't do anything at all. And I won't. *Promise*.'

Chapter 18

Once again they were on their way up to Loch Lomond, with Jimmy driving and she trying to relax in the passenger seat, but this time they had set off from the Byers Road office rather than her new Milngavie home. The morning had been mainly spent interviewing candidates for their receptionist cum administrator post, but none had proved suitable. Frank had popped in to say hello following his meeting at the Bikini Baristas Cafe, and they'd shared a joke or two about waitress Lori's sweet little crush on Jimmy. Much to Maggie's relief, Jimmy had seemed more like himself these past few days, although that did cause her to wonder if she knew what *himself* actually was. Goodness knows, the pair of them had been through plenty of trauma in the last couple of years, but she had Ollie as the immovable anchor in her life, and now she had Frank too. Jimmy had lost Flora, and now with his ex-wife about to re-marry, he had lost all hope too of there ever being a reconciliation. Maggie couldn't help worrying he was drifting like flotsam in the sea, his life being in control of him rather than the other way round.

But then, halfway into their journey, and completely out of the blue, he said something that made her think that perhaps everything would be okay.

'I took your advice Maggie. I joined one of these Facebook groups, ex-service guys with issues. They talk about what they went through, all that sort of stuff. It's good.'

'That's amazing Jimmy.' She reached over and squeezed his arm. 'And have you told them about Belfast? About Naomi I mean?'

'I did. And it felt better. There's a lot of guys who've been through the same thing.'

She gave a sigh of relief. 'You see, I told you there would be. I really do hope it helps.'

'I think it will. It's been pretty helpful so far.

'That's great. So now all we need to do is get you fixed up with a nice girlfriend. I was thinking maybe that little minx at the Bikini cafe.'

He laughed. 'Can I pass on that one? But honestly, I'm okay. I just need to get Flora's wedding behind me and then it's onwards and upwards.'

His words pulled her up short and now she wondered if her expectation of a positive outcome may have been premature. She knew she should say something, tell him that this obsession with the wedding - because she regarded it as nothing less - wasn't healthy and would only lead to further unhappiness. But really, it wasn't her place and she knew it was almost certain to fall on deaf ears in any case. So she just said, 'Yeah, that would be good.' It was hardly profound, but right at that moment she couldn't think of anything better.

They drove in silence for the next few miles, she passing the time by fantasising about hiring a hit-man to put a bullet through the head of Flora's fiancé Hugo. Until she remembered that Jimmy owned a gun, an army-issue pistol sneaked out after he'd come back from Helmand, causing her to stupidly worry if he himself might go and do something crazy. And then she let out a giggle as she recognised the absurdity of it all.

'What's so funny?' Jimmy asked, amused.

'Oh nothing. I was just having a *very* weird daydream that's all. But come on, let's focus on work, shall we? Specifically on Mr Davie Cramond of Premier Construction and the Auchterard Golf Club.'

'Aye, it's going to be interesting what he has to say for himself. Actually, I was quite surprised that he agreed to talk to us. He must be a busy guy.'

Maggie nodded. 'But not too busy to play golf every Friday it seems. Anyway I obviously told him it was in connection with the Juliet McClelland disappearance and he said yes, anything he could do to help.'

'I guess he knows her mother doesn't he? Because there was that photo in the Chronicle.'

She shrugged. 'He's met her, sure. But we can't say if he actually *knows* her in the sense they're friends or anything. Lots of people must meet the First Minister.'

Cramond met them in an opulent wood-panelled lounge that sat alongside the golf club's restaurant, evidently where golfers and guests repaired for coffee after enjoying the fabulous food for which the establishment was noted. Maggie guessed he was in his mid-fifties, just short of six foot tall, and broad-shouldered and slim-hipped. Good looking, definitely, and even though he wore his hair a bit long for her taste, she thought that it suited him. Less tangibly, he seemed to radiate an aura of supreme self-confidence, of a type she'd seen before in men who'd made a great success of their lives. Or, and this she had seen rather more often, in men who liked to give the *impression* they'd made a great success of their lives.

'Welcome to Auchterard Golf Club,' he said pleasantly. 'Take a seat over there and we'll get the steward to fetch us some nice wee drams, or some coffee if you'd prefer. Me, I always like a wee nip after a round. I find it helps you forget the shit four and a half hours you've just wasted. What about you two? Do you play this god-awful game?'

Jimmy smiled. 'I admit to owning a set of clubs Mr Cramond but I keep them locked away under the stairs for good reason.'

'Never mind the Mr Cramond stuff, everybody calls me Davie.' He gave a short laugh. 'Except my ex-wife that is. She calls me a complete bastard, which is probably a fair assessment to be honest. Anyway, what is it I can do for you two?'

'Well,' Maggie said, 'as I explained on the phone, we're a private detective agency and we're working for the family to try and unravel what happened to Juliet McClelland.' She paused for a moment then said quietly, 'Did you know her?'

'What, know Juliet? No, why should I?'

'She worked here in the hotel, for a couple of years in fact. And she was a very beautiful girl, so I think she would have stood out.'

He shrugged. 'Well aye, I learnt she worked here obviously, that was all in the papers at the time of her disappearance. But I don't think I ever bumped into her myself. Mind you, it's a big hotel and I only really use the clubhouse here so it's probably not that surprising.'

'Yes, I can understand that,' Maggie said, weighing up whether she believed him or not. *Probably*, was her initial conclusion, but not *definitely*. No matter, it was possible the next line of questioning would shine a brighter light on the matter.

'We heard from the agency that organises staff for the hotel that Juliet also waitressed from time to time for a gourmet cruise company. And Sandy McDuff up at the hotel suggested that you yourself might have had some hand in organising these cruises. I was just wondering if you could confirm if that is actually the case?'

He gave an amused smile. 'So that wee agency will be the one run by my delightful sister Francis. Has she been telling you all my secrets?'

'None whatsoever,' she said, smiling then shooting Jimmy a knowing look. So Francis Cramond was Davie Cramond's sister then? *Interesting.* 'It was actually one of her staff who mentioned the cruises to us. She told us Juliet liked to get as many shifts on them as she could because they paid extremely well.'

Cramond furrowed his brow as if searching his memory for something buried deep in the past. 'Och aye, I remember now. It was a couple of years back at least but I do vaguely remember one of my mates at the club here telling me about there being some fancy chef involved and persuading me to try one out. It set off from the wee jetty at Inchcailloch as a matter of fact, because I remember we had a few beers at the Tower bar before we left. I just went along for the craic a couple of times but didn't think much of it so I didn't go again. The food was crap and on the two nights we went it was really choppy out there so the other two guys spent the night puking over the edge of the boat. Mind you, we we're all pretty pissed so that might have had something to do with *that*.'

'But it wasn't you who organised them?' Maggie said.

He smiled amiably. 'Nah not me. I mean, how would I have the time for that? But actually, it's kind of coming back to me that it was Sandy McDuff who set them up. He knew a guy with a boat and he must have roped in the chef as well. *He* was French, I remember that much, worked at a Michelin-starred place up in Glasgow. Oh aye, and the other thing I remember about the Frog was he actually turned out to be a rubbish cook. Mind you, we're spoiled because we get nothing but the best at this wee restaurant.'

'And I guess if I were to ask you whether Juliet was one of the servers on any of your trips you would say no?'

'Definitely, I can say that with no hesitation. I remember we had some school lads serving us on our trips which pissed off a couple of the boys who were hoping for a pair of schoolgirls. You know, with the short tartan skirts and the pert wee tits.'

Accompanied by a crude leer, it was a blatantly distasteful remark, but of the type Maggie had been on the end of plenty of times before. Misogynistic behaviour had been rife in her time at Drake Chambers, with the loathsome clerk Nigel Redman by far the worst offender with his blatant sexual innuendos. But today, it gave some indication of how Davie Cramond regarded women, and perhaps went some way to explaining his evident marital difficulties.

'And this golf club mate you mentioned,' Jimmy said, 'the one who got you into it, who was he can I ask?'

'Aye, that was Shuggie Davidson. He was a good golfer actually, big Shug. He played off three, and he was still a bit of a bandit even with that handicap.'

Maggie gave him a sharp look. 'You said *was*. Does that mean he's left the club?'

Cramond laughed. 'Aye, you could say that. Big Shuggie had a heart attack a year ago. He's sadly missed around here I can tell you that. Always first to get his hand in his pocket at the bar and never short of a wee dirty joke.'

'I'm sorry to hear that,' she said. Which was of course what everyone said in these circumstances, even though they didn't know the person in question and thus had no idea whether they were a loss to the world or not. Unkindly she thought that if this dirty-joke-telling Shuggie was anything like his friend, he probably was no loss at all. 'And is there anybody else at the club who might have gone on these cruises who might be able to help us do you know?'

He shrugged. 'Maybe, but it was just me and Shug on the couple I went on. There were a few other guys too but we didn't know them. And I don't think they've been running for a couple of years now. At least if they are I've not heard of it.'

'And the boat guy,' Jimmy said. 'You don't know who he was?'

'Haven't a clue. He had a beard, I remember that. But he was a right miserable bastard. He didn't say much.'

'And what about the boat?' Maggie said. 'You don't happen to remember it's name?'

He shook his head. 'Nah, not something I'd be interested in to be fair. It was just a *boat*, you know, sort of medium-sized, fairly old I think. Wooden, I seem to remember and about forty or fifty feet long, I don't really know. It just looked like any one of these wee tourist boats that float up and down the loch. With a big cabin in the middle where they set out the dining table.'

It was becoming clear to Maggie that they weren't really getting anywhere, either because Cramond didn't actually know anything or because he was being deliberately but cleverly obstructive. But there was one more thing she wanted to ask him before they wrapped up the meeting, something that wasn't directly related to Juliet's disappearance. And something he might not care to talk about.

'You mentioned the cruises set off from Inchcailloch which of course made me think of the terrible tragedy. That must be so difficult for you, what happened that night. And just half a mile from where we're sitting at this very moment.'

He gave her a look of anger mixed with defiance. 'It was an act of *god,* a bloody freak storm. There's been nothing like it in a hundred years. And the world's got climate change in case you haven't heard.'

Although as the media had pointed out at the time, she thought, tens of thousands of buildings across Scotland *didn't* fall down that night. But maybe she was being unduly hard on the guy. If you had something so terrible on your conscience, how *would* you react? Would it break you, even drive you to consider ending it all? Would you be full of contrition and do everything in your power to help the grieving relatives, by setting up a huge compensation fund or something tangible like that? Or would you, like Davie Cramond seemed to be doing, go into denial, convincing yourself that it truly was an act of god, a cruel accident that couldn't possibly have been prevented? Actually, maybe she wasn't being so hard on the guy after all. What if he really didn't give a shit about what had happened? After all, he was still coming here once a week for his nice round of golf and a convivial lunch with his mates.

'I'm sorry to have brought it up,' she said, although she wasn't. 'You've been very helpful and I'm sure Juliet's family will be grateful for your cooperation. But we'll take our leave now if that's okay.'

He shrugged. 'Aye sure. But just let me say before you go, you shouldn't believe any of the shite that guy Patel writes. I've already got my lawyers onto his crappy little rag.'

Knowing Yash, she could imagine what his reaction to *that* would be. *Yeah, bring it on.*

'Good to meet you,' Jimmy said. 'And thanks for your great help Davie. Appreciated.'

Maggie caught her colleague's glance and gave a wry smile. For whatever Davie Cramond had been, he certainly hadn't been of much help.

***

'They've got us going round in circles here,' Jimmy said as they made their way back to the car. 'Davie Cramond said it was Sandy McDuff who organised the cruises but McDuff said the exact opposite.'

Maggie nodded. 'Exactly Jimmy. It's a pity McDuff wasn't in today or we could have heard his side of the story. But of course there's some good that comes out of that because it means that one of them must be being less than truthful. And you know what *that* means.'

He nodded. 'I do. It means that one of them must have something to hide.'

'Exactly. But the thing is Jimmy, even if there's something dodgy going on, there's nothing really to connect it back to Juliet is there? Really, we're just going down this rabbit-hole because we have to. But that's what it will probably turn out to be. Just a rabbit-hole.'

Back at the car, they sat in silence for a full five minutes, Maggie churning the case around in her head and assuming that Jimmy was doing the same.

'We're clutching at straws, aren't we?' she said finally. 'Just like Andrew McClelland said we were.'

He shook his head. 'No no, we're not. Juliet wanted as many shifts as she could get on these cruises, that's what Phoebe Wilson told us. She said the money was amazing, that was her exact words. So we're right to pursue it, definitely.'

And then suddenly it came to Maggie, a question so damned obvious she could kick herself for not thinking of it sooner.

Just exactly how much was *amazing*?

Chapter 19

Back at the New Gorbals nick, Frank had fortified himself with his usual americano - or to be accurate, *americanos* - before embarking on a sweep of the building for his pal DCS Sweeney. First stop had to be the buzzing murder investigation room given that the guy would be up to his armpits in the two Loch Lomond killings. Cautiously pushing open the door, he saw the DCS was on his feet at the front of the room, evidently addressing the troops, who sat lounging at desks or stood in small clumps towards the back of the room. The general gist of the four-letter-expletive-laden epistle was that they were all bloody useless and they couldn't even catch a *beep-beep* cold if they stood out in the rain for a week. This was presumably linked to the fact that three weeks in, they were still struggling for a motive to explain the murder of the boatman Ally Russell, and worse than that, they still hadn't discovered the identity of the second victim. Evidently the purpose of Sweeney's speech was to encourage greater efforts on their part, but Frank knew from looking at some of the faces in the room that it would encourage the exact opposite. Not that he gave a stuff about that of course, although he didn't want wee Lexy McDonald, sitting quietly at the side of the room, being affected by the fall-out if the two investigations fell flat on their collective arses. A couple of DSs were brave enough to ask some clarifying questions, being rewarded by a Sweeney death-stare and no doubt having their cards marked as trouble-makers. Whatever the truth in that, it had the effect of bringing the session to a rapid close, Sweeney tucking his notebook under his arm and marching towards the door, where Frank stood. He stopped abruptly when he saw him.

'I thought I told you to eff off back to London Stewart. But I see you haven't. Why not?'

Frank smiled sweetly. 'I thought of taking your advice sir, because believe me, nothing would give me more pleasure to eff my way back down the M74. But the fact is, if I don't see this wee job through, they won't make my DCI permanent, and quite frankly I want the extra dosh and the pension that comes with it. Nothing wrong with that is there sir?' He paused for a moment. 'Actually sir, I wanted to talk to you about this whole thing.' He paused again. 'You see, I'm as pissed off as you are about all this secrecy, which is why yesterday I told my gaffer and AC Blair that unless I could tell you exactly what I was doing up here, I was going to walk off the job and they could stuff their promotion up their backside. Because it's not right sir, is it? The sneakiness I mean.'

Sweeney gave him a suspicious look. 'You've changed your tune a bit, haven't you?'

Frank shrugged. 'I was never happy with any of it. It was totally deliberate of course, by the UK government I mean. To pick us as their pilot. A bit of political shit-stirring, no more and no less.'

'What's all this *UK government* and *us* stuff? I didn't have you down as a nationalist.'

'Just a proud Scot sir, that's all. As for independence, we couldn't be much worse off, could we?'

'Well I haven't got time for any of that bollocks,' Sweeney sneered. 'Too much golf to play. But I don't like anyone messing about on my patch either.'

'Totally with you there sir. So as I said, I've had a wee word with my gaffers and I'm cleared to tell you exactly what I'm up to. If you've got five minutes?'

'Follow me,' Sweeney said, pushing through the double doors. 'My office.'

Frank smiled. 'I'm right behind you.'

***

All in all the meeting with Sweeney had gone pretty well, mainly because Frank's explanation of what he was up to was both plausible and not too far from the truth either. The story went that

Government Minister Caroline Connor and her crew were looking for a UWIPO scalp, but preferably someone who would not evoke too much public outrage when the story eventually broke. Something that might even have the public nodding their collective heads and saying, *yeah, we really do need this UWIPO initiative to catch all these powerful people with their snouts in the trough, even if it is a terrible invasion of privacy*. So what better than a senior policeman with a penchant for fancy overseas holidays, and even better, a senior cop parachuted into a top Scottish police job from the Met, chosen over a swathe of resentful local candidates? Yep, Assistant Chief Constable Belinda Cresswell, currently trying to sort out the mess that was the Grampian division, was soon going to be rather famous, and no-one north of the border would give a stuff either, irrespective of their political leanings. Now he would just let Ronnie and Eleanor's investigations into Sweeney's financial arrangements run their natural course, in the expectation that something juicy would emerge, and when that happened, he would equip Ronnie with a train-ticket northwards and he could take it on from then. Now, he decided, he would give some more thought to the Andrew McClelland situation. He was just wandering back to his desk when his phone rang. He fished it from his pocket and looked at the screen. Surprised and intrigued in equal measure, he punched the answer button and raised it to his ear.

'*Yash Patel*. Now this is an unexpected pleasure. Long time no speak young Yash. How goes it?'

'*Good Frank good*,' he said in his trademark hundred-words-a-minute style. '*I've been busy up in your homeland as you might have read. Or you might even have seen me on the telly talking about it.*'

Frank laughed. 'I've told you before mate, the Chronicle's got too many long words for me, and I've not really got time to watch telly. But aye, actually I have read all your stuff about the McClelland Tower. It was a terrible tragedy and all this stuff about the government being warned not to build it on Inchcailloch, well that doesn't look good does it? This public enquiry's going to be interesting I think.'

'*A whitewash, that's what it will be. But I'm not going to let that happen. I'm finding out new things every day. Bad things. It's a massive heap of shit.'*

'Well shit's your stock-in trade, so you should be like a pig in it,' Frank said. 'Anyway, what is it I can do for you?'

'Can I buy you a pint?'

'Always. But I'm not in London at the moment. I'm working in Glasgow for my sins.'

'I know. On UWIPO.'

'What? How the hell do you know that? It's supposed to be a bloody secret.'

He heard Patel laugh. *'You can't use the words 'Home Office' and 'secret' in the same sentence Frank, you should know that. Everything they do is controversial so for every initiative there's always an insider who doesn't like it. Which is great for me. Anyway, I'm working out of Glasgow too at the moment, so I can meet you anytime you like. A couple of beers would be nice. Maybe I could even buy you a curry.'*

'I just love your paper's expense account,' Frank said, laughing. 'I'll tell you what. Do you remember my wee brother Jimmy and his boss

Maggie Bainbridge? Well, they're working up here too at the moment and we'd been talking about going for a Ruby on our normal Thursday get-together. Why don't you join us and we can reminisce about old times?'

'*Sounds good*,' Patel said. '*And I'm paying.*'

Frank smiled. 'Aye, of course you are. And before you say anything, this won't worry UWIPO. There's a thousand-quid threshold.'

***

They were just a few streets away from the University, the traditional home of some of the city's most revered Indian eating-houses, and had chosen the most expensive of those on Yash Patel's specific instructions. He wanted something of course. Patel always wanted something, but this no-expense-spared extravagance suggested that this evening he wanted something big. Names, that's what he'd be after, Frank guessing that his Home Office mole had either stopped short of leaking the identities of who had triggered the red flags on the initial UWIPO run, or didn't know them. Actually when he thought about it a bit more, he wouldn't have been surprised if it had been Caroline Connor herself who was responsible for the leak, knowing a bit about how these things seemed to work. But as far as he himself was concerned, there would be no leaks, and if Yash subsequently felt he'd got poor value from his investment in their entertainment, well so be it. The slippery journalist wouldn't be getting anything from him, that was for sure.

They'd been allocated a very nice table with plenty of elbow-room to accommodate the onslaught of side-dishes that Frank hoped were about to come their way, covered by a dazzling white linen tablecloth that he didn't expect would remain unblemished for long. Beers had already been ordered and delivered, and the atmosphere was relaxed and convivial.

'Poppadoms? Onion bhajis? Samosas? The works?' Yash said. 'I've heard all about this place by the way, it gets rave reviews.'

'We've not been before,' Maggie said, smiling, 'We've only been living up here a few weeks so not had a chance to try it yet.'

'Liking it?' Yash said. 'Scotland I mean?'

'Loving it. And my little boy has settled in so well at his new school. Although they do take the mickey out of his accent a bit.'

'What you mean is they *did*,' Frank corrected. 'Now wee Ollie sounds as if he was brought up in Govan. He's got a broader Glasgow accent than me and Jimmy.'

'He does too,' Jimmy said. 'A right wee patter-merchant. Anyway, did somebody say four more beers?'

Yash laughed. 'Coming straight up.' He gestured to a waiter, who sped over to them, acknowledged their order with the faintest of nods, then sped off again.

'Great service here,' Frank said approvingly. 'So then Yash, what have you been up to?'

'You know that already I'm sure. It's all been mainly the Lomond Tower. It shouldn't have been built, and my paper is going to make sure that those responsible face the consequences. Irrespective of what the public enquiry says. Because there's a big trail of shit leading right back to the Government in my opinion.'

'We met Davie Cramond the other day, you know, from Premier Construction,' Maggie said. 'Not the nicest of guys I must say. He seemed strangely undamaged by the whole thing. Said it was an act of god and blamed it on climate change at the same time.'

Yash's eyes lit up. 'You met Cramond did you? Do you think you could get me in there? I could come along with you on your next meeting. Unannounced I mean.'

She sighed. 'I'm not sure there's going to be a next meeting. We got everything we could from him, which was basically two-thirds of nothing at all.'

'No matter,' he said. 'Because it's not really him I'm after. It's the First Minister who I've got in my sights.'

'Because of that photograph?' Jimmy asked. 'The one with her and Cramond?'

'Exactly. You see, the contract was awarded to his Premier Construction outfit just a month after the two of them met at that function. Now don't you think that's an interesting coincidence?'

'But hang on a minute,' Frank said. 'I think you're hinting at sleaze here without any evidence that this Davie Cramond guy employed any funny business to win the contract. And it's no secret that Sheila was absolutely desperate to get the tower built, but she's a really decent woman and wouldn't be involved in anything dodgy. I'm absolutely sure of that.'

'We're not saying there was anything *corrupt*. Just, as you said, that they were hugely keen to get it built as a symbol of national brilliance. A big fancy showcase so they could say to the world *look how clever wee Scotland is*.'

Maggie laughed. 'When you put it that way, it seems more likely she was bribing *him* rather than the other way round.'

Yash smiled. 'Exactly. *Exactly that*.'

'So what are you suggesting?' she said, looking puzzled. 'That the government *actually* bribed him?'

'Imagined in Scotland, designed in Scotland, built in Scotland,' Yash said, giving an ironic smile. 'You must remember the slogan. This was the ultimate vanity project and if it didn't get built, a

lot of important people were going to look like complete dicks. And as we all know, that's not a look that any government is fond of at all, whether it be in Scotland or anywhere else. So what I'm trying to find out is if there were any let's call them *incentives* to overcome any reluctance on anyone's part. Starting with the guy who said it was technically possible in the first place.'

'Who's that?' Jimmy asked.

'A guy called Dougal McCrae. He's a professor at Glasgow Uni. And then we need to see what inducements might have been put in place so that Cramond's firm would take on the project. You see, the government has never released the terms of the contract into the public domain, but my paper has put in a Freedom of Information request for it to be coughed up so that we can see what was in it.'

'What are you looking for exactly?' Maggie said.

'I don't know. But probably something that doesn't make any commercial sense. So huge bonus payments structured into the agreement, or something like that, you know, tied to a successful completion.' He paused for a moment then said,

'You see, it doesn't have to be actual corruption to make it a big story. Reckless use of public funds would do quite nicely for me.' He paused again. 'Now that I think of it, perhaps you could give Davie Cramond a call and ask him straight out. Because I'm assuming he would take your call, since you've met him before? And he would know what was in that contract, definitely.'

She laughed. 'Eh, nice try Yash but no, I don't think we'll be doing that. We're trying to find out what happened to poor Juliet McClelland and her mother Mrs McClelland is our client, so I think we would be on very dodgy moral ground if we were to help you on this. Sorry.'

They were interrupted by the ostentatious arrival of their starters, wheeled to their table on a trolley accompanied by two nervous-looking young servers in long white tail-coats with shining gold buttons. Their uniforms looked so new that Frank wondered if it was their first outing.

'Pile all the dishes in the centre of the table,' he said breezily, 'and just bung us the wee white plates and we'll serve ourselves.' He caught a look of faint disappointment on the face of the younger of the waiters, who evidently had something rather more theatrical in mind.

'Very well sir,' he said, nodding to his companion to commence operations. Covers were whipped off silver salvers and elaborately-arranged serving dishes were placed on the table. Barely a micro-second later, Frank was leaning over and with a brisk *excuse me*, helping himself to a couple of onion bhajis.

'Lovely,' he said, brushing crumbs from around his mouth. 'So this is all very nice, but I'm assuming young Yash that you're looking for something in return for your generous hospitality.'

Yash smiled. 'I was hoping for a name. You know, who you're looking at on this UWIPO thing.' Without giving Frank a chance to answer he continued. 'But I know you're not going to give me that. So all I'm asking on that story is for an unattributed confirmation that a Metropolitan Police undercover team is working on it up here and that they are pursuing a number of lines of enquiry.'

'But you know that already,' Frank said, raising an eyebrow. 'Your Home Office mole told you.'

He nodded. 'But this lets me confirm that the story is true. Gives me an excuse for another article. My editor's been nagging me for more.'

Frank gave him a sceptical look. 'And that's all you want?'

'Well actually, now you ask...'

'All right,' Frank sighed. 'Out with it.'

'The fact is, I'm mainly interested in what's happening on the Ally Russell murder case. You see, I feel quite personally invested in it because he's the guy who took me on to Inchcailloch the very first time. Not exactly Mr Personality, but it was still a shock when I found out he'd been murdered.'

'My pal DCS Sweeney does a regular media conference. You can get everything you need from that.'

'Yeah, but he doesn't say anything about motive or anything like that, you know, the really interesting stuff.'

Frank gave Yash a wry look. 'Have you still got this crazy idea he was killed by the bloody government to discourage other boat guys doing the Inchcailloch trip? Because that's complete and utter bollocks and you know it.'

'No no, I'm thinking I might be on the scent of a *much* better conspiracy theory now,' Yash said. 'You see, Russell drove a Range Rover which wasn't even a year old and I'd always wondered how he could afford a car like that. So I did some research. I spoke to quite a few people who knew him and I think you might be intrigued by some of the things I found out.'

'Oh aye?' Frank said, his tone guarded. 'Like what?'

'Like the fact that he owns - or should I say *owned* - a luxury pleasure-trip boat. That's where all his money came from. That's what a guy at the hotel I stayed in thinks anyway.'

'What?' Maggie exclaimed.

Frank saw her exchange a look with his brother.

'What's the issue?' he said.

'It's our Juliet McClelland case,' she said, sounding excited. 'She did some waitressing on a boat. For some private gourmet cruises. But we've hardly been able to find out anything about them. It's like they never ever existed.'

Yash gave her a smug look. 'I can probably tell you why that is, assuming Russell was the man you're looking for.'

'Why?' Maggie said.

'There was a big incident about three and a half years ago. On one of these booze cruises he used to run. A guy went overboard and was never seen again.'

'Good god,' Maggie said. 'So what exactly happened?'

'Well it's never been *fully* explained, because everyone on that boat was either too pissed to remember or found it convenient not to. But there was an enquiry and he was later charged with gross negligence. And he was bloody lucky it wasn't manslaughter, or else he would have ended up in prison.'

'So what did happen to him then?' Jimmy said.

'He got a whacking big fine and lost his licence to run his little cruises. That was three and a half years ago.'

Frank looked at him uncertainly. 'That doesn't sound much of a conspiracy though. Just a grubby wee human tragedy.'

Yash reached across the table and spooned a helping of spicy onions onto his plate. 'But that's only half the story Frank. Just wait until you hear the rest.'

'We can't wait,' Maggie said.

'We'll need to,' Frank said, glancing over his shoulder. 'Because here come the cavalry with our main courses.'

Maggie gave him a playful dig in the ribs with her elbow. 'Let them do their fancy serving stuff this time please. The young lad looked devastated that he couldn't do it. He'd probably been practising for days.'

He laughed. 'Aye sure. I'm not so hungry now anyway. I'll still eat my main course though, in case you're wondering. I just love a good rogan josh with heaps of pilau rice and a big coriander naan.'

There were a few minutes of relaxed silence as the waiters expertly served up their meal. It was Maggie who spoke first.

'So Yash, don't keep us waiting any longer. Pray tell all.'

He smiled. 'Okay then. So there's two things that I find very interesting. First, the guy who went over the side of Russell's boat that evening. He worked on the Lomond Tower job.'

'So what?' Frank said. 'They had nearly six hundred guys on the site at its peak. No surprise if some of them fancied a wee trip out on the loch in their spare time.'

'But this wasn't just any old guy,' Yash said. 'His name was Paul Adams and he was one of the site managers. A top guy, more or less in charge of the whole construction side of the project.'

'Okay...,' Frank said, struggling to comprehend. 'And your theory is what?'

Yash shrugged. 'I've not got one yet, at least not one that's fully formed. But the thing that is interesting to me is that Ally Russell only seemed to get rich after that incident and after he lost his licence to run his cruising business. You see, the guy John up at my hotel in Ardlui says he was still running cruises even though he didn't have a licence.'

'So he wouldn't have been advertising them either,' Jimmy said. 'Which explains why it's been so hard to track them down.'

'Aye, but it doesn't explain why he's in Range Rover earnings territory does it?' Frank said. 'I don't suppose you've got a theory for *that*.'

Yash shrugged. 'Well he wouldn't have all the expense of licensing and inspections for a start. And he wouldn't have been paying any tax either. So it would be a lot more profitable I suppose.'

'Yes, and these gourmet cruises must have been quite lucrative,' Maggie said. 'I expect the patrons were paying top dollar.'

'But the puzzling thing is,' Yash said, 'and this is just according to John the manager up at that hotel I stayed at, he hadn't been running any cruises for a couple of years now. He'd still been paying his mooring fees at Ardlui marina - again, that's according to John - but the boat hadn't left the jetty in all that time.'

'And yet he was still driving his fancy Range Rover,' Frank mused. 'In fact, he'd recently bought an new one. Now *that's* interesting right enough.'

'What are you thinking Frank?' Yash said, eager as a new puppy.

Frank smiled. 'You've got a guy overboard, a guy who was a big-wig on the Lomond Tower job, and you've got a boatman with a dodgy back-story, a boatman that then goes on to have his head smashed in.' He paused and smiled again. 'You're supposed to be the journalist pal. If you can't come up with a decent conspiracy theory with all *that* to work on, you need to find another job.'

But as the evening drew to a pleasant close, he couldn't help thinking of a truism he'd learned to trust after nearly twenty years on the job. Which was, whenever you came across large dollops of unexplained wealth, you were always looking at something dodgy. And nine times out of ten, your thoughts would turn to the drugs business, which got him wondering exactly what was the nature of these little exclusive cruises that Ally Russell had been running. Aye, much as it pained him, he was going to have to share his thoughts with DCS Sweeney.

Well, maybe.

Chapter 20

The discovery that the murdered Ally Russell might have been the guy running the gourmet cruises had opened up a whole new line of investigation for himself and Maggie, and given that before that they hadn't really been getting anywhere, they ought to have been grateful to Yash Patel of the *Chronicle*. The trouble was, Jimmy thought, Patel was such an irritating little tick with a massive self-regard that made him seriously annoying to spend any time with. But there was no arguing he'd provided a solid lead, that manager guy John up at the wee hotel in Ardlui, and he and Maggie planned to drive up there as soon as they could to quiz the bloke. But before then, there were some loose strands to be tidied up, starting with Miss Francis Cramond of the eponymous staffing agency. Which was where he was heading right now, a walk that would take him less than seven minutes if he got a step on. Just before he'd left the office, he'd overheard Maggie's phone conversation with Mrs McClelland, a delicate affair centred on her missing daughter's menstrual cycle. Afterwards, a quick check of the dates had proved one thing at least. Juliet McClelland hadn't missed her shifts at the Auchterard because of her period. As to the question of how much she was being paid for her stints on the gourmet cruises, well Mrs McClelland could understand why they were asking but would need to talk to her husband first before agreeing to releasing their daughter's bank statements. It occurred to Jimmy that actually they might have been quicker calling in a favour from his brother, asking if his wee pal Eleanor Campbell might employ her dubious hacking skills on Juliet's bank account, but no, that wouldn't be playing the game and Frank would probably tell him to sling his hook in any case.

As he passed a small newsagent's at the bottom of Byers Road, his eyes were drawn to the poster in the window. *Have You Seen This Woman?* They'd been up now for a few days, but so far they'd heard nothing. It was two and a half years since her disappearance so maybe that wasn't surprising, but it was disappointing nonetheless. Looking at the picture again, it served to confirm something that he'd noticed before but which hadn't really registered fully with him. The fact was, Juliet McClelland wasn't just beautiful, but seriously sexy too. The photograph was full-length, taken at a family wedding he thought, and pictured her in a dark red mini-dress, wearing tall stilettos which accentuated her long slim legs. Although he guessed it was a casual snap, it looked strangely posed, like the kind of shot you found in a fashion magazine. She was on her phone, the device pressed against her ear, one hand holding back a mass of dark tresses, her smiling eyes dark and sultry, picked out with a ring of deep navy mascara which made them even more striking. She reminded him a little of his ill-fated *amore* Astrid Sorenson, causing him to recall the powerful and irresistible spell the Swedish temptress had cast on him. Was this what had happened to Juliet McClelland he wondered? Had she cast *her* spell on some man, and that man, overcome with uncontrollable longing and desire, had plucked her off these very streets as she made her way home from the lecture theatre? Perhaps it was just a random encounter, two ships passing in the night, an evil opportunist taking his chance, or maybe he had been studying her, even stalking her for months or years.

Thinking of Astrid inevitably got him thinking of his ex-wife Flora and that got him thinking unhappily about her upcoming wedding to his Uni friend Hugo. Although Hugo hadn't really been a friend, just one of a big crowd they went around with, and even back then Jimmy knew Hugo was sniffing around his girlfriend and would have waltzed right in to usurp him given half a chance. And now, fifteen years later, horrible Hugo was getting that chance. It was, Jimmy now understood, a major cross-roads in his life, and he had never been more certain he had to take a different fork in the road. The problem was, how in god's name was he going to tell Maggie? It was something he'd been putting off for a week or two now, ever since he had come to his decision, but somehow he had not yet found the right moment. Maybe he would talk it over with Frank, try and persuade him to break the news instead. And then he laughed. No, that wouldn't work, not in a month of Sundays. The fact was, it was his decision and his alone and so it was his responsibility to break the news. But then prompted by Juliet's beautiful image, a thought came to him. *Of course, her phone*. This was something he was going to have to talk through with Maggie as soon as he got back.

Now he was approaching the turn into Dumbarton Road and in two minutes he'd be outside the office of Cramond Staffing. Time to focus on the job in hand, to remember what he hoped to learn from the meeting. As he approached their shop-front, he saw that they too were displaying Juliet McClelland's poster in their window. A little bell rang as he pushed open the door, causing two or three of the office staff to look up from their work. He glanced towards Phoebe Wilson, catching her eye and giving her a weak smile. It was a shame they were going to have to renege on their promise to her, but finding out what happened to Juliet surely trumped that, although it didn't make him feel any less bad about breaking her confidence. He saw through the glass wall of her office that Francis Cramond was at her desk and on the phone. Evidently detecting his approach, she smiled and gestured that he should enter, pointing apologetically at the handset as he took a seat at a small conference table. Finishing her call, she got up from behind her desk and walked over, holding out a hand in greeting.

'Nice to see you again Jimmy,' she said, the smile and tone making him think she might be sincere in the sentiment.

'Aye, nice to meet you again too,' he said, returning the smile. 'And I won't take up any more of your time than I have to. I know you're a busy woman.'

'That's not a problem,' she said. 'So how are you getting on with your investigation? Have you made any progress since we last met?'

He paused for a moment before answering, recognising they might be about to enter difficult territory. 'Well, yes and no I suppose. I don't think we're any closer to finding out what happened to her, but we're making some progress in piecing together aspects of her life that might point us in the right direction. Which is really why I wanted to speak to you again Francis.'

She looked at him, eyes narrowed. 'Well of course, I really want to help, but I'm not sure what I can add to what I told you last time.'

He nodded. 'Okay, so this might be quite difficult for you, but we've been looking into the business of these gourmet cruises that we believe Juliet worked on. You do know about them I presume?'

She shuffled uncomfortably in her seat. 'How did you find out about them?' She looked out through the glass in the direction of Phoebe Wilson. 'Although I can guess.'

'We had the information from a number of sources,' Jimmy said quickly. 'Mainly from the concierge at the Auchterard hotel I should say.' He paused for a moment. 'And we had some information too from your brother.'

She gave him an amused look. 'So you've spoken to my Davie have you? I hope you counted your fingers after you shook hands.'

He wasn't sure whether he was expected to laugh or not. Instead he said, 'It's not clear to us who was behind them, or if they are even the slightest bit relevant to Juliet's disappearance. I suppose it's just a loose end we want to tie up. Probably of no consequence, but that's just what we have to do in our line of work.'

She sighed and held her hands up. 'Okay, well I suppose there's no harm in explaining. The truth is, I wanted to squirrel away some cash outside the official accounts of the business. And before you say anything, I wasn't trying to defraud the taxman. I just wanted some money hidden from my pig of a husband so he couldn't get his hands on it when we divorced. There, that's the long and short of it.'

'And who's idea was it, can I ask?'

'I'm not exactly sure. I think it was a combination of Sandy McDuff at the hotel and Ally Russell, the guy who owned the boat. Anyway, McDuff knew about my staffing contract with the hotel and approached me to supply the waiters, and I saw the chance for a little off-the-books revenue stream. He promoted the cruises to his rich American guests as something special to do after a day on the golf course, and charged them top dollar for the privilege.'

Jimmy nodded, staying silent for a brief second as he processed what he'd just learned.

'And Juliet? You got her work on that boat?'

Francis shrugged. 'Yes, I did. Juliet was one of quite a few girls who worked there. We picked the best of them because of how much we were charging the diners, and she was one of the best.'

Out of the blue, a thought came to him. 'But then I think the cruises stopped, and that was not long after Juliet's disappearance. Is that right?'

'Yes it is,' she said. 'I suppose it was just something that had run its course. The boat guy Ally Russell didn't want to do them anymore and that made the decision for us.'

'You know he's dead don't you?' he said. 'Brutally murdered, and right on the lochside.'

She nodded. 'Of course I heard. It's sad of course but I never actually met the man.'

'Really?' Jimmy said. 'That surprises me.'

'I don't know why it should. I was just supplying the girls and Sandy McDuff was my customer. He organised the boat directly with Russell and there was no reason why I should be involved.'

'I guess that makes sense,' Jimmy conceded. 'And the timing of their demise, the cruises I mean. That had nothing to do with Juliet's disappearance?'

She gave him a sharp look. 'No, of course not. Why should there be a connection? As I said, Juliet was just one of several girls we placed there.'

And she was right, he thought. There was no reason at all why there should be a connection, none at all. With more than a hint of dejection he realised they had reached another dead end, crashed into the buffers, gone up a cul-de-sac, however you wanted to describe it. Now they knew pretty much everything there was to know about those gourmet cruises and as far as he could see, that knowledge was going to get them precisely nowhere.

Slowly he got to his feet, giving her a half-smile. 'Look I said I wouldn't keep you too long. It's been helpful, it really has been.' Although truthfully, it hadn't been helpful at all. 'And thanks for putting the poster up in your window. I don't suppose you've had any response though?'

She shook her head. 'It's been a long time, hasn't it?' He guessed what she wanted to say was it was clutching at straws and really there was no hope of anything coming of it. The fact was he thought the same thing too. The whole thing was hopeless, bloody hopeless, and that thought refused to leave his head as he trudged gloomily back to the office.

Until, just as he was reaching the door, another altogether more interesting thought occurred to him. Francis Cramond had said it twice, maybe three times and he had no problem in recalling her exact words. Firstly, *I was just supplying the girls* and then just a few moments later, *Juliet was just one of several girls we placed there. Girls.* And yes, he remembered she mentioned it earlier too. Yet when they had met with her brother Davie Cramond, he had complained in the crudest of terms that on his cruises, they had been waited on by schoolboys.

Somehow, something didn't quite add up and now he had something else to chew over with Maggie, which he hoped to do presently. He pushed open the door and strode in, to find her on her feet and pacing up and down the office, her phone pressed to her ear, one hand behind her head which was nodding vigorously. 'Bloody hell,' he heard her say, and then five seconds later she said it again, this time with even more force. She wasn't on speakerphone but even without that, Jimmy had no difficulty in recognising the equally animated voice on the other end. Just as he was about to shout a cheery greeting to his brother, she ended the call.

'That was Frank,' she said breathlessly. 'And Jimmy, you'll never guess what's happened.' She didn't give him time to try, although somehow he knew what she was going to tell him.

'It's Sandy McDuff. He's been found murdered. Stabbed to death. Up at Loch Lomond.'

Chapter 21

With the gruesome discovery of the McDuff body, everything was going completely mental down at New Gorbals police station. Naturally the local media, a scrum of whom had gathered outside the front door, had been onto it in a flash and it hadn't taken them long to point out the statistical improbability of three killings of strikingly similar MO being unrelated. Now the top brass were asking why the two previous murders had been run as separate investigations when it must have been blindingly obvious to anyone with half a brain that they were connected. Such was the gist of the conversation Frank was having with Lexy McDonald as they enjoyed an incongruously relaxed coffee in the station's canteen.

'So what's happening then?' Frank said, struggling to contain his amusement. 'Is DCS Sweeney now thinking we've got a crazy serial killer on the loose? And is he telling all men with beards to stay indoors and keep away from the bonny bonny banks?'

'Shhh!' she whispered, sounding alarmed. 'You'll get me strung up sir. But I've heard that the Chief Constable is on her way here as we speak and she intends to give a wee speech to the media on arrival. That's what our press officer has been told at least. He's been given an hour to come up with a plausible story so he's bricking himself good and proper.'

He laughed. 'Well they must be worried if her majesty's getting off her arse and leaving her plush big office over at our esteemed Tulliallan headquarters. Because normally it's the little people that get summoned to see her. But aye, I'm looking forward to hearing what she has to say for herself.' He knew of course what the Chief Constable would say, the standard corporate guff the brass trotted out no matter what the circumstances. *We can't say too much at the moment but we are pursuing a number of promising lines of enquiry.* The thing was, who could argue with the statement, other than maybe questioning exactly what *promising* meant?

'And they're also saying sir that DCS Sweeney might get moved off the case and they'll put an ACC on it instead. To signal to the world that the brass are now taking it *very* seriously.'

He looked at her with amusement. 'And who's this *they* Lexy of whom you speak? Or have you got a crystal ball?'

'Tulliallan sources,' she shot back. 'The place leaks like a chocolate watering-can.'

'Ah,' he said, nodding. 'So quite authoritative then. And do your Tulliallan sources have a name by any chance?'

She gave a coy smile. 'You'll never believe it sir. When I tell you.'

'Don't ever play poker Lexy because your face has given it away. Let me see, it wouldn't be ACC Belinda Cresswell by any chance?'

'Got it in one sir.'

'You know she's on my wee list don't you?'

'I do sir. Fancy Caribbean holidays I think you said. Or something like that.'

'That's it. Well at least that's what Eleanor's spreadsheet is telling us.'

She gave him a tentative look. 'The thing is sir...you do know who her partner is, don't you?'

His mind flashed back to when he'd dropped that bloomer with Junior Minister Caroline Connor, when half-joking, he'd suggested that the ACC might have a sugar-daddy. Even thinking about it now, he could feel the colour coming to his cheeks.

'No I don't,' he said meekly. 'Who is he?'

'She,' Lexy said, in a tone dripping with censure. 'The ACC's in a long-term relationship with Felicity Forbes-Brown. You'll never have heard of her I suppose, but she runs a very successful fashion magazine. It's called Fashion First. But the point is sir, that lady is seriously rich. I wouldn't be surprised if she actually *owns* a Caribbean island.'

'Oh is that right?' Frank said, feeling vaguely chastened. 'Aye, so maybe that puts a different light on it.'

And not only that, it got him wondering how reliable Eleanor's UWIPO software actually was. But when he thought about it again, he realised his concerns were probably unfounded. The process was simply flagging up unexplained wealth, doing exactly what it said on the tin. Then it was his job to simply ask those it had identified to explain how they had come by it. In Assistant Chief Constable Creswell's case it seemed that the explanation would be quite straightforward, although her reaction to the intrusion into her privacy was going to be interesting to see.

She laughed. 'Welcome to the modern world sir. Anyway, I'd better be getting back to my big murder enquiry. Three bodies now and we're all waiting with bated breath in case there's another one on the way.'

'Let's hope there's not. But at least everybody will be looking for a link between the victims now, which is a step forward. And that might help you all to figure out who Mr No-Name is.'

'I hope so sir. See you around.'

Comfortably settled, he decided he'd remain in the canteen for his call with Eleanor and Ronnie, whose earlier barely-literate text had suggested they may have some interesting information to impart. His phone rang just as he was sitting down again after fetching another coffee.

'Eleanor, Ronnie, good to hear from you.' This time, he noted they'd opted for an audio-only call, which made him wonder where they were calling from. He suspected Frenchie had sneaked out to the local greasy spoon for one of those Full English breakfasts he was unhealthily partial to. Eleanor would have gone along, albeit reluctantly, because the otherwise traditional menu offered oat milk as a no-cost option with their hot beverages as a half-hearted gesture towards their millennial customers.

'Morning guv. How's things up in Jock-Land?'

'Hey watch your language,' Frank said, laughing. 'But yep, making some progress and of course the weather's always beautiful up here. So what have you got for me? Anything?'

'Yeah, been run off my feet guv but I think I've got somewhere. Oh yeah, and with a bit of help from Eleanor too. That's right Eleanor, isn't it?'

Frank noted the silence at the other end of the line and imagined with amusement the look she was giving Ronnie.

'Well that's great,' he said. 'So come on, tell me more.'

'Right, so first of all this bird Miranda Temple, we've found out who she is. What I mean is, Eleanor's found out who she is.'

Frank laughed. 'I don't think you can call woman birds anymore Frenchie, but I'll let it pass this time. But remind me, who is she again?'

This time it was Eleanor who spoke. *'She's the person at the end of the bank account trail. The person who is getting like six thousand pounds a month from the Andrew McClelland guy.'*

'Okay. But what I mean is *who* is she? What's her relationship to McClelland?'

'So I scanned a basket of databases with some custom SQL code,' Eleanor said. *'Electoral roll, Births, Marriages and Deaths, Criminal Records...'*

'Okay, good,' Frank interrupted, anxious to avoid her spiralling into one of her favoured but convoluted technical explanations. 'And you found her where exactly?'

'She works with him,' French said. *'At the Procurator Fiscal's office. In Edinburgh. She's some sort of administrator.'*

'An office girl then,' Frank said. 'So what are we thinking? An affair maybe? Or is he dishing out child maintenance payments, something like that?'

He heard French laugh. *'We've got a picture of her guv and we know her date of birth too. She's fifty-seven and a size X-X-L by my estimate. But we do know what happened to the money.'*

'What's that?'

'It was getting withdrawn in cash,' Eleanor said. *'All of it.'*

'I thought there was some sort of limit? Three hundred quid a day or something like that?'

'There is. So it was being withdrawn on twenty consecutive days. That's like one day after another.'

Frank laughed. 'Surprisingly enough, I know what consecutive means. But am I hearing some past-tensing going on here? It was *getting* withdrawn in cash, that's what you said.'

'Yeah guv, I thought you knew,' French said. *'It all stopped about two months ago. Nothing since.'*

'And I guess we don't know what she was doing with all those readies,' Frank said, not waiting for their answer. 'No, of course we don't. But it's quite a dedicated mission to go to the cash-line nearly every day for a month, month-in-month-out.' He paused for a moment. 'So Frenchie, I think that's got to be *your* first mission up here in Jock-land. And just as a tip, I wouldn't use that word up here unless you want a broken nose. So get your backside round to King's Cross tomorrow morning, get on the first Edinburgh train and see what this Miss Miranda Temple has to say for herself.'

'No problem guv,' French said, *'I'll be right on it.'*

'Good, good, we're making some progress here. So what about my mate DCS Sweeney? Anything to report there Frenchie?'

'Yeah, we've found a couple of things that might be interesting. So those expensive motors first of all. Like we said, the Super just seems to have the use of them, he doesn't own them. We got onto the DVLA registration database and they're shown as being owned by a company. An outfit called GC Prestige Automobiles. They're car brokers, if you know what that is?

Frank shook his head. 'I don't think I do. Enlighten me.'

'They're sort of middle-men guv. They generally have a website where if you're in the market for a fancy motor you can go on and search for the one you're looking for. They've got contacts with the prestige dealers all over the country and so they always know who's keen to shift some stock. They phone round with your requirements and do a bit of haggling to get you the best deal. Normally they're just one-man bands, some guy with a telephone and a car-pound and a lot of contacts in the motor trade. They make their money by taking a cut from the deal.'

'And this GC outfit, they're one of these one-man-bands too?'

'Sure guv. It's run by a guy called George Cramond. We looked at his website. He's got his mug-shot on it.'

'Cramond did you say?' Frank couldn't conceal his astonishment. 'Bloody hell.'

'Do you know the geezer then guv?' French said, sounding surprised.

'I don't *know* the geezer, but I know the name.' But it couldn't be any more than a bizarre coincidence, he thought. It wasn't the most common name by any means, but there were still plenty of them around. Right now there was one of them playing for the Scotland rugby team, and of course they had a whole suburb in Edinburgh named after them. Still, if this was a coincidence, it was a bloody bizarre one.

'I tell you what Ronnie, since you're run off your feet, I'll give this George Cramond a wee ring myself. Anything else? What about Sweeney's old cases?'

'Eleanor did the heavy lifting on this one guv, so I'll let her speak for herself.'

'It wasn't like exactly difficult,' Eleanor began, which made Frank smile. She was a bit of an unreliable witness when it came to difficulty he had found, it being measured more by how much praise she was looking for rather than the complication of the task itself. But he knew what his role in the play was.

'I bet it was,' he said, feigning sincerity. 'You're always too modest.'

'No, it really was easy. And Lexy helped me. It was mostly her actually. But she said it was nothing really because he was on mainly one case for more than two years.'

And then he remembered. *Of course.* Sweeney had been in charge of investigating those Glasgow serial killings and he was the guy who had nailed the evil narcissist Denis Northcote, a case that had consumed half the resources of Police Scotland for the best part of three years.

'And then I hacked the court databases to see if DCS Sweeney's name appeared on any of the proceedings.'

'What do you mean hacked? I thought these records were available on line anyway?'

'But you need to apply for a login and password and that takes ages, Eleanor said, matter-of-factly. *'Besides, it was like interesting to test their security.'*

'Don't tell me,' Frank said, laughing. 'They'll be getting a wee e-mail from your mate Zak soon suggesting they need to hire someone to check out their cyber defences.'

'Well they do,' she said. *'They're like terrible. A five-year old could breach them. I ran an SQL injection and it bust their password firewall first time.'*

'Aye, that's the thing, you just can't trust these password firewalls, I've always found that. So anyway, what did you uncover with this masterly hack? Anything interesting?'

He smiled when she answered, recognising a line she'd used in the past. *'I found some things. I don't know if they're interesting or not.'*

'He nailed an organised car-theft ring,' French interjected. *'You know, these geezers that nick the Mercs and Beemers to order and ship them off to Albania and the likes. He was on that one for nine months before the Northcote case. They all got eight years.'*

Frank sighed. 'Aye, but if he caught them and got them put away he obviously wasn't on the take from them, was he? Anything else?'

'Just the one other thing that I thought was interesting. He represented the police at a Fatal Accident Enquiry. Some geezer who fell off a boat on Loch Lomond and drowned.'

'What?' Frank spat out the word, unable to hide his astonishment. 'Bloody hell. So tell me Frenchie, what was that all about?'

'They managed to fish out his body, and when the pathologist got him on the slab there was some concern about an injury to his head. So the police were called in to investigate. But the story from the bloke who owned the boat was that the victim was pissed and had fell over and hit his head earlier in the night. And then later this guy started messing about. Apparently he climbed onto a

fishing platform at the back of the boat and toppled into the water.'

'And Sweeney represented the police did he? And what did he have to say for himself?'

'He said after they'd made their enquiries, the police found no evidence of foul play. The Sherriff accepted it and ruled that it was an accident that could have been prevented if the boat operator had had proper safety procedures in place.'

'Aye, I know all about that. That boat was owned by Ally Russell, the guy who was murdered a few weeks back. Correction, *one* of the guys who was murdered.'

Now Frank's head began to swim as the sheer crazy complexity of the situation threatened to overwhelm him. After thanking Eleanor and Ronnie for their help, he hung up and, operating on dazed auto-pilot, meandered back to the canteen's serving counter to grab his third caffeine injection of the morning. To call this thing twisted would be the understatement of the millennium, and a lot of it wasn't even related to his own UWIPO investigation. It was the *connections* that were doing his head in, loose though they might be. A guy falls overboard on Loch Lomond, on a boat owned by Ally Russell, who himself is murdered a couple of years later. Not long after Russell's killing, two more guys are murdered and dumped on the lochside, the similarity of the MOs being a significant connection in themselves. And then there was the surprising involvement of his UWIPO target DCS Sweeney, albeit that was a bit tentative. Then there was the emergence of this guy George Cramond, the prestige car broker who shared a surname with Davie Cramond, the bloke whose firm had built the ill-fated Lomond Tower. He consoled himself with the thought that at least the situation with the Miranda Temple woman seemed a little more straightforward. For some reason she was the recipient of six grand a month from Andrew McClelland, and had been tracked down by Eleanor Campbell's magic despite McClelland having made obvious efforts to hide the trail behind a web of offshore accounts. Tomorrow Ronnie French would be asking Miss Temple some awkward questions which he hoped would shed a spotlight on what *that* was all about.

But getting back to the four guys who'd met their ends up at Scotland's most famous loch. Sure, the Sheriff had agreed with Sweeney that the death of guy number one had been an accident, but the pathologist had had sufficient doubts to call in the cops at the outset. So Frank was going to do a wee bit of digging, finding out who this guy was and whether *he* had any obvious connections to the rest of the stuff that was going on. A quick call back to wee Eleanor and he would have the Sheriff's report on his laptop in a jiffy.

Feeling better, he decided he might as well hang about in the canteen until lunch. Picking up his phone, he did a swift survey of the room, googled *GC Prestige Automobiles* then punched the *call* button. After ringing a dozen times, it flipped over to answerphone, a broad Glaswegian voice identifying itself as the proprietor before launching into a stream of excruciating and extended sales patter. Eventually though, there was the opportunity for the caller to leave a message. Which Frank did.

'Mr George Cramond I presume,' he said laconically. 'I'm Detective Chief Inspector Frank Stewart with the Metropolitan Police. I want to ask you a few wee questions about your business with Detective Chief Superintendant Peter Sweeney. So give me a call back at your earliest convenience.'

Chapter 22

The news of Sandy McDuff's brutal murder had cast a gloomy shadow over Bainbridge & Stewart, and so Maggie had arranged that the next morning she and Jimmy would head straight to the Bikini Barista Cafe in order to chew things over. They'd arrived at the cafe at about the same time, and as she'd anticipated, Lori, the young waitress they'd met last time and who had become completely besotted by Jimmy, had instantly appointed herself to be their server.

'Morning! What can I get youse?' she asked brightly, the question addressed at both but her eyes only on Jimmy. She raised her pencil to her lips. 'Don't tell me. Two americanos with hot milk and two bacon rolls with brown sauce. Or would you prefer a wee square sausage? Aye, I think you would.'

Jimmy shot the girl a smile. 'Was that just a good guess or are you a mind-reader?'

She laughed. 'My sister says I've got psychic powers. She says I always seem to know what she's going to wear to a party and I get there first. But no, the sausages are great here, honest they are. They come from a butcher so they do.'

'Good to know,' Maggie said, smiling as she recognised her inadvertent use of one of Frank's favourite sayings. But looking across at Jimmy, she noticed he wasn't smiling.

'Is there anything the matter?' she asked. *And then it all came out.*

'I've been meaning to speak with you Maggie,' he said, not looking at her. 'It's about the partnership.' He paused for what seemed an age. 'The thing is, I don't think it's for me. I'm really sorry.'

'Okay,' she said, not immediately catching on to what he was trying to tell her. 'I'm quite happy to keep it as it was if you prefer, that's not a problem. In fact, I rather liked being your boss.' It was a lame attempt at humour, and she recognised immediately how desperate it sounded.

'No, it's not that,' he said quietly. 'I want to...no, I *need* to do something different Maggie. I've been talking to an old army mate. A guy I connected back with through that Facebook group I told you about, you know, the mental health thing. Stew Edwards his name is. We go way back. He was with me all the way through my Helmand tours.'

'So...so are you saying you're *leaving*? She could feel her face start to flush as she'd tried to process what he had just said. 'You mean permanently, or do you just want a few weeks off? Because that can easily be arranged. Like a sabbatical.'

He shook his head. 'No, I'm sorry Maggie, it's something I've really got to do. Stew and me have been talking about this for a while and we decided the time was right. What it is, we're planning to set up an outdoor centre where we can take damaged people into the mountains, take them outside themselves, let the power of nature help with their healing. We've found a little place to rent as a base up near Braemar and we're going to take our Mountain Instructors badges in January.'

She could feel herself shaking inside, her nervous system evidently struggling to deal with the shock. 'But, but...so *soon*?' was all she could think of to say.

'Aye, I'm sorry,' he said, sounding regretful and sad at the same time. 'But I won't leave you in the lurch, of course I won't. I'll obviously see Juliet's case through and it'll be a few months until the new venture is fully up and running, so I'll still be able to do a couple of days a week for you until then. If you'll still want me that is?'

These five words had the effect of a shot of adrenalin injected into a cardiac-arresting patient. *Still want me? Still want me?* Still want the man who had *literally* saved her life when she had been plunged into the darkest despair, when she was threatened with losing everything that was dear to her?

'You absolute fool Jimmy,' she said, half-laughing, half-crying. 'Of course I'll still want you. *Always*.'

'Thank *god* for that,' he said, his relief palpable. 'And anyway, you're going to be stuck with me, aren't you? Or have you forgotten that little matter of your wedding? When I become your official brother-in-law?'

She laughed. 'No, how could I? Frank won't let me, he's always going on about it.'

'He's the luckiest man in the world to have won the heart of a woman like you. And he knows it too.' It was said with such force that she was momentarily taken aback by the sweet sentimentality of its message.

'It's me that's the lucky one,' she said, her face beginning to flush again. 'God, if I hadn't decided to go to that recruitment fair that day I wouldn't have met either of you. I remember thinking at the time it was too expensive and I only went because Asvina told me I had to look like a proper business if I wanted to get Ollie back.'

'Well I'm bloody glad you did. Perhaps it teaches us we should trust in fate. Even if it's not always kind to us at first.'

Unnoticed, Lori had materialised with their order. Evidently sensing something was going on, she gave them a curious look and said, 'You sure you guys are alright?'

Wiping the remnants of a tear from her cheek Maggie said, 'Yes Lori we are, or at least we will be after we've had this lovely breakfast. Thank you.'

'Nae bother,' she said. 'And I'll be around if youse need anything else.'

'Appreciate that,' Jimmy said, nodding and giving the girl another smile, which Maggie was not exactly sure was wise. But that was him all over. Jimmy was the nicest guy in the world, not counting his brother of course. Now she was beginning to feel better, the shock thankfully beginning to recede as quickly as it had come, to be replaced by an overwhelming feeling of gratitude that she had the Stewart brothers in her life.

'Look, I really wish you all the best with your venture,' she said to him. 'I'm sure you and Stew will make a big success of it. Although when I think about it, I actually hope you fall flat on your face and come running to me pleading for your old job back.'

He laughed. 'That's not going to happen, at least I hope not. And as for Stew, he's a bit of a nutcase. But he's brilliant with people and he can navigate a mountain pass with his eyes shut. So I think we'll be fine. But come on Maggie, this isn't earning us our big fat fee. Time to get to work, don't you think?'

She glanced at her watch and gave it a tap. 'Don't forget that Mrs McClelland is scheduled to call us at nine-thirty five, hopefully to tell us how much Juliet was getting paid for her shifts on the boat.'

'That precise?' he said, laughing. 'Mind you, I suppose her days are jam-packed with stuff.'

Maggie nodded. 'Yeah, I guess so, she's certainly a busy woman. Anyway, to work. And bloody hell, a lot's happened in the last twenty-four hours, hasn't it?'

'Aye, it's been totally crazy,' he agreed. 'Sandy McDuff's murder has really shocked me you know. I mean, it's no more than a couple of days since we were talking to him.'

'Yeah it's so weird,' she said, frowning, 'but you know, I couldn't help wondering if his murder is connected to *us*.'

'What?' he said, sounding sceptical. 'No way. What could we have to do with it?'

'We've been digging into these gourmet cruises, and all our enquiries were pointing to McDuff being the guy who set them up.'

'Well sure, I think that's a done deal as far as I'm concerned,' Jimmy said. 'Francis Cramond was pretty honest about the whole thing. McDuff came up with the idea, she supplied the staff and it was all done on a cash basis because Ally Russell had lost his licence to run passenger cruises on the loch and *she* wanted to hide a pile of cash because she was planning to divorce her husband. And remember, her brother Davie also told us he thought it was Sandy McDuff who was their instigator.'

'Except now we can't get Sandy's version of the story, can we? No-one can.'

He shook his head. 'No, that's crazy. What, are you trying to say one or other of the Cramonds got McDuff killed just so he couldn't talk to *us*? I'm sorry Maggie but that's just mad.'

'Maybe it's mad, but don't forget the boat guy Ally Russell is dead too. It's all very convenient if someone wanted to hide something. You must admit that.'

He looked unconvinced. 'Perhaps, but hide what? That the food was actually crap and they were served by schoolboys? No, it's all a bit too improbable for me. I'm sorry.'

She shrugged. 'Okay, well let's agree to disagree for the time being and park that one for later. But you said there were a couple of other things that were bothering you. What were they?'

'It was the poster that brought the first one to my mind. Juliet was on the phone, wasn't she, in that picture? And that got me thinking. Surely the police must have accessed her phone records at some point during the original investigation? I mean, no-one goes anywhere without their phone these days and especially not someone her age. And those records would have let them track her movements on the evening in question.'

'You're *right*,' Maggie said. 'I should have thought it would have been the first thing they did, you know, get onto her mobile provider and get her location data.'

'Exactly,' Jimmy said, nodding. 'So did they or didn't they? That would be something which would be good to know. But I'm not sure how we can find that out.'

'We'd need to ask the police I suppose. But I've got an idea. Why don't we ask Mrs McClelland when she calls? We can give her a quick update on progress too...

'There hasn't been any,' he interrupted, shooting her a wry look.

'I know, but let's skate over that for now. We can tell her about our concerns regarding Juliet's phone records, and then ask her if she can help with an approach to the police. I guess she could ask the Chief Constable, you know, go right to the top.'

'Well perhaps,' he said, sounding doubtful again. 'Or we could just ask Frank to do us a wee favour? Don't forget the original investigation was run out of New Gorbals police station so there's probably plenty of cops still there who worked on it. Someone would know whether they looked at her phone stuff or not.'

'True,' she said. 'Yeah that's worth trying first I guess.' She stole a glance at her phone. 'Nine thirty-three. Sheila will be calling us in a minute.'

'Two minutes if you want to be exact,' he laughed. But at that precise moment, her phone rang.

She nodded at Jimmy and gave a silent thumbs-up. 'Ah Mrs McClelland, thank you so much for calling us back. I know you must be terribly busy.' She glanced around the cafe, and satisfying herself that they wouldn't be overheard, slipped it onto speakerphone. 'I've got Jimmy with me here too.'

'Okay fine,' McClelland said, the words clipped and business-like. And then she paused, long enough for Maggie to wonder if she was still on the line. *'So as we discussed, I spoke to my husband about the matter. We considered it very carefully but I'm afraid we have decided that Juliet's financial affairs must remain private.'*

'But...' It wasn't the response Maggie had hoped for and for a moment she struggled to find the words. Finally she said, 'Well of course I have to respect your decision, naturally. But can I just ask why? Because I think it would have been very helpful to our investigation. No, more than that. Incredibly helpful.'

'We have our reasons, good reasons. But I'm afraid you'll have to leave it at that. Andrew and I have made our decision. As I said, we need to respect Juliet's privacy.'

From the First Minister's tone, Maggie could tell there was little hope of changing her mind. But that didn't mean she wasn't going to try.

'Mrs McClelland, I'm sorry for being persistent but can I ask if it is something specific...' Quickly she pulled herself up short. No, *is there something specific that you're trying to hide*, which is what she was going to say, that was unlikely to go down well. Instead she said, 'What I mean is, is there something specific that is causing you such concern? Because perhaps if you shared it with us, we might be able to help you and your husband.'

There was a silence at the end of the line and then McClelland said, *'Everyone thinks that Juliet is dead, but we still cling to the hope that she may just have chosen to disappear. So my husband and I don't believe we have the right to disclose her private affairs. That's the reason and I'm afraid our decision is final.'*

Maggie looked at Jimmy and gave a resigned shrug. The fact was, the likelihood of Juliet turning up alive was next to zero, but she wondered if she would feel the same as the McClellands were she ever to be in the same position. The thought of losing Ollie sent a cold shiver down her spine, and she knew that if, heaven forbid, something similar ever happened to her precious boy then she would never *ever* give up hope of a happy outcome, no matter how impossible the situation. Every parent would feel the same and there was no reason why the important and greatly respected leader of a country should feel any different.

'I understand Mrs McClelland,' she said finally. 'We know it must be agony for you and your husband and for Mr Paterson too. And we're still trying to do everything we can to find out what happened.' But as she said it, a wave of despair began to descend as it dawned on her how hopeless the situation was. At the same time it struck her that finding out how much Juliet was being paid for her shifts on that boat was probably immaterial anyway and would have got them no further. Really, there was nothing for it but to end the conversation and try to regroup. Pausing for a second she said, 'But thank you. And we'll obviously keep you up to date with any developments.'

Afterwards, neither of them spoke for a full minute, and when Maggie did speak, she couldn't hide the mix of bitterness and despondency that now seem to be enveloping her.

'Developments?' she said angrily. *'What* developments? There haven't been any bloody developments, and there aren't going to be any either. The whole thing is impossible, it really is.' It wasn't like her, she knew that, but this wasn't a normal day, and now she began to suspect she hadn't made such a swift recovery from Jimmy's bombshell as she'd thought.

'I don't agree,' Jimmy said calmly. 'Remember, we've been here before with other cases, plenty of times. There's always a point where everything looks bleak and then suddenly something turns up that changes the whole outlook.'

She gave him a doubtful look. 'Yeah maybe, but I don't see that in this one. I really do think we're facing defeat. You know, I'm beginning to think we should throw in the towel. Tell the client that we've gone as far as we can and we'd just be wasting their money if we carried on.'

He frowned. 'Bloody hell, is this what's going to happen to the force of nature that is Maggie Bainbridge when I'm not around to gee you up? Come on, I've never heard you speak like that before.'

But you've not walked out on me before she thought, immediately regretting the tinge of bitterness and glad she hadn't said anything dumb that gave that bitterness away. Yeah, the truth was this new situation was going to take some getting used to. Instead she said, smiling, 'Well okay smart-arse, if you're so clever let's have some ideas from you. Come on, out with them.'

He laughed. 'Well for a start, let's do a bit of brainstorming around what we've just heard from Sheila McClelland. And I'll throw the first idea into the ring, and before you say anything, remember the rules of brainstorming. Any idea is fair game, no matter how mad it seems.'

She gave a thumbs-up. 'Okay, I agree. Shoot.'

'Okay, so what if Juliet had got herself pregnant and had decided to have an abortion, and the payment to the clinic was showing up on her bank account? That might be something a loving parent might want to cover up. What do you think?'

'Yes, that's not bad,' she conceded, 'although if I might be a trifle pedantic, I think you'll find you can't actually get *yourself* pregnant. So that means of course there would have to be a man involved. And what if that man's name showed up on her account and it was someone in the public eye? Someone who might provoke a scandal if it all came out?'

He nodded. 'Aye, I like that too. So what else?' He paused for a moment, screwing up his face as he evidently tried to come up with something. 'Perhaps she was badly in debt and the account was showing some huge overdraft. Or maybe she had a drug problem and was having to shell out big dollops of cash to fund her habit.'

'Two good suggestions,' Maggie said. 'Or maybe she'd secretly joined the Tory party and her monthly subscriptions were showing up on her account.'

He grinned. 'Aye, that would be hilarious and definitely something her mum might be embarrassed about. But doesn't all of this mean we really *do* need to get this information somehow? Couldn't we ask her real father to do something? Because he could apply for a court order or something like that, although I'm a bit rusty on the law surrounding that sort of thing.'

'Yes, me too. But even if there's a legal route, there's about a nine-month backlog in the courts at the moment and even if we got a court slot the McClellands would be bound to oppose it. So I'm not sure that would work if I'm being totally honest. At least not in our timescale.'

'Aye you're right. What if we added it to the list of favours we want from Frank?' he said, a note of caution in his voice. 'That wee Eleanor Campbell could get us what we need no bother I would imagine.'

She shook her head. 'She could of course, but that would be illegal. The Product Security and Telecommunications Infrastructure Bill I think you'll find covers it. The police can do this stuff as part of an official enquiry but I wouldn't want to ask Frank to do it off the books so to speak.'

'Aye you're right,' he said, sounding deflated. 'You know, maybe we *are* reaching the point where we need to turn this over to Frank in an official capacity, or at least ask for his help. Because that's what his wee Department does after all. Cold cases and all that sort of stuff. It's their speciality.'

'Yes I know it is, and yes you might be right. Although I don't think it's something he can just barge his way into is it? His Department 12B generally gets *invited* in, and usually only as a last resort, when the guys who've cocked up the original investigation can't keep it locked away out of sight any longer. I don't see Police Scotland extending that invite, even if we got the First Minister to encourage them.'

'That's true,' Jimmy said, nodding, 'but remember, we also want to find out whether Juliet's phone records were or weren't used to track her movements. That's not something we can do without a favour from Frank.'

'I know, I know. But that one's different, that's just a simple yes or no. He can ask around at his police station or get DC McDonald to do it for him.'

'And if the answer's no?'

She gave a grimace. 'I don't know. But we can worry about that when we know one way or the other. But whilst we're exploring possibilities, you said there was something else that struck you after your visit to Francis Cramond. What was it?'

He shrugged. 'It was probably nothing. But when she was talking about supplying staff to the cruises, she only talked about girls. Three time she mentioned it, and not once did she say 'staff'. No, every time she said 'girls. Which I thought was a bit odd.'

'But is it so strange?' Maggie said, thinking out loud. 'I guess these rich golfers from around the world would be ninety-nine percent male, and I suppose most of them would be on a boys' trip and would have left their wives and girlfriends back home. I don't condone it, but you can imagine they'd prefer a pretty girl to serve them rather than some spotty youth.'

And then out of the blue, a random phrase came into her mind, something she'd heard a couple of the misogynistic cretins who used to work with her at Drake Chambers say, although they were talking about rugby not golf. *What happens on tour stays on tour.*

'You know Jimmy,' she said excitedly, 'this has been bloody staring us in the face for ages now and we've just been too dumb to see it. Or at least *I* have.'

'What do you mean?' he said, puzzled.

'What I mean is, what if it wasn't just fancy food that was being served to these high-rollers on Ally Russell's boat?'

Chapter 23

As it turned out, wee Lexy McDonald's source in Tulliallan headquarters had been bang on the money. To a flurry of media publicity, Assistant Chief Constable Belinda Cresswell had been appointed to head up the expanded Loch Lomond murder enquiry, now formally encompassing the killings of Ally Russell, Sandy McDuff and the still-unidentified third victim. The media being what it was - particularly those outlets on the right of the political spectrum who liked to imagine the hand of outrageous wokeness in everything in public life - much of the story focussed on Cresswell's sexuality and its role in her rapid promotion up the career ladder. Naturally her life partner, prominent, photogenic and seriously rich magazine owner Felicity Forbes-Brown, also featured heavily in the coverage. Whatever the rights and wrongs of all of that, and there was plenty could be said on either side of the argument in Frank's opinion, ACC Cresswell was now installed in New Gorbals police station, and, by chance, in an office directly opposite his own.

As for DCS Sweeney, unceremoniously shoved aside by the brass so that they could give the impression that they were actually doing something positive, it seemed to Frank he had taken the indignity rather better than might have been expected. But of course, he knew exactly why that was. Sweeney fully expected Cresswell's moment in the sun to be short-lived, knowing as he did that DCI Frank Stewart's UWIPO guns were fully trained on her. Which probably explained the smug look on his face as he strolled into Frank's office, closing the door firmly behind him.

'Well this is all going tickity-boo, isn't it Stewart?' he said brightly as he took a seat opposite Frank's desk. 'Belinda's here and looking very pleased with herself after all these TV appearances. She's milking it, isn't she? She thinks she's on Britain's Got Talent but what she doesn't know is she's about to get the big *no* from the panel. And then it'll be bye-bye Belinda.'

'So you're not bothered then sir?' Frank said. 'Because I would have thought it was a bit of a humiliation for you, getting kicked off the case. That's what everybody around here is saying anyway.'

Sweeney gave a dismissive smile. 'Do you think I give two flying monkeys what anybody around here thinks? The fact is, I'm glad to be out of it. The public don't give a stuff about the murder of a few old guys and frankly neither do I, which means this investigation is going to go rapidly down the plughole. Me, I'm just looking forward to a ringside seat when lesbo Belinda falls flat on her arse. In fact I can't wait. So when are you making your move, that's what I'm here to find out?'

His derogatory language shocked Frank but it didn't surprise him. He said, 'We've got to go through due process sir, as you know. I'm getting my DC up from the Smoke to do some fact-checking and when we're satisfied with that we'll make our move. Don't you worry about that sir.' *And if you call her lesbo Belinda again, I'm going to report you.* He was within an inch of saying it, but decided just this once to keep his powder dry.

'Well get your arse in gear and stop pissing about, okay?' Sweeney got up, opened the door, and pointed. 'See, her office is just across the corridor so what's keeping you? And it looks like she's in too. Strike whilst the iron is hot, that's what they say.'

'Thank you for your excellent advice sir,' Frank said, smiling sweetly. 'And of course I'll keep you fully informed of developments as and when they arise.'

Aye, and there would be plenty of developments coming down the line and not of the kind Sweeney was going to welcome. Although right now there was something that was a bit odd too, something that Frank didn't fully understand. Because now that the prestige car dealer George Cramond was aware that the police were interested in him, it might be assumed that news of that interest would have got back to Sweeney. And yet Frank had heard not a peep. The bent DCS was obviously getting the use of these fancy motors for *something*, either as a reward for some dodgy service rendered or - and as Frank thought about it some more, the more likely scenario - to keep quiet about something he knew. Yes, that was a more plausible explanation for why Sweeney had evidently not been told yet of this sudden police interest. The bad guys, whoever they were, would be seriously worried that he might blab and so were nervously weighing up how to handle this unwelcome development. That might all become clear later this afternoon when he and Ronnie French paid George Cramond an unannounced visit.

Talking of ACC Cresswell, it *had* been in Frank's mind to make a wee call on her too, but not on this occasion to unveil that the machinery of the state had been spying on her and was very interested in all these wee luxury holidays she was evidently so fond of. That was likely to be a tricky conversation and he was in no mood to have it until he was sure of his facts. No, what he wanted to talk about was entirely connected to her murder enquiry, to alert her to the possibility that in fact she should be looking at four killings not just three.

He took a quick glance at his watch, which caused him to reconsider. If he got caught up in an extended conversation with the ACC, he'd miss his arranged pick-up of Ronnie French, who was scheduled to tool into Queen's Street station within the half hour. Nope, Cresswell would have to wait until tomorrow. His mind made up, he set off down to the front desk to borrow a set of wheels, hoping the duty sergeant would not be his default arsy self and would thus provide him with what he wanted - a marked patrol car with the nice big orange stripe down the side and the wee blue light on top.

By luck it was a young constable on the desk this morning, someone Frank hadn't seen before. He looked about twelve years old.

'Morning son,' he said. 'I'm DCI Stewart with the Met. I need a marked patrol car. What've you got?'

The youth gave an eager smile, turning to examine the bank of keys hanging on a board behind him. 'An Astra or a Beemer 5-Series sir.'

Frank nodded. 'That'll do.'

'The Astra or the Beemer?'

'Do you need to ask? Come on, hand them over.'

It was only a five or ten minute drive up to the station, especially since the marked car gave him no-questions-asked access to the restricted area around the entrance. He parked up in the taxi rank, leaving the BMW unlocked as he went in search of his corpulent colleague. French's train had evidently just arrived, a stream of mid-afternoon travellers emerging through the barriers into the concourse, Frank speculating Sherlock Holmes-style on their likely occupation based on their appearance. Students, business folk and, he noted slightly sourly, public servants, a category that had swelled in both numbers and importance in recent years. Towards the rear of the throng he spotted his DC, conspicuously scruffy in a creased grey suit, an off-white shirt unbuttoned at the collar, thin navy tie hanging at an angle several degrees away from the vertical. Would he be identified as a detective, Frank wondered, should any other observer be engaged in the same 'spot the occupation' parlour game as himself? Quite possibly, but from about four decades earlier. The fact was, Ronnie French would have been a shoo-in for a part in *The Sweeney*, had he answered 'actor' rather than 'policeman' when asked at school what he wanted to be when he grew up.

'Afternoon guv,' French said affably. 'And just to let you know in case you've got anything planned for me, I'm pretty knackered meself. Had to set the bloody alarm for half five to catch that bloody train up from King's Cross.'

Frank laughed. 'But you had four and a half hours to catch up on your kip on the way up, so excuse me if I don't extend my sympathy. And aye, I do have something planned for you. But on the way, you can tell me all about your interview with Miss Miranda Temple.'

Soon he was threading the patrol car westwards along St Vincent Street, picking up the urban motorway network and crossing the Clyde on their way out towards the airport.

'Where are we heading guv?' French asked as they steamed along the outside lane, nervous motorists checking their speedometers and moving aside as they spotted the marked car in their rear-view mirrors.

'Paisley, but I don't suppose that means anything to you. But anyway, to Miss Temple.'

French shrugged. 'Well I'll tell you what guv, that was the strangest thing in the world.'

'What do you mean?'

'The old bird didn't have a bloody clue what I was talking about. And she was genuine, one hundred percent. Honest, she really didn't have any idea what I was on about. Obviously I didn't mentioned our geezer Andrew McClelland's name or anything like that. I just said we were investigating the potentially illegal movement of funds into her bank account and she just about fainted with the shock.'

'And you're absolutely sure about that? That she knew nothing about it?'

'Yeah guv, like I said, one hundred percent. Eleanor had got me a copy of one of the bank statements. It was from Santander and it had Miranda's name and her pukka address on it, and it showed the money being transferred in and the cash being drawn from the holes in the wall. But she was adamant she knew nothing about it.'

'So what do you think's going on?' Frank said. 'Any ideas?'

'Someone's pinched her identity guv, that would be my bet. Definitely.'

'McClelland do we think? But how would he have managed that?'

French shrugged. 'Not my area of expertise guv, but our guy McClelland's a big cheese in this Procurator Fiscal organisation, so he'll have access to all the personnel records I would guess. And Miranda told me she'd joined the Civil Service forty years ago and back then proof of identity would have been old-school.'

'Meaning?'

'Meaning that you would have needed to provide a copy of your Birth Certificate when you accepted a job.'

'Which will still be in her file.'

'Exactly guv. And with one of them and a Photoshopped utility bill and a payslip you'd be able to open a bank account with no questions asked.'

'Bloody hell, you're right Frenchie,' Frank said, feeling his excitement rising. 'But the question is, *why*? Why, if it is Andrew McClelland who's behind all this palaver, has he gone to all this trouble?'

'Yeah, that's what I was thinking too guv. So are we going to haul him in for questioning, see what he's got to say for himself?'

Frank shook his head. 'Eventually, but we've got a fair amount to do first to be sure of our ground. I'm thinking out loud here, but for a start it would be great to get some evidence that it's actually him who's making these cash withdrawals.'

'That's easy-peasy guv,' French said. 'All these cashlines have got CCTV. I'll have a word with the bank in the morning, get them to send us the clips.'

'Brilliant, that'll be a good start. So, let's now have a wee think about what we're going to say to Mr George Cramond. We'll be there in five minutes.'

***

GC Prestige Automobiles was located at the end of a pot-holed cul-de-sac on a run-down industrial estate not far from the airport. It occupied an open plot, secured by a rusting metal-railing fence topped by barbed wire, the double entrance gates currently lying open, allowing Frank to drive straight in and at speed. Spinning the steering-wheel he braked sharply, throwing up a shower of gravel as the car came to a halt outside the Portakabin which evidently housed the sales and administration functions of the firm. In contrast with the unprepossessing surroundings, the yard was packed with expensive motorcars, most it seemed wearing a current-year registration plate.

'I thought these guys were middle-men?' he asked French. 'I didn't know they held this much stock. There must be a million-quid's-worth here at least. Probably more.'

French shrugged. 'These guys know a bargain when they see one. He probably got them on the cheap. Well, cheap-ish, compared to their normal price I mean.'

'Aye maybe. Anyway, let's wander over and see if he's in.'

Frank pushed open the door of the cabin and strolled in. A man dressed casually in jeans and sweatshirt sat at a desk punching away at a laptop computer.

'Hello can I help you?' he said, without looking up.

'You can if you're George Cramond. Here, let me show you my warrant card.' He slipped the card out of an inner pocket and thrust it in front of the man. 'Actually, I've been wondering why you haven't been returning my calls.'

'Haven't I?' the man said, unconvincingly. 'I don't remember you calling me.'

'Well you won't if you're not George Cramond. If you are him, then you've ignored at least five of my calls, which is very rude in my opinion.'

'Yeah I'm Cramond,' the man admitted. 'But I've been busy, that's all. Sorry.'

'Aye well it's not a problem because we're here now. By the way, this is my colleague, Detective Constable French. We're with the Metropolitan Police.'

'What, from London?' Cramond said, sounding surprised.

'Yep. And I told you that too when I left my wee message. We're from a specialist team that's investigating corruption in public office on behalf of the UK Government. Just so you know who we are.'

Cramond seemed to relax a little. 'I don't see what that's got to do with me. I'm just a wee car dealer.'

'And a very generous one it seems to me,' Frank said. 'By the way, me and DC French here were wondering if you're any relation to Davie Cramond, of McClelland Tower infamy.'

'It was that bloody freak storm that blew it down in case you hadn't noticed,' he said sharply. 'And aye, Davie's my big brother.'

'Thought he might be. So my question relates to these three motors you own that are currently in the sole custody of my colleague DCS Peter Sweeney. Remind me what they are again DC French?'

French responded instantly. 'There's a BMW X5 SUV, a Mercedes SL350 and a Tesla Model S guv. Total dosh value over one hundred and eighty grand.'

'Thank you Detective Constable. So Mr Cramond, what's this all about then?'

The man shuffled uncomfortably. 'He's just a mate from the golf club who likes his motors.'

'A mate from the golf club eh? Well that's nice. So you thought you'd lend him nearly two hundred grand's worth of motor just to be pally? Costing you what, about forty grand a year in depreciation? All I can say is I wish I was your mate too.'

'So what?' Cramond said, summoning some defiance. 'The last time I looked it wasn't against the law.'

'Not for you maybe,' Frank said, giving a cold smile. 'But it might be for your golf buddy, especially now we've got some lovely new laws at our disposal. By the way, I meant to ask, what's your handicap?'

Cramond was silent for a moment and then said, mumbling, 'I don't actually play the game myself.'

'You hear that DC French?' Frank said. 'Mr Cramond doesn't actually play golf. Ah, so I take it he's your *brother's* golf buddy and it was Davie who asked you to set up this wee scam for him. Am I right or am I right?'

'How's it a scam?' Cramond said, defiant again. 'Somebody's insured to drive some of my motors, so what? I do it all the time for my mates.'

Frank gave him a cynical look. 'Aye, that's the kind of generous guy you are. But what I find interesting is that despite my five phone calls to you it seems DCS Sweeney has still not been told that we're on to him. So why's that, I've been asking myself?' He paused for a moment. 'I'll tell you what I think Mr Cramond and you can tell me if I'm warm or if I'm cold. And you can play the game too DC French, if you want to.'

'I'm in guv,' French said, nodding.

'Good. So here's what I think. I think our dodgy DCS knows something that would be seriously disadvantageous to your brother and probably you as well should it come out into the open. And ever since my phone call, you've been absolutely shitting yourselves in case Sweeney finds out, decides the game's up and thinks it would be better for him if he just came clean. Now you and your brother can't make up your minds whether to keep stumm in the hope that it all just blows away, or whether you need to do something to shut him up before he blabs.' He paused again, shooting Cramond a smile. 'How am I doing George? Getting warm?'

'That's bollocks,' Cramond said, but it wasn't convincing.

'No I don't think it's bollocks,' Frank said. 'But we're all going to find out soon enough aren't we? Because no-one's going to be able to keep this a secret much longer. But I'll ask you anyway George. What does your brother's golfing pal know or what has he done to merit being the beneficiary of such outstanding generosity?'

Cramond looked uncomfortable but said nothing. So Frank tried again.

'Come on George, what's it all about?'

'No comment.' His words were mumbled such that they were barely audible. But Frank heard them all right.

'Well well,' Frank said, giving a wry smile. '*No comment eh?* Whenever I hear that, I know we've definitely got something to worry about.' He nodded at French. 'Anyway, I think what we'll do here is charge you with obstruction of a police officer going about their lawful duties and then we'll cart you off with us and install you in a nice comfortable cell at our nick. You can have a wee overnight stay, but don't worry, they do a nice breakfast and you can share a shower with some of our other friendly guests before we question you some more in the morning. How does that sound George? All right?'

He gave them a resigned look then shrugged. 'Davie asked me to do it. He owed the guy a favour. I don't know what that was. I just supplied the motors.'

Frank beamed back a smile. *'Excellent* George, thanks *so* much for your co-operation. So we'll be in touch in due course. And don't worry, we'll see ourselves out.'

***

On the drive back to town, neither of them said much, French on account of weariness after his early start, Frank because his brain was churning crazily as a million thoughts and theories battled for attention. What was this favour Sweeney had done for Davie Cramond that meant he had been enjoying the use of these cars for two years or more? It reminded him that they needed to follow up on that Paul Adams guy, the bloke who'd gone overboard on one of Ally Russell's cruises and the one whose death Sweeney had investigated. Was that it Frank wondered, was there something dodgy about that incident, something the DCS had turned a blind eye to? But no, there was something else, something obvious that he was missing. *What the hell was it?* Perhaps something about dates, but he couldn't think exactly what. And then suddenly it came to him. He leant across and gave French an elbow in the ribs, causing the snoring DC to wake with a start.

'Sorry Frenchie, but can you just remind me exactly when this started? When Sweeney first took out the insurance on these motors I mean?'

French stretched out, rubbed his eyes and failed to suppress a yawn. 'Sure guv. It was about two years ago. In the June I think. Yeah, that was it, definitely.'

Which, Frank recalled, was exactly two months after Juliet McClelland was reported missing.

Chapter 24

The rain was crashing down from the heavens, the wipers of the little Golf set to maximum speed but making little impression. The gathering puddles on the A82, the busy road that ran up the western side of the loch, were already turning into small lakes, although she wouldn't have even considered slowing down on their account had not Jimmy scared her with talk of something he called aquaplaning. He looked across from the passenger seat and gave her a sardonic smile. 'It'll still be there when we get there, don't worry.'

Maggie nodded. 'I know. But I'm desperate to find out if my crazy theory is right or not.'

'Well maybe if you told me what it is I might be able to pass judgement. Instead of me having to play this daft wee guessing game of yours.' She saw him glance at the speedometer. 'Oh and by the way, sixty-five miles an hour is just perfect if you want to sail into the next crash barrier, never mind the fact that the speed limit along here is only sixty and there's cameras every hundred yards. Just saying.'

'Yes, I know, sorry,' she said, easing her foot off the accelerator, 'but...'

'Aye, I know,' he interrupted. 'You want to find out whether your mad idea is right or not.'

They drove in silence for the next few miles, partly because the foul weather made concentration imperative, partly because her head wouldn't stop churning around the half-formed theory which she hoped would be proved correct, or at least given some supporting evidence after their visit to Ardlui Marina. Stupid, ridiculous, nuts, it was all of these things and more, but the one and only solid concrete fact they had definitely seemed to fit - the fact there was something in Juliet McClelland's bank account her family desperately wanted to hide from them.

They were interrupted by a ping from Jimmy's phone. He reached into his pocket and fished it out.

'Voicemail,' he said, punching in the code to retrieve the message then switching to speakerphone. It was a woman's voice, Scottish and educated, the words breaking up occasionally but without losing the sense of what she was saying. And a voice that Maggie instantly recognised.

'Hello, I assume this is Bainbridge and Stewart? This is Dr Becky Johnson. I've tried to call a couple of times this morning but couldn't get through. Look, I've been seeing these posters of Juliet everywhere, and now I've got something to tell you. Well perhaps something to confess is a better

way of putting it. Anyway, you can get me on this number. Bye.'

'Bloody hell,' Maggie said, giving him an excited look. 'Dr Becky Johnson? Bloody hell.'

He laughed. 'That's twice you've said that.'

She nodded. 'She's the sexy flat mate, remember? The one that stole Juliet's boyfriend. He's a right arsehole by the way. So come on, call her back. This sounds bloody important.'

He thrust the phone briefly in front of her so she could see it. 'Hardly half a bar of signal. I think we'll wait until we get there. They'll probably have wi-fi in the hotel so we can do an internet call.'

'Come on, try anyway. Call her.'

He shrugged. 'Okay boss, but I don't hold out much hope.'

He tapped the phone to call her back. After a few seconds, it tripped over to voicemail. *'Hi, this is Becky, I'm not...'* He hung up and shot Maggie a look that said *see I told you*.

'Fair enough,' she said, disappointed. 'We'll get her later. But I wonder what it is she wants to confess. Because that call sounded bloody ominous to me.'

He shrugged again. 'No point in speculating. And I wouldn't get our hopes up too much. It was two years ago remember, so her recall might be less than perfect.'

'Yeah, maybe.' And he was right to be cautious of course, but Maggie couldn't help thinking that it was a sign that the tide might finally be turning in their investigation. There always was a moment when all the disparate threads came together, when all the half-formed theories and half-baked ideas suddenly began to point in the same direction. And every time, it was preceded by a strong but inexplicable feeling in her gut. Today, she thought she might be having that feeling.

Glancing over, she saw Jimmy was studying the map on his phone. 'Yash said not to confuse his place with the big Ardlui hotel right on the lochside. His hotel was some smaller place on the left side of the main road. It's called Loch View although he said you had to strain your eyes a bit to actually see the water because there's a big tin boat shed on the opposite side of the road that blocks it. But anyway, it's only three-quarters of a mile now according to the sat-nav.'

The Loch View Hotel turned out to be a whitewashed affair, constructed in a traditional style that she had recently read about in the Homes section of the Chronicle. Scottish Baronial, that's what it was apparently, characterised by a profusion of ornamental turrets and fake castellations. This one might have been a rather nice home in the Victorian era, in the days before the supermarkets' articulated lorries thundered by on their way up to Fort William and beyond, but now it was distinctly low-rent in appearance, its aesthetic spoiled by a series of unattractive flat-roofed extensions that seemed to have been added in haphazard fashion. The car park was of black ash, pot-holed and heavily weed-infested, and hosted only two other cars that morning. Maggie wondered exactly what Yash Patel must have made of it when his taxi dropped him off that night after his nightmare journey up from London. It certainly wouldn't have been complimentary that was for sure and he wouldn't have been shy about saying it either.

Jimmy gave a grimace as they pulled up. 'See what our Tourist Board have to put up with? It looks a bit like Fawlty Towers. Or maybe worse.'

She laughed. 'You're too young to remember that show surely? Even I was only about six months old when it was on.'

'My dad loved it. It was about the only thing the old grump ever found funny. He still watches the re-runs.'

'You're talking about my almost-father-in-law now don't forget,' she said in a mock scolding tone. 'And he's very nice. So is your mum.' Which of course was what any daughter-in-law was expected to say, even though Frank and Jimmy's parents were actually pretty horrible, that view formed instantly and perhaps unfairly on the first occasion she had met them. Snobbish and judgemental just about summed them up, which went a long way to explain the strained relationship they had with their two sons. But that didn't matter, because it was Frank she was marrying not them, and now, *hallelujah*, the wedding was less than nine months away.

'At least we get to park at the door,' he said, grinning. 'So shall we just make a run for it? Because this rain's on for the day by the looks of things.'

It was just a few steps to the entrance, the door of sturdy oak construction with a frosted glass window engraved with the hotel's name. A threadbare tartan carpet covered the spacious entrance hall and led to an elegant wood-panelled staircase. The reception desk was unattended, a sign directing visitors to ring the brass bell that sat on the counter. To the left, another sign pointed to the lounge bar from where wafted the muted sound of conversation. Ignoring the bell, they headed leftwards. An elderly man and woman, seemingly the sole customers, were sitting on high stools at a bar, chatting to a middle-aged barman of smart appearance, wearing a dark green tartan waistcoat over a dazzling white shirt. With some amusement, Maggie recognised the barman's accent, a rich Cockney that reminded her of Frank's colleague Ronnie French. Or, less agreeably, of the snivelling Clerk of Drake Chambers, Nigel Redmond.

'Ello folks,' he said pleasantly. 'What can I get for you? Staying for lunch? Because if you are, I just need to tell you we've got a coach party of Yanks in at half-one, one of them glens and lochs tours. Couldn't have picked a better day for it could they, poor sods? So it would be handy if you got your order in before then. My missus is in the kitchen on her own today and she's already having a meltdown. And by the way, I'm John Watkins. I own this place for my sins.'

'Actually John we're here for business, not leisure I'm afraid,' Maggie said, smiling. 'But that doesn't mean we won't be having lunch though. I'm Maggie Bainbridge and this is my colleague Jimmy Stewart. We're private investigators and we're here in connection with Ally Russell.' She had thought it better not to mention Juliet at this stage, and anyway what she told him was true. Their visit to Ardlui chiefly concerned the murdered man.

'You knew him I think?' she continued. 'A friend of ours from a newspaper said you had put him in touch with Mr Russell and he had taken him out to Inchcailloch on his boat.'

The man shrugged. 'He drunk here love, that was all. We didn't socialise or nothing.' He gave a bitter laugh. 'You don't have time for socialising when you run a place like this, believe you me. It's full-on, day-in, day-out.'

'We heard he was involved in a terrible tragedy a couple of years back,' Jimmy said, 'when one of his passengers was drowned. We wondered if it had affected him at all?'

Watkins gave another shrug. 'Can't see I noticed any difference mate. Ally liked a drink before the accident and he liked one afterwards too. But he did lose his licence to take passengers out on the loch of course.'

'That must have caused him some problems,' Maggie said. 'With it being his livelihood and all that.'

'You think so? Not that I noticed. All he did afterwards was sell one of his boats for a packet then started doing the private stuff with the one he kept. Everybody around here knew what was going on.'

'And nobody reported him?'

'Why should they, he weren't doing nothing wrong. You only need a licence if you're taking fare-paying passengers. Nothing to stop you taking a few mates out on your boat, know what I mean love? No, there were no flies on him, let me tell you that. Smart guy was our Ally.'

'But then someone murdered him,' Jimmy said wryly.

'Yeah, tragic that,' Watkins said. 'Ally had his faults but he didn't deserve that, no way.'

'So what did he do with his time?' Maggie asked. 'Was he a family man or did he go fishing or what?'

Watkins shook his head. 'Nah, he didn't do much really. See, he got divorced about ten years back but he never talked about it much. He just did his boat trips and then came in here most nights, had three or four pints and a couple of drams. He just lived up the road a bit, a couple of miles away.'

'And he drove here and back did he?' Maggie asked, raising an eyebrow.

'Yeah, that was Ally all over,' Watkins said, laughing. 'Didn't give a shit about nobody.'

'And do you have any theories John, about why he was killed?'

'Nah,' he said. 'The police asked me the same thing of course, but no, no idea at all. As I said, he was in here a lot but I didn't really get to know him personal-like. That's the art of the great landlord,' he continued self-importantly. 'You want to be matey but you don't pry.'

'I guess not,' Maggie said.

'But actually, there was one thing,' Watkins said, sounding cagey. 'Something me and the missus used to laugh about.'

'What was that?' she asked, interested.

'So once a month Ally would take a trip up to Glasgow. Always on a Sunday and he always went easy on the drink the night before just to make sure he still wasn't over the limit in the morning.'

'So what was that all about?' Jimmy asked.

Watkins reduced his voice to a whisper. 'Me and the missus, we thought he might be shagging somebody up there if you pardon my French. Someone married, is what we thought. Because he was always a bit secretive about it. In fact me and the missus thought that maybe it was the husband what done him in. You know, this guy caught them at it or something and took his revenge.'

'Did you mention this to the police?' Jimmy said.

Watkins shrugged. 'Nah, it was just me and Agnes letting our imaginations run away with us. We like to watch all them crime dramas when we get a chance.'

Maggie laughed. 'Yes, I like them too. In fact sometimes I think me and Jimmy are actually in one. But anyway, the real reason we're here is to look at Ally's cruise boat. I believe it's still moored at the marina.'

'What, the *Joan Greig*? Yeah, it's still here. It's tied up on the jetty next to the boat shed across the road.'

She gave him an uncomprehending look. 'It's called the Joan Greig is it? Why's that? Or should I say, who was she?'

Jimmy smiled. 'It's a play on words I think. A guy called John Greig played for Glasgow Rangers football club in the sixties. He was a legend. Still is.'

'I'll take your word for it. So John, what will happen to that boat now do you know? Has he got any relatives who might inherit it?'

Watkins shrugged. 'As I said, Ally got divorced about ten years ago and there's no kids or anything, so I've no idea. It's just been sitting there since he got killed.'

'Okay then,' Maggie said. 'We're going to wander across now and take a look. And we'll try to get back before your coach party arrives. I wouldn't want Jimmy here missing out on his lunch.'

Outside, the rain was still hammering down, drumming a rhythmic pattern on the roof of the Golf as they paused in the entrance porch, contemplating their strategy.

'We could drive round I suppose,' Jimmy said, 'but we'd still have quite a walk from their car-park I think.'

'Yeah, I know,' Maggie said ruefully. 'Let's just go for it shall we?'

He nodded. 'Aye, onwards and upwards. Or should I say onwards and across-wards. Let's go.'

As luck would have it - bad luck that was - the road was heavy with traffic in both directions and it took them nearly five minutes to get across. Now completely soaked, they sprinted up the narrow path which ran up the side of the corrugated boat-shed, and as Watkins had correctly informed them, led straight onto the jetty that hosted the *Joan Greig*. Maggie had formed an impression of the craft in her mind which turned out to be reasonably accurate. The hull looked to be constructed out of some kind of varnished wood and still glistened through the raindrops despite moss and algae beginning to take hold. The boat was a bit longer that she'd expected though, perhaps forty or maybe even fifty feet in extent, with a glazed passenger cabin situated centrally and stretching to thirty feet at least, the interior not visible due to closed roller-blinds on every window. A steel platform with handrails that facilitated passenger access from the jetty was still in place, the centrally-located double entrance doors three steps below the edge of the hull. Nimbly skipping down the steps, she tried the door handle. It was locked.

She gave Jimmy a knowing look. 'It's what you would expect of course. But we haven't come all this way for nothing.'

He grinned. 'Stand aside madam.' He gripped the handle and gave it a pull. The twin doors rattled loosely in their frame. He pulled it again with more force and this time they sprung open. 'There we go. Easy-peasy and no damage done either. So I guess we're going in?'

She nodded her assent, then stepped into the cabin and began to look around. The first impression was of a quiet up-market elegance, the floor in polished wood laid in parquet style, a large central dining table in a rich dark red mahogany, the well-stocked bar at one end also constructed of gleaming polished wood. But then that impression was shattered when she caught sight of the images that were screen-printed onto a few of the lowered roller blinds.

'Bloody hell Jimmy, have you seen these?' she said, unable to hide her distaste.

He smiled, looking faintly embarrassed. 'How could you miss them? Although they are pretty classy I suppose. Not the hard-core porno stuff at least.'

'They're still women in their underwear. And those poses are bloody provocative. This wasn't a bloody Marks and Sparks catalogue shoot was it?'

She took in the scene once more, knowing almost certainly now that her crazy mad theory was correct, one-hundred-percent. Now she just needed the final proof, and she was pretty damn sure she knew what she was looking for.

'Jimmy, over there. That door, next to the bar. Can you take a look and see what's behind it?'

He nodded and strode over, then pushed it open and stuck his head through the gap. 'Looks like the kitchen Maggie. Quite a fancy one too if I'm any judge. Which I'm not by the way. A massive range and a big stainless steel work area. Top-end.'

Yes, well it would need to be top-end she thought, if they had some big-name Michelin-starred chef serving up cordon bleu dishes. But interesting though that was, it wasn't what she was looking for. Then suddenly she saw it. Another door, reflected clearly in the large mirror that hung behind the bar, tucked away in a corner directly behind her. *This must be it.*

Her heart pounding, she spun round and slowly made her way towards it. But she didn't want to open it or go into the room alone.

'Jimmy,' she said, reducing her voice to a whisper, for what reason she could not quite understand. 'I'd like us to do this together. If that's okay.'

'Your hunch is right isn't it?' he said. 'The crazy theory is suddenly not so crazy after all.'

She nodded slowly. 'I think so. But I don't want it to be, really I don't. For Juliet's sake.'

'Well we better find out, hadn't we? I'll go first if you want.' Without waiting for her to answer he took a step forward and grabbed the handle. The door opened outwards and at a glance Maggie could see it was exactly and depressingly as she had been expecting. A bedroom, but a bedroom dressed and decorated for sex, not sleep. A king-size bed draped with black satin sheets, a silver chrome metal headboard to which were attached two pairs of handcuffs. On the wall behind the bed hung more pictures, but these ones very much more explicit. On a bedside table, an empty bottle of champagne and two glasses. Next to them, a small china dish, empty, but Maggie was pretty sure she knew what it would have contained.

'Bloody hell,' she heard Jimmy saying. 'So this was what was going on was it? This explains all the secrecy I guess. But what a right little shagging palace this is.'

She raised an eyebrow. 'That's one way to describe it I suppose.'

'But *Juliet*,' he said, disbelieving. 'Are we saying *she* was involved in this? Because it seems incredible, a girl like her.'

'But you said it yourself didn't you? That she was incredibly alluring, not just beautiful. A lot of men would pay a lot of money to sleep with a girl like that. Maybe this is where that dream could come true, if you were rich enough.'

And as she said it another terrible and depressing thought threatened to overcome her. A girl like Juliet could awaken uncontrollable passions in even the most sane of men, causing them to do crazy things like have mad dangerous affairs or even walk out on much-loved wives and children, an atom bomb of lust exploding inside them. And if that lust was not sated, if it was coldly rejected, then there were men in this world who would just go ahead and satisfy it anyway, and then either dispassionately or in a blind panic, commit murder to cover their heinous crime. Perhaps that was what happened to Juliet on the elegant streets of the West End of the city, and maybe this whole enterprise, sordid though it was, had nothing to do with her disappearance at all.

She sat down on the edge of the bed feeling distinctly queasy and took a deep breath, aware as she was of her pulse racing. 'I need a drink Jimmy. Let's go back to the hotel. And would you mind if you drive back? Because actually, I *need* two drinks.'

He gave her a sympathetic smile. 'Aye of course, no problem. I'd feel a lot safer in the driving seat anyway, no offence to your piloting skills. And I'm sure our man John will lend you a towel to dry yourself off.'

It was just like him she thought, to try to make her feel better, even at a time like this.

'Yeah, and I hope he's got a hairdryer too. I must look a frightful mess.'

'Aye, you do,' he said, laughing. 'But still very lovely.'

'Idiot. But at least we don't have to bother running on the way back because honestly, how can we get any wetter?'

* * *

The coach carrying the American tourists had just pulled in as Maggie and Jimmy were traipsing across the sodden car-park. As they reached the entrance porch, they were passed by owner John travelling in the opposite direction and carrying a large and already-erected golf umbrella, surely a forlorn gesture with the rain falling so heavily. He gave them a resigned look then said, 'My missus is holding the fort in the bar for five minutes. If you're quick you can get your lunch order in before the hoards descend. And I'd recommend the bacon and brie ciabatta. Agnes does it lovely.'

As her husband had predicted, Agnes Watkins was behind the bar when they entered the lounge. She was a rosy-cheeked and robustly-built woman perhaps just touching forty years of age, wearing a chequered chef's apron, her red hair almost totally concealed by a matching hat.

'You're just in time folks,' she said, smiling and revealing a soft Highland accent. 'Are you eating or is it just a wee drink you're wanting?'

Maggie returned the smile. 'We've been recommended the bacon and brie Mrs Watkins.

And please, a double brandy. And I'd love a towel if you have one.'

'No bother,' the woman said pleasantly. 'I'll bring you one through in a minute. And you sir, you're having the ciabatta too? And the brandy?'

Jimmy gave her a rueful look. 'I'd love a wee whisky but I'm the designated driver today so just a coke for me. But aye, I'll have the ciabatta too. And do you have the code for your wi-fi please? I assume you have it.'

'Loch View, all one word, all lower case. Right, let me get that towel first and then I'll get onto the drinks and lunch.'

'Nice woman,' Jimmy said after she'd gone. 'So let's see if we can get hold of your Doctor Becky. You met her, didn't you?'

'I did, at the hospital where she works,' Maggie said, nodding. 'Pretty, but pretty full of herself too. She reminded me of a couple of girls I knew at school. Snakes in the grass, that's what we used to call them. And actually, I don't think Becky exactly took to me. So it would be better if you made the call I think.'

She watched as he punched in the wi-fi code, nodding silently to himself as it evidently connected without issue. 'Right, here we go,' he said, giving a thumbs-up then switching to speaker-phone. It rang for a few seconds before being answered.

'Is that Becky? This is Jimmy Stewart from Bainbridge and Stewart Private Investigators. You called earlier and left a message.'

'Yes, I did. Thanks for calling back.' The woman paused for what seemed an age before continuing. 'Look, I've been thinking about this thing for forever. But your poster made me think I really needed to do something now.'

'Okay,' Jimmy said slowly, 'but I'm not sure I'm completely with you.'

'I followed her that night. After the lecture. Back to our flat.' The words were blurted out, as if Becky was desperate not to be associated with them.

'Oh-kay', he said again, this time stretching the word out. Maggie gave him an admiring look, impressed by his coolness. She would have spat out a *bloody hell,* no doubt about that. In fact, she very nearly did.

'Why was that?' Jimmy continued. 'Why did you follow her I mean?'

'Because I hated her. And I know it's a horrible phrase and I know you shouldn't speak ill of the *dead, but she was a right little prick-tease. Rob was totally obsessed with her.'*

Unable to restrain herself, Maggie jumped in. 'Hi Becky, it's Maggie Bainbridge. But I thought it was Rob who had finished with Juliet? Or did I misunderstand him?'

'There was no Rob and Juliet,' she said bitterly, *'although he wished there had been. Okay, maybe they did it once when she was drunk and feeling sorry for him, but this wasn't some great romance. But he wouldn't stop going on about her, even when he was supposed to be with me. I needed to do something to make it stop, it was affecting my mental health.'*

'So why that evening?' Maggie asked quietly.

'She did something, in the lecture theatre, that afternoon,' Becky said plaintively. *'And I know she knew I'd seen it too. She put her hand on the inside of his thigh and then slid it up. All the way up. It was sickening for me. So I decided there and then I would have to say something.'*

'So what did you do?'

'Do? I didn't do anything, that's the point. As I said, I meant to have it out with her at the flat before she left for her shift at the hotel, but her taxi had just arrived as she got there. And before I

could get to her I saw her run out of the close and get in.'

'What?' Maggie said, astonished. 'You *saw* her get in the taxi? So why the hell didn't you say anything to the police at the time?'

'How could I?' she said. *'Everybody at Uni knew I hated her and I'd followed her, hadn't I? The police are imbeciles and I didn't want them putting two and two together and making five. And I had my career to think about.'*

'What about her poor bloody family?' Maggie exploded. 'Didn't you think about *them*? If you'd come forward earlier the police might have had a chance of finding her.'

'I know I know,' the doctor said, sounding close to tears, *'but I was young and stupid and actually I was glad she disappeared. It's a horrible thing to say but I hoped she'd been murdered, I really did.'*

'But now finally, you've decided to do the right thing,' Jimmy said, sounding a lot more sympathetic than he ought to in Maggie's opinion.

'Yes,' the woman said, then paused for a moment. *'What will happen to me? Will you tell the police?'*

And at that moment, Maggie knew exactly what they had to do. This thing had suddenly got way too big for her little firm, much as she might hate to admit it. So once she was done with this reprehensible woman, she was getting straight on the phone to her lovely Frank Stewart.

'Tell the police Becky?' she said, her tone bitter and judgemental at the same time. 'Of course we're going to bloody tell the police. *Everything*.'

Chapter 25

Down at New Gorbals police station, things had moved at breakneck speed in the aftermath of Maggie's astounding phone call. In fact, half way through the call, Frank had had to appeal to his brother to intervene such was the torrent of words she was sending his way, driven he could tell by a mixture of outrage and urgency. But eventually he was able to make out the gist of what she was saying to him, and bloody sensational it was too. Juliet McClelland hadn't disappeared on the streets of Hillhead that night but had in fact got into the taxi as was her normal routine, which then sped off to deliver her to the Auchterard Hotel where she was due on shift one hour later. Except she wasn't going there at all, but instead to perform sordid but lucrative duties on board the murdered Ally Russell's boat, the *Joan Greig*. Two minutes after the call had ended, Frank had been across the corridor and in the office of Assistant Chief Constable Belinda Cresswell, and barely four hours after that and despite it being very late in the evening, the basement interview rooms of the station had been witnessing a frenzy of activity.

In Interview Room 3, the largest of those available, ACC Cresswell had personally taken charge of the grilling of DCS Peter Sweeney, a man with a lot of questions to answer, all of them difficult. Like why he had decided to lump Juliet's disappearance in with those of the other murdered women, despite the stark differences, the principle one being that the serial killer Denis Northcote was a narcissistic bastard who wanted his victims to be found, and quickly, so that he could bask in the media attention. Like why had he not bothered to ask for Juliet's mobile phone records when it would have shown she *had* got into that taxi after all. And how could a guy on an adequate but moderate senior police officer's salary afford all these upmarket motor cars he liked to swan around in?

Next door in Room 4, the owner of Lomond Minicabs had been forlornly denying that he had ordered his illegal immigrant driver to tell the police that he'd waited outside Juliet's flat for nearly twenty minutes but she hadn't turned up, and equally forlornly denying that he had either been paid or threatened by person or persons unknown to do it. DC Lexy McDonald, patiently in charge of the interrogation, had remained relaxed, judging that the man would not be able to hold this line for much longer. And after less than one hour, her judgement had proved correct, and she knew everything.

Later that evening, back at their new-ish Milngavie home and after Ollie had been put to bed, Maggie and Frank had talked and talked, trying to knock some shape into the convoluted jumble of facts that were now beginning to emerge in both their investigations, investigations that now seemed to be tangling together in a very interesting and surprising fashion. But despite - or maybe because of - considerable lubrication of their little grey cells by chardonnay and single malt respectively, no sense could be made of it all. Frank wasn't bothered though. They were getting close, he could sense it in his bones, and soon there would be that magical *eureka* moment. There always was.

And now this morning they could finally concentrate on unravelling First Husband Andrew McClelland's little cash trail. Crammed into his small office were Detective Constables Ronnie French and Lexy McDonald, the former looking faintly hung over after evidently blowing his dinner expenses in the bar of his hotel, the latter bursting with annoying perkiness as ever. Unusually, Maggie and Jimmy were there too, on account of them being summoned into the station by ACC Cresswell so that she could learn first-hand everything they had found out about the Juliet McClelland case. On the video call was Eleanor Campbell, broadcasting from her favoured dank corner of Atlee House and sporting a surly demeanour which signalled to Frank she was operating as normal. Lexy and Maggie occupied his office's two spare chairs whilst Jimmy and Ronnie lounged against a wall. He noted with some amusement that DC McDonald had barely taken her eyes of his brother since he'd walked in. Jimmy could do a lot worse than team up with the spirited Islander, he thought, although matchmaking wasn't really his thing. Something to talk through with Maggie, since matchmaking very much *was* her thing.

'Right then guys,' he said, trying to match Lexy's vim, 'this is going to be an exciting wee session I can tell you. First off Eleanor, I need to check that you've got all your databases and network aliases and dark web connections and asymmetric protocols all present and correct. The usual stuff is what I mean. So how's it looking?'

Lexy let out a laugh then checked herself with a hand over her mouth. Eleanor didn't laugh.

'None of that meant anything,' she said in a serious tone. *'It's like you were on Doctor Who or something.'*

'I know,' Frank said, grinning. 'Just wanted to start the meeting on a light note. But seriously, have you still got an access-all-areas backstage pass to all that MI5 and MI6 stuff? Because as you well know, it saves us a lot of time and more importantly, a lot of tedious paperwork.'

'Zak has got me beta access,' she said stiffly. *'That's like everything.'*

'Zak?' he said, puzzled. 'I thought he'd gone private?'

'His company's now a government agency,' she said in her everyone-should-know-that tone. *'They've been co-opted to the administration as technical associates.'*

Exactly what that meant he didn't know and didn't want to know either. What was important was that wee Eleanor could access the stuff they needed from the comfort of her laptop.

'Good to know,' he said, smiling. 'So first of all Ronnie, I think you've tracked down the location of the cash machine from whence most of the dosh was being extracted?'

'Yep guv,' he said, laconic as always. 'The machines have all got a unique code and it was on the statement I got. But the whole scheme is bloody crazy isn't it? It takes whoever more than half the month to get six grand's worth of cash out in three hundred pound lumps. Not exactly criminal mastermind stuff is it? Why don't they just go to their branch and withdraw it in one go?'

'Aye, but that would invite awkward questions, what with money-laundering regulations and all that stuff. But it also underlines the scheme was bloody important to the *whoever*, important enough to go to all that trouble. Speaking of which, let's see if we can find out exactly who this *whoever* is. Over to you Eleanor I think?'

Unexpectedly she smiled. *'I'm like there already. Just sharing my screen......now.'* Instantly their screen filled with a typical grainy CCTV image, showing a cashpoint on a city street somewhere, taken from an aerial viewpoint, probably a camera attached to a building across the street. *'This was from six months ago, but we've got like trillions of captures to choose from.'*

'And where's this exactly?' Frank asked Ronnie.

'A street called Cow Gate in Edinburgh guv.' Suddenly he pointed at the screen. 'Look, there we go.'

At that moment a man appeared on camera, the shot catching him removing his bank card from a pocket, giving a furtive look over his shoulder then punching in his PIN.

'Bloody hell,' Maggie said.

'Well well well,' Frank said, feigning surprise. 'If it's not Mr Andrew McClelland himself.'

'You knew it would be him, didn't you sir?' Lexy said.

He shrugged. 'Odds on, wasn't it? But what a bloody palaver to have to go through, day-in, day out.'

'Looks like it's his lunchtime routine sir,' Lexy said, pointing to the timestamp at the top left-hand corner of the screen. 'Twelve-thirty. The Procurator's office is just round the corner so it wouldn't take him five minutes to nip out.'

'Aye, that's right. So the question now is, what the hell is he *doing* with all that cash? Six grand's worth we think.'

'He must be giving it to someone guv,' Ronnie said. 'That's my guess.' He gave a self-deprecating smile as he realised what he had just said.

Lexy laughed. 'Brilliant deduction Sherlock. But I think you've got a plan on how to find out who, haven't you sir?'

Frank grinned. 'Indeed I have. So Miss Campbell, am I correct in thinking that the mobile phone guys have to keep call records for a year?'

'Like yeah,' she said. *'And longer for a person of interest. Terrorists mainly.'*

'Well I don't think Mr McClelland is one of them, but that doesn't matter because a year will be enough for us. So how do we look at this stuff exactly?'

'We can draw like a map of his movements,' Eleanor said. 'And then you can see where he's been. On your screen in real time.'

'We can maybe restrict it at first to the days when he's not having to do his wee cashpoint runs,' Lexy said. 'Which now that I think about it, occur on almost every working day of the month.'

'Weekends then, when he's not at the office,' Ronnie said, then laughed. 'Yeah I know guys, I'm a detective genius.'

'Off you go then Eleanor,' Frank said. 'Show us what you've got for him at the weekends.'

They watched as her fingers flew over the keyboard, her eyes not once leaving her screen. 'I'm looking for like GPS correlations,' she said. 'Patterns of movement.' She paused for a moment. 'Yeah, got it.'

'Got what?' Frank said impatiently.

She ignored him and kept tapping. 'Every fourth Saturday in the month. It's like he's got a routine.' Frank gave Lexy a sharp look that signalled no sarccy comments please.

'So this is five months ago.' She gave a theatrical prod at the enter button and their screen filled with a map, on which was traced a blue thick blue line.

'They live in the West End, up in Hyndland,' Lexy explained, pointing at the start of the blue line. 'I mean that's the McClelland's own house, not the government's official residence in Edinburgh. He must go back there at weekends I suppose. I'm not sure whether the First Minister would go with him.'

'But do you see where he's going?' Maggie said, excitedly. 'Look, at the top of the screen.'

'Bloody hell,' Jimmy said. 'Ardlui.'

'What's that all about?' Frank asked, puzzled.

'That's where Ally Russell lives - sorry, lived,' Maggie said. 'I mean, that must be who he was going to see. Who else could it be?'

'And he stops on the way. Every time,' Eleanor said. She moved her mouse to highlight a point on the route. *'It's a supermarket. On the big road up to Loch Lomond.'* She peered at her screen for a second. *'Dum-barton it says.'*

'Aye, that's on the way right enough,' Jimmy said. 'Grabbing some breakfast I suppose'.

'Yeah, maybe,' Maggie said. 'But the same place, every time? Sounds a bit odd to me.'

Eleanor interupted them, sounding uncharacteristically apologetic. *'Actually, there's*

some more. I had the time filter set wrong. Soz.'
She banged down on the *enter* button and the
blue line was instantly extended. *Across the loch.*

'Hey, looks like our guy takes a boat trip once
he gets there guv,' Ronnie said, laughing. 'I
suppose he wants value for money from his six
grand. Mind you he could probably buy his own
bloody boat for that.'

'What, he goes to *Inchcailloch*? Maggie said
incredulously. 'Why the hell is he going there?
Eleanor, is this just a one-off or does he do that
every time?'

*'I told you, I ran a GPS correlation search
across multiple time windows,'* Eleanor said,
unsmiling. *'It links across a hundred or more
waypoints and only retrieves exact matches.'*

'I think that means yes, he goes there every
time,' Frank said. 'But you're right. Why is Russell
taking him there every month?'

'It must be something bloody important for six
grand,' Ronnie said. 'That's some hire fee.'

'Hang on,' Maggie said suddenly. 'Jimmy, do
you remember what John Watkins told us?'

'Who's he?' Frank asked.

'He's the owner of the Loch View hotel, remember the guy I told you about last night. Anyway, when we were up there he told me and Jimmy that Ally Russell went to Glasgow every month. On a Sunday. They thought he was seeing a woman.'

'That's the day after he always met with McClelland,' Lexy said. 'It's got to be connected, surely?'

'Six grand's a lot to spend on a bird,' Ronnie said. 'She must be one hell of a woman, that's all I can say.'

'He was paying someone else,' Maggie said, blurting out the words. 'He *must* have been. This is something huge, isn't it? Everyone going to such enormous trouble, month-in, month-out.'

'I could track him too,' Eleanor said, butting in. *'If I get his mobile number.'*

Frank leapt to his feet, causing his wheeled office chair to bang against the wall. 'The murder guys will have it. In fact I remember seeing it written on their big whiteboard. Back in a jiffy.'

***

Eleanor said she needed an hour to set things up, so they repaired to the New Gorbals canteen for bacon rolls and coffee, babbling excitedly on the way down the corridor. Central to the conversation was that Andrew McClelland was handing over six grand a month to Ally Russell, six grand that he could barely afford, and there was speculation if he was needing hand-outs from his First Minister wife to bridge the gap. What the *hell* was this all about, that was the big question? And with Russell being a murder victim and two, maybe three other killings to worry about too, what was the connection? Maggie, Jimmy and Frank could agree that although it was a big horrible messy blancmange, somewhere, somehow it was all related and that there were just a couple more pieces in the jigsaw required before it all fell into place. The trouble was, right now they didn't know where to find these pieces.

'Right,' Frank said, looking at his watch, 'this speculation is all very interesting, but we'd better get back or wee Eleanor will be having a fit.' They trooped back up the corridor, each carrying refills in cardboard cups, Ronnie and Lexy sharing some private joke that Frank suspected was directed at him. The feisty forensic officer was waiting for them online, and rather than being irritated by their somewhat late return, he thought she was looking pleased with herself.

'Got good news for us then Eleanor?' Frank said in anticipation.

She shrugged. *'I know where he goes. I don't know if it's good news or not.'*

'That's exciting Eleanor,' Maggie said in a kindly tone. 'So don't keep us in suspense. Where *does* he go? Or where *did* he go I suppose is more accurate.'

'Somewhere called Strathblane and then to a hotel in Glasgow. The Caledonian Central.'

'Right, interesting,' Jimmy said. 'And do we know how long he stayed at each?

'Not long. Twenty minutes in Strathblane and about an hour in Glasgow.'

'Doesn't sound as if he was seeing a woman then,' Ronnie said. 'I mean if I was running around with six grand in my pocket I'd want more than an hour's worth.'

Frank shook his head. 'You really are the modern man Frenchie. But aye, I would agree with you on this occasion. So what was he doing? I don't even know where Strathblane is.'

'It's in the Campsie Hills,' Jimmy said, 'and actually more-or-less en-route between Loch Lomond and Glasgow.'

'Okay,' Frank said, 'and Eleanor, are we able to narrow down the exact location in this Strathblane place?'

She nodded. *'I can triangulate to a few metres. But it's only got a few streets anyway. Wait a second. '* She clicked on the map to zoom in. *'There it is. Kirkview Avenue.'*

'Brilliant,' Frank said. 'And do we know which house, or is that too much to ask?'

'There aren't as many cells in the countryside. So no, I can't nail it down to a house. But I can access the last Electoral Roll for the street.' Without waiting for his assent, she started clicking away on her keyboard. *'There it is. For the 2019 election. Thirty-one homes, sixty-seven voters.'*

'Bloody hell, that was quick,' he said, peering at the screen. 'So guys, do we recognise any of the folks on this list?'

'I do. I do,' Lexy almost screamed, jabbing at the screen. 'It's the McClelland Tower consultant guy, look. Number seven. Professor Dougal Charles McCrae and Mrs Rhona Anne McCrae. There can't be more than one Prof McCrae, can there?'

'Right guys,' Frank said, jumping up. 'Maggie, Jimmy, you two come with me. Ronnie and Lexy, get round to that hotel and see what you can find out. Seems like you're looking for any connection to that bloody tower, but let me know as soon as you find out anything. I just hope they've still got that big BMW available for us, because we need to be there in a hurry.'

***

Their phone satnavs had predicted forty-one minutes for the fourteen mile journey and had proved accurate, even though they'd had to settle for a Peugeot rather than Frank's fast motor of choice. En-route he had dismissed Maggie's concerns about the irregularity of a couple of private eyes accompanying him on official police business, and now they were descending the steep incline into Strathblane village, with just a minute to run until they reached their destination. An earlier phone call had established that Mrs McCrae would definitely be in residence.

'She was a bit evasive about her husband, wasn't she?' Maggie said. 'Didn't you think that was a bit strange? That she didn't seem to know where he was?'

'I suppose it's a bit of a shock when the police call you up out of the blue and tell you they want to see you right away,' Jimmy said.

'Anyway, we'll find out soon enough,' Frank said. 'We're nearly there.'

They pulled straight on to the short drive of the house, it being of the type the estate agents would describe as an executive family residence. Rhona McCrae was holding open the door as they arrived. She was about mid-forties, slim and tall with long auburn corkscrewed hair. The curls looked natural, the colour less so. What was obvious though was that she had been crying, and if the evidence of her breath was anything to go by, drinking too.

'Mrs McCrae?' Frank said, showing his warrant card. 'I'm DI -sorry DCI - Frank Stewart. These are my colleagues who work for a firm of investigators who've been helping us out with a police matter, Maggie Bainbridge and Jimmy Stewart. Can we come in for a wee minute?'

She nodded. 'Come through to the living room. Would you like tea or coffee?'

'No thanks, we won't be taking up much of your time, because it was your husband we really wanted to talk to. So where is he this morning?'

'I'm not sure,' she said, sounding evasive. 'He didn't tell me where he was going this morning. When he left the house I meant. At half-past seven. I expect he's gone to work.'

Frank gave her a questioning look but didn't immediately respond. Because one thing he'd learned in twenty years of policing was that lying convincingly wasn't as easy as it looked. And Rhona McCrae was lying, he had spotted that immediately.

'Aye well nae bother,' he said placidly. 'I'm sure we'll catch up with your husband later. But whilst we're here, do you mind if we ask you a couple of questions?' Without waiting for an answer he continued, 'It's about Ally Russell. He's the guy who visited you once a month on a Saturday. Poor chap's dead now, but I suppose you know that, seeing as you knew him so well. We just wondered what these wee visits were all about? Can you help me with that?'

She stared at the floor without speaking for a few seconds. Then eventually she said. 'He was just a friend of my husband. I didn't actually know him very well myself.'

'And what was the reason for them being pals?' Frank asked. 'Did they play golf or go fishing or something? Or were they at school or uni together?'

She paused again. 'I don't really know. They were just friends.'

Frank nodded. 'And they must have been *really* great mates, because Ally came here every month to hand over a nice big wad of cash to your husband, didn't he? Dougal, that's his name isn't it? So what I want to know Mrs McCrae is did you ever ask your lovely Dougal why he was getting all this money from a guy you hardly knew? Because your story sounds like a massive big pile of crap to me if I'm being honest.'

It was all it took, and he felt a bit bad about it for a moment, but it needed to be done. *All it took for her to break down in tears.*

'I don't know anything about it, but Dougal got really scared when Ally and then that other man he knew got murdered. And then when there was a third murder, that's when he decided he had to...had to *run away*. He was really scared.'

'Wait a minute,' Frank said sharply. 'Did you say *that other man he knew*? So does he know who the second murder victim is? Because *we* bloody don't.'

'He guessed,' she said, sobbing. 'After the body was found and the man went missing from his work. That's when he guessed.'

'So hang on. You say this guy went missing from his work? Where was this?'

She gave a sad shrug. 'I don't know exactly. He was a chef, at a big hotel up in Glasgow. He was French, I knew that,' she added pathetically. 'Anton Girard his name was.'

'Bloody hell,' Frank said, shooting an incredulous look at Maggie and Jimmy. 'Guys, we need to call Lexy and Ronnie and tip them off about this.' Turning back to the woman he said, 'So Mrs McCrae, where's your husband now? Because you need to tell us, and right away.'

'Is he in danger?' she said, unable to hide her fear. 'Is he going to get killed like the others? Because he thinks he is.'

'You tell me,' Frank said, exasperated, 'because *I* don't have a bloody clue what's going on here. But I expect your Dougal will be able to fill us all in when we find him. So come on Mrs McCrae, where the hell is he?'

**

'Skye?' Jimmy said as they drove away from the house. 'Are we going there now to pick up the good Professor? It's only about four hours drive if you put your foot down and they've got that bridge now.'

Frank laughed. 'I assume you're joking. Nah, we'll get the local boys to whizz round to that sister of his and pick him up. They can ask him a few questions then send him down to us when they're done. Anyway, looks like victim number two was a chef at the Caledonian eh? That's a turn-up for the books. I just wonder why nobody's reported him missing.'

Jimmy shrugged. 'Maybe he'd only been in the job a few months, you know, came over from France and was living on his own. But he would have been the guy who was doing the cooking on these gourmet jaunts of Ally Russell's. That's the connection we've been looking for, probably.' He turned and looked over his shoulder. 'So what do you think Maggie? Is that the connection?'

'Sorry Jimmy, what?' It was evident that she hadn't been listening. Then suddenly she blurted out. 'Turn around Frank. We need to go to Dumbarton. Right now. It's only twelve miles. Come on, turn around.'

He looked at her, puzzled. 'Why the hell do we want to go there? It's a right dump.'

'Because I think I've worked it out. *Everything*. But this will prove it.'

He knew there was no point in arguing with her so he didn't. 'Fair enough. And I guess you're not going to tell us what this madness is all about?'

'I will when we get there. If I'm right.'

'Which you will be,' Jimmy said. 'As per normal.'

And as it turned out, she was right. Because there it was, exactly as she had expected, sitting in the middle of a run-down strip of shops next to the supermarket that Eleanor had identified from her mobile phone tracking. The one that Andrew McClelland seemingly always stopped at on his way up to Ardlui. A neat little shop, its simple name spelled out in elaborate lettering above its window and door. *Flora's Flowers.*

Now, tomorrow being Saturday, they would be taking a trip to the abandoned island of Inchcailloch for what would undoubtedly be a very interesting day out.

Chapter 26

You weren't allowed to even blow your nose without a risk assessment these days, that had been Frank's jaundiced view when he tried to get permission to commandeer one of the fast patrol boats Police Scotland kept on the Loch. But luckily with Assistant Chief Constable Belinda Cresswell now installed as top cop at New Gorbals, the complicated but necessary sign-offs were completed in double-quick time, even if it was a Friday night with everyone desperate to disappear off to the pub. And now here they were at ten-thirty on a cold Saturday morning, powering up from Balloch Pier en-route to the island of Inchcailloch. Maggie was wearing a thick fleece and a bobble hat which went some way to keeping out the biting chill, but she couldn't help looking enviously at the brace of uniformed constables who accompanied them, snug in their well-insulated hi-viz jackets. As well as the pilot, on board with her were Jimmy, Frank and Lexy - Ronnie French having opted out claiming a dubious propensity to sea-sickness - and the aforementioned uniforms.

'So you think he'll be here?' Jimmy said, shouting over the roar of the engine to make himself heard. 'Now that we've gone to all this trouble?'

She shrugged. 'Probably. Maybe. I don't know. But it's Saturday. It's his day.'

'Two minutes guys,' the pilot yelled. 'And sorry for the choppy ride. That's Loch Lomond for you.'

The boatman slid his craft alongside a substantial concrete jetty, it's robustness suggesting it was built primarily to serve the construction of the Tower. On it at fifty-feet intervals stood stout warning signs proclaiming *Property of the Scottish Government. Public Access to the Island Forbidden.*

'Okay Maggie, do we know where we're going?' Frank said once they'd landed.

'The north side, that's where Yash said he saw it. So where's that exactly?'

'That way I think,' Jimmy said, pointing ahead. 'It's only about half a kilometre and there's a path, skirts round the side of the wreckage according to my map.'

'Great,' Maggie said. 'Shouldn't take more than ten minutes then.'

She heard Frank shouting over to the boatman. 'Hey pal, is there any other way on to the island? Another jetty or something?'

The man yelled back. 'Aye, up on the north side as it happens. It's pretty wrecked though. We couldn't land there, no way. Not with a big boat like this.'

Frank raised a hand in acknowledgement. 'But I think you should pootle round there anyway, because my guess is that's how our guy will have got onto the island. If he's bloody here at all of course. But aye, get round there in case he tries to do a runner. But don't forget to come back for us.'

Maggie caught Lexy staring open-mouthed at the ruins and walked over to her. 'It's a sombre scene, isn't it?' she said softly. 'Especially when you think of all these poor people who lost their lives.'

Lexy nodded. 'I'd only ever seen it from the shore and somehow it didn't seem real. It's so much more horrible this close up.' She paused for a moment. 'But this is what this case is all about Maggie isn't it? Everything connects back to this bloody tower.'

Maggie gave a half-smile. 'Yeah, perhaps. But it's just the old time-honoured human failings that are really at the heart of it. Lust and greed and the fact that people will always do whatever it takes not to get found out after they've done something dreadful. But come on, we'd better get moving.'

Jimmy was leading the way and setting a cracking pace, head down as he followed the route on a large-scale map on his phone. They were skirting to the western side of the wreckage, the tower having crashed down on the opposite side and rendering the eastern paths impassable. Now the twisted metal shards rising up from inadequate foundations caught the wind, whistling a mocking melody that seemed to say *we knew this would happen but you wouldn't listen.* Behind him, Maggie struggled to keep up, all the while wondering how she would react if the killer was there, and how she would contain her disappointment if he wasn't.

And then, as they rounded a bend of the path, she saw him. Standing head bowed in contemplation over the grave, incongruous in a bright red walking jacket, hands clasped behind his back. Maggie shouted from thirty yards away, unable to control her anger and revulsion. 'It's all over Andrew. All over. We know what you did.'

Taken by surprise, Andrew McClelland turned to face them, momentarily frozen to the spot. *And then he ran.* Jimmy was the first to react, setting off at a sprint, leaving the path to take a direct route across the thick bracken in an attempt to cut off McClelland's route to the shore. The other man, fit but twenty years older, stood no chance, Maggie watching hawk-eyed as her colleague blocked off the killer's path to the old wooden jetty. Somewhere in the distance she heard the roar of an outboard motor, as McClelland's boatman evidently decided the game was up for his client. She wondered if it might be piloted by Davie Cramond, but then quickly dismissed the idea. He was too smart for that. The mastermind perhaps, but as for getting his hands dirty, that was unlikely.

But irrespective of who was in charge of the speedboat, its unscheduled departure meant that there was now nowhere to run for McClelland, cast adrift on this tiny island of little more than a square mile in area. However that evidently didn't mean he was going to go down without a fight, as she saw him remove something that had been concealed inside his jacket, something she saw glint in the watery sunshine. Recognising what it was, she yelled a warning as Jimmy got closer. 'Jimmy, Jimmy, he's got a knife! He's hiding it behind his back. Please, be careful!' Then she remembered the MO of the three murder victims, all viciously stabbed to death. McClelland was a powerful guy, and now he had nothing to lose. She screamed at the two uniformed officers, who seemed reluctant to get involved. 'You've got to help him, *go*!' And then out the corner of her eye, she spotted Frank and Lexy creeping along the path, closing in on McClelland from behind, crouching down in the hope of concealing their approach.

'Frank Frank, *please* be careful,' she was about to yell, then checked herself, fearful of alerting McClelland to their presence. And then suddenly she thought, *what the hell am I doing, standing on the touchline as if I was the bloody manager of a football team?* Throwing off her hat, she raced across the bracken, retracing Jimmy's steps until she was standing at his shoulder.

'Maggie, for God's sake, get back,' Jimmy yelled, stealing her a glance. 'No offence, but this is a job for professionals. And that goes for you too,' he added, jabbing a finger in Frank and Lexy's direction. Alerted to their presence, McClelland turned his head whilst still holding the knife in front of him, ready to strike. *Which gave Jimmy his opportunity.* He launched himself into a classic rugby tackle, catching McClelland below the knees and causing him to crash to the ground. But the killer was still holding the knife, and although winded, was making an effort to get back on his feet. Until, that was, he felt the crunch of a second tackle, this one strictly illegal under the rules of the game, two sinewy arms clamping around his neck and sending him crashing to the ground once more, the weapon flying from his grasp.

'Bloody good work wee Lexy,' Frank shouted, ripping out a pair of handcuffs from the pocket of his padded bomber jacket. Now Jimmy had McClelland pinned to the ground, allowing Frank to slam his wrists together and click the handcuffs in place.

'Right then pal,' he said, giving a grim smile. 'Let's see if I can get this right without having to look at my words. Andrew McClelland, I am charging you with the murder of Juliet McClelland. You do not have to say anything, but anything you do say.....'

It took an age for him to go through the charge sheet, once Conspiracy to Murder had been added in respect of the three Loch Lomond victims. Maggie watched patiently and with grim satisfaction, biting her lip to stop her saying to McClelland what she desperately wanted to say. But she knew that wouldn't help anyone, and it would make Frank angry too and she didn't want that. Instead she thought with sadness about how cruel a hand fate could deal you if it wanted to, and how utterly ghastly had been the hand dealt to Juliet McClelland.

And how utterly, utterly lucky she was that fate had dealt her Frank Stewart.

Chapter 27

It had become somewhat of a tradition that they would get together for a nice dinner after a case had reached a satisfactory conclusion, and with this one being by a country mile the most complex and twisty they had ever been involved in, then it was only fitting that the celebration should be something special too. Frank had fancied another curry at that place near the University, but Junior Minister Caroline Connor had firmly suggested the posh Caledonian Central as more appropriate, and since it was she - or at least the Government - who were picking up the tab, Maggie was happy to accede to the request.

So here they were, gathered in an opulent private room and with a free bar to boot. Present were Maggie, Frank, Jimmy, Lexy McDonald, Ronnie French, Eleanor Campbell, Yash Patel - who had made sure he was seated right next to Connor, looking to bag an exclusive from the Minister - Connor herself of course, her assistant Giles Harkness, ACC Belinda Cresswell and Frank's boss DCI Jill Smart.

'Quite a party this is,' Frank was saying, looking relaxed as he moved onto his third pint of the evening, 'and my main course was totally epic. The steak was absolutely cooked to perfection. What about yours Jimmy-boy?'

'Same,' his brother said, giving a thumbs-up. 'I had it rare and with those cheesy French potatoes. Superb.'

Across the table, Maggie gave Jimmy a fond look, then with a sinking feeling remembered that soon he would be leaving her little firm for his new adventure. God, that was going to be difficult but it wasn't as if she wasn't going to see him again. That realisation made her feel better, and in any case tonight wasn't the occasion to be maudlin. And then her thoughts were interrupted by the zing of a teaspoon being tapped against a wine glass.

Caroline Connor was on her feet and evidently about to make a speech, waiting patiently for the hubbub of conversation around the table to subdue. Not that patiently as it happened, Maggie noting the withering look she shot in the direction of her assistant Giles, who seemed rather smitten by the charms of Jill Smart and had not noticed his boss had stood up. Finally cottoning on, he raised a hand in silent apology.

'Well ladies and gentlemen, this is a red-letter occasion is it not? My government is all about celebrating success and my goodness, don't we have a *big* success to celebrate here?' Maggie caught Frank's eye and exchanged a smile. She knew the cynical thought that would be going through his head. *Aye, **your** success dear. Your wee*

Unexplained Wealth project has delivered the goods and the public aren't going to be shedding any tears for who it's caught in its net. But this wasn't an occasion to be churlish, Maggie thought, reproaching herself. Let her have her moment in the sun.

'So I raise my glass to all of you,' Connor continued, 'for playing your part in keeping Britain free from the corruption that blights so many other nations and for bringing a ghastly murderer to justice. And in such a complicated set of circumstances too. Which is why I'm going to ask the lovely Maggie to explain to us exactly how it all fitted together.' She paused to take a sip from her wine glass. 'And I think we are all going to have to concentrate *very* hard,' she added, raising a laugh from her audience. 'So Maggie, over to you.'

'Thank you Caroline.' Maggie stood up and gave a self-deprecating smile. 'I'm not so used to this as you are, so bear with me if I ramble a bit.' That wasn't quite true of course, she knew that, having been a barrister, albeit a hopeless one, for nearly twenty years, but it was the kind of thing you were expected to say. 'So really, it was the cursed Lomond Tower that was at the heart of everything in this case. And to understand its central role in the drama, you need to go back seven or eight years when the project first surfaced. Now I should say from the start that

Sheila McClelland, whom I admire very much incidentally, has been a terrible victim in this case, not a perpetrator. But if she does have any grounds for regret, it was in her great drive to see the tower built as a showcase for what Scotland and the Scottish people could achieve. It's been called a vanity project and that very much was what it was.'

'Aye, pride comes before a fall if you pardon the tasteless pun,' Frank said.

Maggie smiled. 'So when Europe's leading construction engineers said that the tower couldn't be built, well that was like a red rag to a bull for Mrs McClelland and her government. Wee Scotland will show you, that was the attitude, and it was that spirit of defiance that set off the terrible chain of events.'

'And that's where Davie Cramond came in,' Jimmy said.

'Exactly,' she nodded. 'Cramond was a golfing buddy of Mrs McClelland's husband Andrew, and it was him who persuaded Cramond he should bid for the contract. We don't yet know the full details of what was discussed, but we do know, thanks to Yash and his paper's Freedom of Information request, that the contract was very unusual indeed.'

'That's right,' Yash Patel said. 'Because most contracts like this are stuffed with penalty clauses for lateness and quality and all that kind of thing.'

'And this one wasn't?' Connor asked.

Patel shook his head. 'The opposite. Nothing at all about meeting the timescale for a start. But it did have a massive bonus built in if the Tower was completed successfully. Five - million -pounds,' he added, spelling out the words for maximum impact. 'That just shows how desperate McClelland's government was to get the thing built.'

Maggie nodded. 'So then of course Davie Cramond was going to do anything to build that tower, anything at all. Naturally his first job was dealing with that inconvenient report by the Cambridge expert Professor Elizabeth Bates.'

'The one that said you couldn't build such a structure on Inchcailloch because of that Highland Boundary Fault thingy?' Frank asked.

'That's the one. But that wasn't a problem for Cramond. He just went out and found his own expert. Professor Dougal McCrae of Glasgow University, who he commissioned to write a contrary report that said that actually Elizabeth Bates was wrong and it could be built after all. We think McCrae was paid about twenty thousand pounds for his trouble, which helped overcome his doubts about the thing.'

'And that set a bit of a pattern, didn't it?' Jimmy said. 'Because having taken Cramond's money, the Professor was compromised. That happened to quite a few people in this case.'

'It did,' Maggie said. 'And it was Davie Cramond who was orchestrating everything. He was the mastermind if you will. So the contract was awarded to great fanfare and construction started. At first, everything was wonderful. There were a host of excellent new jobs created and they started by building a splendid new bridge over to the island from Balmaha. Just about every week a smug politician would pop over from Edinburgh for a photo-opportunity and the project was attracting positive headlines all over the world.'

'I'm sensing an *and then*,' Caroline Connor said, giving a wry smile.

Maggie nodded. 'Afraid so. And then it was time to start the piling for the foundations. That's when everything started to go pear-shaped, exactly as Professor Elizabeth Bates had predicted. I'm no expert, but as I understand it, the rock was either too hard or too soft and they were struggling to pour enough concrete to support the structure. But meanwhile our Professor McCrae had set up a little firm to do the legally-required

Building Regulations sign-offs, and low and behold, doesn't he just go and win the contract for the Lomond Tower inspections.'

'A case of poacher turned gamekeeper,' Jimmy said. 'That was shocking, wasn't it?'

'Exactly. And that's when the conflict started. You see, the chief site manager was an experienced old hand called Paul Adams, who'd worked on the North Sea rigs and knew a thing or two about construction on difficult ground. So when McCrae's firm started to sign off on shoddy work, he kicked up a right old fuss. Threatened to go to the media if he wasn't listened to.'

'And so Cramond got involved again,' Jimmy said. 'As you would if your five million quid bonus was under threat.'

'That's right,' Maggie said. 'We can't know the full details of what went on between them, but the upshot was, Cramond invited Adams to come for a cruise on a mate's boat. *We'll have a few beers, something nice to eat, do a bit of fishing, have a wee chat. I'm sure we can sort all this out without any bother.* That would have been the gist of it.'

'But Adams never came back,' Jimmy said.

'No, he didn't. According to the fatal accident enquiry, he got blind drunk and went over the side. The police were asked to investigate by the

Fiscal's office but came to the conclusion there was no foul play involved.'

Frank nodded. 'And by some remarkable coincidence, the copper who did the investigation was another of Cramond's golfing mates. My pal DCS Peter Sweeney.'

'Well he won't be playing any golf for a long time now,' ACC Cresswell said. 'Not unless they've built a course inside HMP Barlinnie.'

Maggie smiled. 'No he won't. But then Cramond began to think he could use Ally Russell's little cruise boat to do some schmoozing of anybody else who might be planning to shoot their mouths off about what was going on on the site. At first I think it was genuinely just fine food and fine wines they were providing, and that's why they fully-equipped the kitchen on the Joan Greig and hired that expensive French chef. It was a pretty low-key operation, maybe three or four times a year. But then at some point he must have thought, wouldn't it be nice if we got a couple of really pretty girls to do the serving, special-looking girls who wouldn't mind dressing up in sexy waitress uniforms if the money was right.'

'Which is where his sister Francis Cramond came in. She was already supplying lots of staff to the Auchterard Hotel and was able to pick out the prettiest ones to work on the gourmet cruises.'

'And then it all got very sordid I'm afraid,' Jimmy said. 'Because then Cramond starts thinking that if *sex* was on offer he would really have a powerful hold over these guys who were kicking up a fuss. Entice them into that wee bedroom, take a few photographs, show the pictures to them, tell them what would happen if they didn't keep their mouths shut.'

She nodded. 'That's right. And then, Juliet McClelland enters stage left, if you'll forgive the theatrical metaphor. She was a beautiful girl, but seriously mixed-up after her dysfunctional upbringing. If we believe Becky Johnson her ex-flatmate - and in mitigation I must say we have had some quite differing views on this - then Juliet was used to using her sexuality to her advantage. If that was true, then we can presume that when she was offered eye-watering amounts of money to participate in Cramond's malevolent scheme she had no moral scruples. She was just thinking of the cash and that fancy flat in the West End.'

'And in any case, we don't think actual sex took place,' Jimmy said. 'This was a classic honey-trap operation. The victim was photographed in a compromising position but before any...' He paused, looking embarrassed. '...well, you know what I'm talking about.'

'We do indeed,' she laughed. 'So then we come to the fateful evening when everything started to go wrong for everyone involved. We know Davie Cramond was a ruthless operator who wasn't going to leave any stone unturned in making sure he got his hands on that juicy five million pound bonus. At some point he begins to think, *who knows too much, who do I need to take care of properly? There's that Professor guy. I've been paying him plenty but he's a bit of a wimp and he might blab at any minute. And what about my so-called mate Andrew McClelland? I gave him a pile of sweeteners to get me some meetings with his missus so that I could smooth-talk her into giving me the contract, but he's a slippery snake and I don't trust him as far as I can throw him.*

'So he invites the pair of them to come on one of his wee cruises?' Frank said. 'Is that what happened?'

'Exactly. But that evening Cramond is fatefully unaware that the girl his sister has supplied is Juliet McClelland. For obvious reasons the girls didn't use their own names. As far as Cramond was concerned, it was a girl called Amber who was on duty, if I can use that horrible phrase. The evening proceeds in its normal hedonistic fashion, with food, champagne and cocaine being imbibed as if it's going out of fashion. And then at some point Cramond says *we've got a wee treat for you Andrew*, nodding in the direction of the bedroom door.'

'Oh god, that's horrible, ' Caroline Cramond said, covering her mouth with her hand. 'Really sick.'

Maggie nodded sadly. 'Yes indeed. So McClelland is pretty drunk and high on cocaine, and crazy with pent-up desire too. And then he walks into that bedroom and is confronted by his step-daughter in her underwear.'

'That's like *gross*,' Eleanor said, exchanging a horrified look with Lexy.

'And at that moment all he can think of is the effect on his reputation if this ever got into the public eye, if Juliet decided to talk. In a blind panic, he strikes out, catching his step-daughter with a sledge-hammer blow from his fist, causing her to collapse onto the bed, out cold.'

'At least that's what out police pathologist reckons happened after she examined the body,' Frank said.

Maggie nodded. 'Then, in some crazed moment of clarity, McClelland realises if she is dead, she can't talk.'

'So he smothered her with the pillow,' Jimmy said, 'holding it down until she had drawn her last breath.'

'And now of course they have a body to deal with,' Maggie said. 'We can only imagine what the atmosphere must have been like on that boat when the others realised what he had done. The obvious course of action would have been to throw Juliet's body over the side, but McClelland, sick with a remorse that wrecked his judgement, wouldn't allow that. Crazily, all he could think of was what his wife would say if she ever found out, about how little he thought of his step-daughter that he could just toss her away like she was garbage.'

'He'd *murdered* her for god's sake,' Connor said, aghast. 'What, did he think he would get a little pat on the back for not just chucking her into the loch?'

Maggie shrugged. 'I know. Against their better judgement, they agree to go along with his mad scheme. I suppose they thought it was the only way to stop him completely cracking up and leaving them all in the shit. So they pull the boat into the old jetty at Inchcailloch, drag her out of the cabin and bury her body on the island. By now it's the early hours of the morning and they manage to do it without being seen.'

'And then the cover up starts,' Jimmy said. 'Big time.'

'Exactly,' Maggie said. 'First of all Cramond gets his mate DCS Sweeney on board, promising to make it worth his while.'

'The fancy motors,' Frank said.

She nodded. 'That's it. So Sweeney lumps Juliet's investigation in with the hunt for the serial killer who's been stalking the east end of the city. He knows that her telephone records will show her true movements that night so he makes sure that no-one on the case is allowed to look at them. Meanwhile, Cramond gets his sister to pay off the taxi-driver and the firm's owner and the narrative then is unchallenged, that the taxi turned up and waited for twenty minutes but Juliet didn't appear. So everyone is looking for her in the city when in fact they should have been looking up at Loch Lomond.'

'Aye that's right,' Jimmy said. 'And now, Cramond and McClelland have some other big problems to deal with, namely the witnesses to the crime who were onboard the boat that night. Professor McCrae, Ally Russell and Anton Girard the chef. But we're guessing Cramond wanted nothing more to do with the affair after setting up Sweeney, and told McClelland he was on his own from now on. So the murderer set up this crazily elaborate scheme to pay them to keep quiet. He must have thought using the offshore accounts then paying in cash would stop anyone being able to trace what was going on.'

'But it wasn't,' Maggie said. 'Mainly thanks to Eleanor and Ronnie here.'

'Aye, good solid police work guys,' Frank said, raising his glass.

'And then something changed,' she continued. 'Maybe McClelland was running out of money or maybe one of the witnesses, probably Russell, started to turn the screw and demand more. And so he thought, I've killed once, what's stopping me doing it again?'

'First Russell and then Anton Girad,' Jimmy said. 'Lured to the lochside on some pretence and then knifed to death.'

'But what about the third victim?' Jill Smart asked. 'What was his name? Sandy something?'

'Sandy McDuff,' Maggie said. 'And I'm afraid his death was probably because of us. And it wasn't McClelland that killed him either. That was Davie Cramond who did that one.'

'Aye it was,' Jimmy said. 'When we met with Cramond at the golf club, he was pretending that he didn't know anything about the gourmet cruises. He said that it was Sandy McDuff who was behind them when in fact that guy had nothing to do with them at all.'

'So when we said we would talk to McDuff about it, he knew he had to do something, and fast. And with the two earlier murders being accomplished by a brutal stabbing, he had ready-made MO to create the perfect copy-cat killing. Same method, same location. It was odds-on that the police would think it was the same person that carried them out.'

'But you figured it all out for us Maggie,' ACC Creswell said appreciatively. 'We owe you a very big thank you for that. And now two very bad men are in custody and facing a very long stretch.'

Maggie gave a modest smile. 'Not just me, although I'd love to take all the plaudits. Jimmy of course, and Frank and Lexy and Ronnie. And last but not least, Eleanor, our hacker supreme.'

'Ethical hacker,' Eleanor corrected, 'and I'm government-approved.'

Frank shot a wry smile in the direction of Caroline Connor. 'Aye, we know all about government-approved hacking don't we?'

'I think we've seen that the ends justify the means,' Connor said primly. 'And democracy is protected as a result. No-one can argue with that.'

'If you say so,' Frank said, laughing. 'But aye, I suppose you could call it a result. So maybe we need your government expense account to crack out the single malts and raise our glasses in celebration.'

'And who will we be toasting sir?' Lexy asked.

'All of us. As Maggie said, it's been a great team effort.'

Maggie looked around the room at the happy expressions and gave a wry smile. Yes, it was true that it had been a great team effort, but now with Jimmy's bombshell decision, that team was about to be broken up. After everything she had gone through barely two years earlier, when it seemed her world would be destroyed forever, she had learned that the human spirit was capable of recovering from the very worst that fate could throw at you. It was a new chapter, that was all. This time next year she would be married to the man she loved and settled into a completely new life. She glanced across the table, first at Caroline Connor and then at Jill Smart, two beautiful and successful women more or less her own age, but neither wearing rings on the third finger of their left hands. Was that by choice she wondered, or had life just not worked out the way they might have wanted? It seemed hard to imagine that either of them would envy her, but surely they must feel the march of time in the same way she had, the hormones driving a powerful desire to have a child before it was too late. In her case, that had led her into her disastrous marriage to Phillip. Maybe Caroline and Jill weren't so dumb.

And what of that other phenomenally successful woman, First Minister Sheila McClelland? Maggie had come to admire her in the short time she had known her, this woman so dedicated to public service, with a humility and humour that set her apart from almost every other politician she knew. But a woman who, like her, had made a disastrous marriage and whose only other mistake was driven by a great but misguided love and pride she had for her country.

She saw Frank was smiling at her. 'I know what you're thinking about,' he said softly. 'She'll never be the same again, will she? I mean, how could she be after all that's happened to her?'

Maggie nodded. 'It was that bloody tower, wasn't it? At the heart of everything. That's what we've always known.'

'Aye it was. But she'll always be loved for her great service to her wee nation and we can only hope that's of some comfort to her .'

'We did our job,' Jimmy said. 'We found out what happened to Juliet. Not knowing would have been worse for her.'

'It's all about choices in the end, isn't it?' It was a cliché, Maggie knew that, but that didn't make it any less true. There was Sheila McClelland, her life shattered by two of them, and Jimmy, still in mental turmoil since his ill-fated affair more than two years ago.

And then there was Frank. Lovely, sweet Frank, who had chosen *her*.

Epilogue

It was crazy, mental, totally nuts, he knew it was, of course he did. And yet here he was, ex-army Captain Jimmy Stewart on another mission. Yes, here he was, crouched down in the heather, his binoculars trained on the sturdy wooden doors of Lochmorehead's quaint sixteenth-century church. *Binoculars* for god's sake! What the *hell* was he thinking? But these doors lay no more than a hundred metres away, a hundred metres that, flat-out, could be covered in less than fifteen seconds.

The bridegroom and all the guests were already inside, bloody Hugo in full Highland dress, a rig-out that Jimmy had to admit suited him. He was a good-looking bastard, no-one would argue with that, but Flora was the most beautiful woman in the world and she was hardly going to settle for anything less. Jimmy gave a quiet grin as he glanced at his watch. Six minutes past two and the Rolls-Royce carrying Flora and his ex-father-in-law still hadn't pulled up outside the door. That was his ex-wife all over of course. They'd often joked, unoriginally, that she would be late for her own funeral. Now here she was, late for her own wedding. Or perhaps she wasn't late. Perhaps she'd changed her mind, couldn't go through with it, knowing that she could only ever be married to one man, and that man wasn't super-smug Hugo in his bloody kilt.

And then he heard the crunch of gravel on the drive and knew *that* particular hope was about to be dashed. As the car approached at a stately pace, Jimmy focussed his binoculars on the nearside rear window. That, unfortunately, turned out to be the side occupied by Flora's father. With some dismay he realised her arrival and her short walk to the church door would be concealed by the gleaming white wedding car. But actually that didn't matter, because now he had a decision to make. *Fight or flight. Action or inaction.* It was the kind of decision he'd had to make many times in his army days, but back then *flight* just meant living to fight another day. Today, if he chose that option, that would be the end of it. *For good.*

The car had now drawn up. In a moment, the chauffeur would be at the rear door and opening it for the bride. So if he didn't want an embarrassing scene in the church, he would have to make his move now. *One hundred metres to cover, fifteen seconds to do it in.* He thought about what Maggie had said at the celebratory dinner, that life was all about choices. Sure it was, and now he had just a few seconds to make the biggest one he'd ever make in his life. And then another saying came to mind, this one perhaps not so common as to qualify as a cliché. *It's better to regret what you did than what you didn't do.* Which, he realised with dismay, could be taken both ways in this current situation. But then suddenly it all became clear and he knew what he must do. Replacing his binoculars in their carry-case, he got to his feet.

And then after a moment's hesitation, he turned on his heels, and without as much as a glance over his shoulder, he began to walk away.

A BIG THANK YOU FROM AUTHOR ROB WYLLIE

Dear Reader,

A huge thank you for reading *The Loch Lomond Murders* and I do hope you enjoyed it! For indie authors like myself, reviews are our lifeblood so it would be great if you could take the trouble to post a star rating on Amazon.

If you did enjoy this book, I'm sure you would also like the other books in the series -you can find them all (at very reasonable prices!) on Amazon. Also, take a look at my webpage - that's robwyllie.com

Thank you for your support!

Regards
Rob

Printed in Great Britain
by Amazon

34297907R00215